Photo by Charles H. Davis

CHRISTOPHER MORLEY, AUTHOR OF SHANDYGAFF, WHERE
THE BLUE BEGINS, THUNDER ON THE LEFT, ETC.

814
m864s

33954

CHRISTOPHER MORLEY

SHANDYGAFF

A number of most agreeable
Inquirendoes upon *Life & Letters*,
interspersed
with *Short Stories & Skits*,
the whole most Diverting
to the Reader

GARDEN CITY, NEW YORK
GARDEN CITY PUBLISHING CO., INC.
1927

COPYRIGHT, 1918, BY DOUBLEDAY, PAGE
& COMPANY.   ALL RIGHTS RESERVED.
PRINTED IN THE UNITED STATES AT THE
COUNTRY LIFE PRESS, GARDEN CITY, N. Y.

814
M 864 s

33954

10/30/39

TITLES AND DEDICATIONS

I WANTED to call these exercises "Casual Ablutions," in memory of the immortal sign in the washroom of the British Museum, but my arbiter of elegance forbade it. You remember that George Gissing, homeless and penniless on London streets, used to enjoy the lavatory of the Museum Reading Room as a fountain and a shrine. But the flinty hearted trustees, finding him using the wash-stand for bath-tub and laundry, were exceeding wroth, and set up the notice

> THESE BASINS ARE FOR
> CASUAL ABLUTIONS ONLY

I would like to issue the same warning to the implacable reader: these fugitive pieces, very casual rinsings in the great basin of letters, must not be too bitterly resented, even by their publishers. To borrow O. Henry's joke, they are more demitasso than Tasso.

The real purpose in writing books is to have

the pleasure of dedicating them to someone, and here I am in a quandary. So many dedications have occurred to me, it seems only fair to give them all a chance.

I thought of dedicating the book to
CLAYTON SEDGWICK COOPER
The Laird of Westcolang

I thought of dedicating to the
TWO BEST BOOK SHOPS IN THE WORLD
Blackwell's in Oxford and
Leary's in Philadelphia

I thought of dedicating to
THE 8:13 TRAIN

I thought of dedicating to
EDWARD PAGE ALLINSON
The Squire of Town's End Farm
Better known as Mifflin McGill
In affectionate memory of
Many unseasonable jests

I thought of dedicating to
PROFESSOR FRANCIS B. GUMMERE
From an erring pupil

I thought of dedicating to
FRANCIS R. BELLAMY
Author of "The Balance"
Whose Talent I Revere,
But Whose Syntax I Deplore

I thought of dedicating to
   JOHN N. BEFFEL
   My First Editor
Who insisted on taking me seriously

I thought of dedicating to
   GUY S. K. WHEELER
   The Lion Cub

I thought of dedicating to
   ROBERT CORTES HOLLIDAY
   The Urbanolater

I thought of dedicating to
   SILAS ORRIN HOWES
   Faithful Servant of Letters

But my final and irrevocable decision is to dedicate this book to
   THE MIEHLE PRINTING PRESS
   More Sinned Against Than Sinning

—

For permission to reprint, I denounce The New York *Evening Post*, The Boston *Transcript*, The *Bellman*, The *Smart Set*, The New York *Sun*, The New York *Evening Sun*, The *American Oxonian*, *Collier's*, and The *Ladies' Home Journal*.

Wyncote, Pa.
November, 1917.

SHANDYGAFF: a very refreshing drink, being a mixture of bitter ale or beer and ginger-beer, commonly drunk by the lower classes in England, and by strolling tinkers, low church parsons, newspaper men, journalists, and prizefighters. Said to have been invented by Henry VIII as a solace for his matrimonial difficulties. It is believed that a continual bibbing of shandygaff saps the will, the nerves, the resolution, and the finer faculties, but there are those who will abide no other tipple.

> *John Mistletoe:*
> *Dictionary of Deplorable Facts.*

CONTENTS

SHANDYGAFF

SHANDYGAFF

A QUESTION OF PLUMAGE

KENNETH STOCKTON was a man of letters, and correspondingly poor. He was the literary editor of a leading metropolitan daily; but this job only netted him fifty dollars a week, and he was lucky to get that much. The owner of the paper was powerfully in favour of having the reviews done by the sporting editor, and confining them to the books of those publishers who bought advertising space. This simple and statesmanlike view the owner had frequently expressed in Mr. Stockton's hearing, so the latter was never very sure how long his job would continue.

But Mr. Stockton had a house, a wife, and four children in New Utrecht, that very ingenious suburb of Brooklyn. He had worked the problem out to a nicety long ago. If he did not bring home, on the average, eighty dollars a week, his household would cease to revolve. It simply had to be done. The house was still being paid for on the installment plan.   There were plumbers' bills, servant's wages, clothes and schooling for the children, clothes for the wife, two suits a year for himself, and the dues of the Sheepshead Golf Club—his only extravagance.   A simple middle-class routine, but one that, once embarked upon, turns into a treadmill.   As I say, eighty dollars a week would just cover expenses.   To accumulate any savings, pay for life insurance, and entertain friends, Stockton had to rise above that minimum.   If in any week he fell below that figure he could not lie abed at night and "snort his fill," as the Elizabethan song naïvely puts it.

There you have the groundwork of many a domestic drama.

Mr. Stockton worked pretty hard at the newspaper office to earn his fifty dollars.   He skimmed faithfully all the books that came in, wrote painstaking reviews, and took care to run cuts on his literary page on Saturdays "to give the stuff kick," as the proprietor ordered.   Though he did so with reluctance, he was forced now and then to approach the book publishers on the subject of advertising.   He gave earnest and honest thought to his literary department, and was once praised by Mr. Howells in *Harper's Magazine* for the honourable quality of his criticisms.

But Mr. Stockton, like most men, had only a

certain fund of energy and enthusiasm at his disposal. His work on the paper used up the first fruits of his zeal and strength. After that came his article on current poetry, written (unsigned) for a leading imitation literary weekly. The preparation of this involved a careful perusal of at least fifty journals, both American and foreign, and I blush to say it brought him only fifteen dollars a week. He wrote a weekly "New York Letter" for a Chicago paper of bookish tendencies, in which he told with a flavour of intimacy the goings on of literary men in Manhattan whom he never had time or opportunity to meet. This article was paid for at space rates, which are less in Chicago than in New York. On this count he averaged about six dollars a week.

That brings us up to seventy-one dollars, and also pretty close to the limit of our friend's endurance. The additional ten dollars or so needed for the stability of the Stockton exchequer he earned in various ways. Neighbours in New Utrecht would hear his weary typewriter clacking far into the night. He wrote short stories, of only fair merit; and he wrote "Sunday stories," which is the lowest depth to which a self-respecting lover of literature can fall. Once in a while he gave a lecture on poetry, but he was a shy man, and he never was asked to lecture twice in the same

place. By almost incredible exertions of courage
and obstinacy he wrote a novel, which was published, and sold 2,580 copies the first year. His
royalties on this amounted to $348.30—not one-
third as much, he reflected sadly, as Irvin Cobb
would receive for a single short story. He even did
a little private tutoring at his home, giving the sons
of some of his friends lessons in English literature.

It is to be seen that Mr. Stockton's relatives,
back in Indiana, were wrong when they wrote to
him admiringly—as they did twice a year—asking
for loans, and praising the bold and debonair life
of a man of letters in the great city. They did
not know that for ten years Mr. Stockton had
refused the offers of his friends to put him up for
membership at the literary club to which his
fancy turned so fondly and so often. He could
not afford it. When friends from out of town
called on him, he took them to Peck's for a French
table d'hôte, with an apologetic murmur.

But it is not to be thought that Mr. Stockton
was unhappy or discontented. Those who have
experienced the excitements of the existence where
one lives from hand to mouth and back to hand
again, with rarely more than fifty cents of loose
change in pocket, know that there is even a kind
of pleasurable exhilaration in it. The characters
in George Gissing's Grub Street stories would

have thought Stockton rich indeed with his fifty-dollar salary. But he was one of those estimable men who have sense enough to give all their money to their wives and keep none in their trousers. And though his life was arduous and perhaps dull to outward view, he was a passionate lover of books, and in his little box at the back of the newspaper office, smoking a corncob and thumping out his reviews, he was one of the happiest men in New York. His thirst for books was a positive bulimia; how joyful he was when he found time to do a little work on his growing sheaf of literary essays, which he intended to call "Casual Ablutions," after the famous sign in the British Museum washroom.

It was Mr. Stockton's custom to take a trolley as far as the Brooklyn bridge, and thence it was a pleasant walk to the office on Park Row. Generally he left home about ten o'clock, thus avoiding the rush of traffic in the earlier hours; and loitering a little along the way, as becomes a man of ideas, his article on poetry would jell in his mind, and he would be at his desk a little after eleven. There he would work until one o'clock with the happy concentration of those who enjoy their tasks. At that time he would go out for a bite of lunch, and would then be at his desk steadily from two until six. Dinner at home was at seven, and after that he worked persistently in his little den under the roof until past midnight.

One morning in spring he left New Utrecht in a mood of perplexity, for to-day his even routine was in danger of interruption. Halfway across the bridge Stockton paused in some confusion of spirit to look down on the shining river and consider his course.

A year or so before this time, in gathering copy for his poetry articles, he had first come across the name of Finsbury Verne in an English journal at the head of some exquisite verses. From time to time he found more of this writer's lyrics in the English magazines, and at length he had ventured a graceful article of appreciation. It happened that he was the first in this country to recognize Verne's talent, and to his great delight he had one day received a very charming letter from the poet himself, thanking him for his understanding criticism.

Stockton, though a shy and reticent man, had the friendliest nature in the world, and some underlying spirit of kinship in Verne's letter prompted him to warm response. Thus began a correspondence which was a remarkable pleasure to the lonely reviewer, who knew no literary men, although his life was passed among books. Hardly dreaming that they would ever meet, he

had insisted on a promise that if Verne should ever
visit the States he would make New Utrecht his
headquarters. And now, on this very morning,
there had come a wireless message via Seagate,
saying that Verne was on a ship which would
dock that afternoon.

The dilemma may seem a trifling one, but to
Stockton's sensitive nature it was gross indeed.
He and his wife knew that they could offer but
little to make the poet's visit charming. New
Utrecht, on the way to Coney Island, is not a likely
perching ground for poets; the house was small,
shabby, and the spare room had long ago been
made into a workshop for the two boys, where
they built steam engines and pasted rotogravure
pictures from the Sunday editions on the walls.
The servant was an enormous coloured mammy,
with a heart of ruddy gold, but in appearance she
was pure Dahomey. The bathroom plumbing
was out of order, the drawing-room rug was fifteen
years old, even the little lawn in front of the house
needed trimming, and the gardener would not be
round for several days. And Verne had given
them only a few hours' notice. How like a poet!

In his letters Stockton had innocently boasted
of the pleasant time they would have when the
writer should come to visit. He had spoken of
evenings beside the fire when they would talk for

hours of the things that interest literary men.
What would Verne think when he found the
hearth only a gas log, and one that had a peculiarly
offensive odour? This sickly sweetish smell had
become in years of intimacy very dear to Stockton,
but he could hardly expect a poet who lived in
Well Walk, Hampstead (O Shades of Keats!), and
wrote letters from a London literary club, to
understand that sort of thing. Why, the man
was a grandson of Jules Verne, and probably had
been accustomed to refined surroundings all his
life. And now he was doomed to plumb the subfusc depths of New Utrecht!

Stockton could not even put him up at a club, as
he belonged to none but the golf club, which had no
quarters for the entertainment of out-of-town
guests. Every detail of his home life was of the
shabby, makeshift sort which is so dear to one's
self but needs so much explaining to outsiders.
He even thought with a pang of Lorna Doone,
the fat, plebeian little mongrel terrier which had
meals with the family and slept with the children
at night. Verne was probably used to staghounds
or Zeppelin hounds or something of the sort, he
thought humorously. English poets wear an
iris halo in the eyes of humble American reviewers.
Those godlike creatures have walked on Fleet
Street, have bought books on Paternoster Row,

have drunk half-and-half and eaten pigeon pie at
the Salutation and Cat, and have probably roared
with laughter over some alehouse jest of Mr.
Chesterton.

Stockton remembered the photograph Verne
had sent him, showing a lean, bearded face with
wistful dark eyes against a background of old
folios. What would that Olympian creature think
of the drudge of New Utrecht, a mere reviewer
who sold his editorial copies to pay for shag
tobacco!

Well, thought Stockton, as he crossed the
bridge, rejoicing not at all in the splendid towers
of Manhattan, candescent in the April sun, they
had done all they could. He had left his wife
telephoning frantically to grocers, cleaning women,
and florists. He himself had stopped at the
poultry market on his way to the trolley to order
two plump fowls for dinner, and had pinched
them with his nervous, ink-stained fingers, as
ordered by Mrs. Stockton, to test their tenderness. They would send the three younger children to their grandmother, to be interned there
until the storm had blown over; and Mrs. Stockton was going to do what she could to take down
the rotogravure pictures from the walls of what the
boys fondly called the Stockton Art Gallery. He
knew that Verne had children of his own: perhaps

he would be amused rather than dismayed by the incongruities of their dismantled guestroom. Presumably, the poet was over here for a lecture tour —he would be entertained and fêted everywhere by the cultured rich, for the appreciation which Stockton had started by his modest little essay had grown to the dimension of a fad.

He looked again at the telegram which had shattered the simple routine of his unassuming life. "On board Celtic dock this afternoon three o'clock hope see you. Verne." He sneezed sharply, as was his unconscious habit when nervous. In desperation he stopped at a veterinary's office on Frankfort Street, and left orders to have the doctor's assistant call for Lorna Doone and take her away, to be kept until sent for. Then he called at a wine merchant's and bought three bottles of claret of a moderate vintage. Verne had said something about claret in one of his playful letters. Unfortunately, the man's grandfather was a Frenchman, and undoubtedly he knew all about wines.

Stockton sneezed so loudly and so often at his desk that morning that all his associates knew something was amiss. The Sunday editor, who had planned to borrow fifty cents from him at lunch time, refrained from doing so, in a spirit of pure Christian brotherhood. Even Bob Bolles.

the hundred-and-fifty-dollar-a-week conductor of
"The Electric Chair," the paper's humorous
column, came in to see what was up. Bob's
"contribs" had been generous that morning, and
he was in unusually good humour for a humourist.

"What's the matter, Stock," he inquired genially, "Got a cold? Or has George Moore sent in
a new novel?"

Stockton looked up sadly from the proofs he was
correcting. How could he confess his paltry problem to this debonair creature who wore life lightly,
like a flower, and played at literature as he played
tennis, with swerve and speed? Bolles was a
bachelor, the author of a successful comedy, and
a member of the smart literary club which was
over the reviewer's horizon, although in the great
ocean of letters the humourist was no more than a
surf bather. Stockton shook his head. No one
but a married man and an unsuccessful author
could understand his trouble.

"A touch of asthma," he fibbed shyly. "I
always have it at this time of year."

"Come and have some lunch," said the other.
"We'll go up to the club and have some ale.
That'll put you on your feet."

"Thanks, ever so much," said Stockton, "but
I can't do it to-day. Got to make up my page.
I tell you what, though——"

He hesitated, and flushed a little.

"Say it," said Bolles kindly.

"Verne is in town to-day; the English poet, you know. Grandson of old Jules Verne. I'm going to put him up at my house. I wish you'd take him around to the club for lunch some day while he's here. He ought to meet some of the men there. I've been corresponding with him for a long time, and I—I'm afraid I rather promised to take him round there, as though I were a member, you know."

"Great snakes!" cried Bolles. "Verne? the author of 'Candle Light'? And you're going to put him up? You lucky devil. Why, the man's bigger than Masefield. Take him to lunch—I should say I will! Why, I'll put him in the col-yum. Both of you come round there to-morrow and we'll have an orgy. I'll order larks' tongues and convolvulus salad. I didn't know you knew him."

"I don't—yet," said Stockton. "I'm going down to meet his steamer this afternoon."

"Well, that's great news," said the volatile humourist. And he ran downstairs to buy the book of which he had so often heard but had never read.

The sight of Bolles' well-cut suit of tweeds had reminded Stockton that he was still wearing the threadbare serge that had done duty for three winters, and would hardly suffice for the honours to come. Hastily he blue-pencilled his proofs, threw them into the wire basket, and hurried outdoors to seek the nearest tailor. He stopped at the bank first, to draw out fifty dollars for emergencies. Then he entered the first clothier's shop he encountered on Nassau Street.

Mr. Stockton was a nervous man, especially so in the crises when he was compelled to buy anything so important as a suit, for usually Mrs. Stockton supervised the selection. To-day his unlucky star was in the zenith. His watch pointed to close on two o'clock, and he was afraid he might be late for the steamer, which docked far uptown. In his haste, and governed perhaps by some subconscious recollection of the humourist's attractive shaggy tweeds, he allowed himself to be fitted with an ochre-coloured suit of some fleecy checked material grotesquely improper for his unassuming figure. It was the kind of cloth and cut that one sees only in the windows of Nassau Street. Happily he was unaware of the enormity of his offence against society, and rapidly transferring his belongings to the new pockets, he paid down the purchase price and fled to the subway.

When he reached the pier at the foot of Fourteenth Street he saw that the steamer was still in midstream and it would be several minutes before she warped in to the dock. He had no pass from the steamship office, but on showing his news-paperman's card the official admitted him to the pier, and he took his stand at the first cabin gangway, trembling a little with nervousness, but with a pleasant feeling of excitement no less. He gazed at the others waiting for arriving travellers and wondered whether any of the peers of American letters had come to meet the poet. A stoutish, neatly dressed gentleman with a gray moustache looked like Mr. Howells, and he thrilled again. It was hardly possible that he, the obscure reviewer, was the only one who had been notified of Verne's arrival. That tall, hawk-faced man whose limousine was purring outside must be a certain publisher he knew by sight.

What would these gentlemen say when they learned that the poet was to stay with Kenneth Stockton, in New Utrecht? He rolled up the mustard-coloured trousers one more round—they were much too long for him—and watched the great hull slide along the side of the pier with a peculiar tingling shudder that he had not felt since the day of his wedding.

He expected no difficulty in recognizing Fins-bury Verne, for he was very familiar with his photograph. As the passengers poured down the slanting gangway, all bearing the unmistakable air and stamp of superiority that marks those who have just left the sacred soil of England, he scanned the faces with an eye of keen regard. To his surprise he saw the gentlemen he had marked respectively as Mr. Howells and the publisher greet people who had not the slightest resemblance to the poet, and go with them to the customs alcoves. Traveller after traveller hurried past him, followed by stewards carrying luggage; gradually the flow of people thinned, and then stopped altogether, save for one or two invalids who were being helped down the incline by nurses. And still no sign of Finsbury Verne.

Suddenly a thought struck him. Was it possible that—the second class? His eye brightened and he hurried to the gangway, fifty yards farther down the pier, where the second-cabin passengers were disembarking.

There were more of the latter, and the passage-way was still thronged. Just as Stockton reached the foot of the plank a little man in green ulster and deerstalker cap, followed by a plump little woman and four children in single file, each holding fast to the one in front like Alpine climbers, came down the narrow bridge, taking almost ludicrous care not to slip on the cleated boards.

To his amazement the reviewer recognized the dark beard and soulful eyes of the poet.

Mr. Verne clutched in rigid arms, not a roll of manuscripts, but a wriggling French poodle, whose tufted tail waved under the poet's chin. The lady behind him, evidently his wife, as she clung steadfastly to the skirt of his ulster, held tightly in the other hand a large glass jar in which two agitated goldfish were swimming, while the four children watched their parents with anxious eyes for the safety of their pets. "Daddy, look out for Ink!" shrilled one of them, as the struggles of the poodle very nearly sent him into the water under the ship's side. Two smiling stewards with mountainous portmanteaux followed the party. "Mother, are Castor and Pollux all right?" cried the smallest child, and promptly fell on his nose on the gangway, disrupting the file.

Stockton, with characteristic delicacy, refrained from making himself known until the Vernes had recovered from the embarrassments of leaving the ship. He followed them at a distance to the "V" section where they waited for the customs examination. With mingled feelings he saw that Finsbury Verne was no cloud-walking deity, but one even as himself, indifferently clad, shy and perplexed of eye, worried with the comic cares of a family man. All his heart warmed toward the poet, who stood in his bulging greatcoat, perspiring and aghast at the uproar around him. He shrank from imagining what might happen when he appeared at home with the whole family, but without hesitation he approached and introduced himself.

Verne's eyes shone with unaffected pleasure at the meeting, and he presented the reviewer to his wife and the children, two boys and two girls. The two boys, aged about ten and eight, immediately uttered cryptic remarks which Stockton judged were addressed to him.

"Castorian!" cried the larger boy, looking at the yellow suit.

"Polluxite!" piped the other in the same breath.

Mrs. Verne, in some embarrassment, explained that the boys were in the throes of a new game they had invented on the voyage. They had created two imaginary countries, named in honour of the goldfish, and it was now their whim to claim for their respective countries any person or thing that struck their fancy. "Castoria was first," said Mrs. Verne, "so you must consider yourself a citizen of that nation."

Somewhat shamefaced at this sudden honour, Mr. Stockton turned to the poet. "You're all coming home with me, aren't you?" he said. "I got your telegram this morning. We'd be delighted to have you."

"It's awfully good of you," said the poet, "but as a matter of fact we're going straight on to the country to-morrow morning. My wife has some relatives in Yonkers, wherever they are, and she and the children are going to stay with them. I've got to go up to Harvard to give some lectures."

A rush of cool, sweet relief bathed Stockton's brow.

"Why, I'm disappointed you're going right on," he stammered. "Mrs. Stockton and I were hoping——"

"My dear fellow, we could never impose such a party on your hospitality," said Verne. "Perhaps you can recommend us to some quiet hotel where we can stay the night."

Like all New Yorkers, Stockton could hardly think of the name of any hotel when asked suddenly. At first he said the Astor House, and then remembered that it had been demolished years before. At last he recollected that a brother of his from Indiana had once stayed at the Obelisk.

After the customs formalities were over—not without embarrassment, as Mr. Verne's valise when opened displayed several pairs of bright red union suits and a half-empty bottle of brandy—Stockton convoyed them to a taxi. Noticing the frayed sleeve of the poet's ulster he felt quite ashamed of the aggressive newness of his clothes. And when the visitors whirled away, after renewed promises for a meeting a little later in the spring, he stood for a moment in a kind of daze. Then he hurried toward the nearest telephone booth.

As the Vernes sat at dinner that night in the Abyssinian Room of the Obelisk Hotel, the poet said to his wife: "It would have been delightful to spend a few days with the Stocktons."

"My dear," said she, "I wouldn't have these wealthy Americans see how shabby we are for anything. The children are positively in rags, and your clothes—well, I don't know what they'll think at Harvard. You know if this lecture trip doesn't turn out well we shall be simply bankrupt."

The poet sighed. "I believe Stockton has quite a charming place in the country near New York," he said.

"That may be so," said Mrs. Verne. "But did you ever see such clothes? He looked like a canary."

DON MARQUIS

THERE is nothing more pathetic than the case of the author who is the victim of a supposedly critical essay. You hold him in the hollow of your hand. You may praise him for his humour when he wants to be considered a serious and saturnine dog. You may extol his songs of war and passion when he yearns to be esteemed a light, jovial merryandrew with never a care in the world save the cellar plumbing. You may utterly misrepresent him, and hang some albatross round his neck that will be offensive to him forever. You may say that he hails from Brooklyn Heights when the fact is that he left there two years ago and now lives in Port Washington. You may even (for instance) call him stout. . . .

Don Marquis was born in 1878; reckoning by tens, '88, '98, '08—well, call it forty. He is burly, ruddy, gray-haired, and fond of corn-cob pipes, dark beer, and sausages. He looks a careful blend of Falstaff and Napoleon III. He has conducted the Sun Dial in the New York *Evening Sun* since 1912. He stands out as one of the most penetrating satirists and resonant scoffers at folderol that this continent nourishes. He is far more than a colyumist: he is a poet—a kind of Meredithian Prometheus chained to the roar and clank of a Hoe press. He is a novelist of Stocktonian gifts, although unfortunately for us he writes the first half of a novel easier than the second. And I think that in his secret heart and at the bottom of the old haircloth round-top trunk he is a dramatist.

He good-naturedly deprecates that people praise "Archy the Vers Libre Cockroach" and clamour for more; while "Hermione," a careful and cutting satire on the follies of pseudokultur near the Dewey Arch, elicits only "a mild, mild smile." As he puts it:

A chair broke down in the midst of a Bernard Shaw comedy the other evening. Everybody laughed. They had been laughing before from time to time. That was because it was a Shaw comedy. But when the chair broke they roared. We don't blame them for roaring, but it makes us sad.

The purveyor of intellectual highbrow wit and humour pours his soul into the business of capturing a few refined, appreciative grins in the course of a lifetime, grins that come from the brain; he is more than happy if once or twice in a generation he can get a cerebral chuckle—and then Old Boob Nature steps in and breaks a chair or flings a fat man down on the ice and the world laughs with all its heart and soul.

Don Marquis recognizes as well as any one the value of the slapstick as a mirth-provoking instrument. (All hail to the slapstick! it was well known at the Mermaid Tavern, we'll warrant.) But he prefers the rapier. Probably his Savage Portraits, splendidly truculent and slashing sonnets, are among the finest pieces he has done.

The most honourable feature of Marquis's writing, the "small thing to look for but the big thing to find," is its quality of fine workmanship. The swamis and prophets of piffle, the Bhandranaths and Fothergill Finches whom he detests, can only create in an atmosphere specially warmed, purged and rose-watered for their moods. Marquis has emerged from the underworld of newspaper print just by his heroic ability to transform the commonest things into tools for his craft. Much of his best and subtlest work has been clacked out on a typewriter standing on an upturned packing box. (When the *American Magazine* published a picture of him at work on his packing case the supply man of the *Sun* got worried, and gave him a regular desk.) Newspaper men are a hardy race. Who but a man inured to the squalour of a newspaper office would dream of a cockroach as a hero? Archy was born in the old *Sun* building, now demolished, once known as Vermin Castle.

"Publishing a volume of verse," Don has plaintively observed, "is like dropping a rose-petal down the Grand Canyon and waiting to hear the echo." Yet if the petal be authentic rose, the answer will surely come. Some poets seek to raft oblivion by putting on frock coats and reading their works aloud to the women's clubs. Don Marquis has no taste for that sort of mummery. But little by little his potent, yeasty verses, fashioned from the roaring loom of every day, are winning their way into circulation. Any reader who went to *Dreams and Dust* (poems, published October, 1915) expecting to find light and waggish laughter, was on a blind quest. In that book speaks the hungry and visionary soul of this man, quick to see beauty and grace in common things, quick to question the answerless face of life—

> Still mounts the dream on shining pinion,
>   Still broods the dull distrust;
> Which shall have ultimate dominion,
>   Dream, or dust?

Heavy men are light on their feet: it takes stout poets to write nimble verses (Mr. Chesterton, for instance). Don Marquis has something of Dob-sonian cunning to set his musings to delicate, aus-tere music. He can turn a rondeau or a triolet as gracefully as a paying teller can roll **Durham** cigarettes.

How neat this is:

TO A DANCING DOLL

Formal, quaint, precise, and trim,
    You begin your steps demurely—
There's a spirit almost prim
    In the feet that move so surely.
So discreetly, to the chime
Of the music that so sweetly
    Marks the time.

But the chords begin to tinkle
        Quicker,
And your feet they flash and flicker—
        Twinkle!—
Flash and flutter to a tricksy
        Fickle meter;
And you foot it like a pixie—
        Only fleeter!

Not our current, dowdy
        Things—
"Turkey trots" and rowdy
        Flings—
For they made you overseas
In politer times than these
In an age when grace could please,
        Ere St. Vitus
Clutched and shook us, spine and knees;
Loosed a plague of jerks to smite us!

But Marquis is more than the arbiter of dainty elegances in rhyme: he sings and celebrates a robust world where men struggle upward from the slime and discontent leaps from star to star. The evolutionary theme is a favourite with him: the grand pageant of humanity groping from Piltdown to Beacon Hill, winning in a million years two precarious inches of forehead. Much more often than F. P. A., who used to be his brother colyumist in Manhattan, he dares to disclose the real earnestness that underlies his chaff.

I suppose that the conductor of a daily humorous column stands in the hierarchy of unthanked labourers somewhere between a plumber and a submarine trawler. Most of the available wheezes were pulled long ago by Plato in the *Republic* (not the *New Republic*) or by Samuel Butler in his Notebooks. Contribs come valiantly to hand with a barrowful of letters every day—("The ravings fed him" as Don captioned some contrib's quip about Simeon Stylites living on a column); but nevertheless the direct and alternating current must be turned on six times a week. His jocular exposal of the colyumist's trade secret compares it to the boarding-house keeper's rotation of crops:

MONDAY. Take up an idea in a serious way. (ROAST BEEF.)
TUESDAY. Some one writes us a letter about Monday's serious idea. (COLD ROAST BEEF.)

WEDNESDAY.   Josh the idea we took up seriously on Monday.
(BEEF STEW.)

THURSDAY.   Some one takes issue with us for Wednesday's
josh of Monday's serious idea.   (BEEFSTEAK PIE.)

FRIDAY.   We become a little pensive about our Wednesday's
josh of Monday's serious idea—there creeps into our copy
a more subdued, sensible note, as if we were acknowledging
that after all, the main business of life is not mere hare-
brained word-play.   (HASH OR CROQUETTES WITH GREEN
PEPPERS.)

SATURDAY.   Spoof the whole thing again, especially spoofing
ourself for having ever taken it seriously.   (BEEF SOUP
WITH BARLEY IN IT.)

SUNDAY.   There isn't any evening paper on Sunday.   That
is where we have the advantage of the boarding-house
keepers.

But the beauty of Don's cuisine is that the
beef soup with barley always tastes as good as, or
even better than, the original roast.   His dry
battery has generated in the past few years a
dozen features with real voltage—the Savage
Portraits, Hermione, Archy the Vers Libre Cockroach, the Aptronymic Scouts, French Without a
Struggle, Suggestions to Popular Song Writers,
Our Own Wall Mottoes, and the sequence of
Prefaces (to an Almanac, a Mileage Book, The
Plays of Euripides, a Diary, a Book of Fishhooks,
etc.).   Some of Marquis's most admirable and
delicious fooling has been poured into these Pref-

aces: I hope that he will put them between book-covers.

One day I got a letter from a big engineering firm in Ohio, enclosing a number of pay-envelopes (empty). They wanted me to examine the aphorisms and orisonswettmardenisms they had been printing on their weekly envelopes, for the inspiration and peptonizing of their employees. They had been using quotations from Emerson, McAdoo, and other panhellenists, and had run out of "sentiments." They wanted suggestions as to where they could find more.

I advised them to get in touch with Don Marquis. I don't know whether they did so or not; but Don's epigrams and bon mots would adorn any pay-envelope anthology. Some of his casual comments on whiskey would do more to discourage the decanterbury pilgrims than a bushel of tracts.

By the time a bartender knows what drink a man will have before he orders, there is little else about him worth knowing.

If you go to sleep while you are loafing, how are you going to know you are loafing?

Because majorities are often wrong it does not follow that minorities are always right.

Young man, if she asks you if you like her hair that way, beware. The woman has already committed matrimony in her own heart.

I am tired of being a promising young man. I've been a promising young man for twenty years.

In most of Don Marquis's japes, a still small voice speaks in the mirthquake:

If you try too hard to get a thing, you don't get it.

If you sweat and strain and worry the other ace will not come—the little ball will not settle upon the right number or the proper colour—the girl will marry the other man—the public will cry, Bedamned to him! he can't write anyhow!—the cosmos will refuse its revelations of divinity—the Welsh rabbit will be stringy—you will find there are not enough rhymes in the language to finish your ballade—the primrose by the river's brim will be only a hayfever carrier—and your fountain pen will dribble ink upon your best trousers.

But Don Marquis's mind has two yolks (to use one of his favourite denunciations). In addition to these comic or satiric shadows, the gnomon of his Sun Dial may be relied on every now and then to register a clear-cut notation of the national mind and heart. For instance this, just after the United States severed diplomatic relations with Germany:

This Beast we know, whom time brings to his last rebirth
Bull-thewed, iron-boned, cold-eyed and strong as Earth. . .
As Earth, who spawned and lessoned him,
Yielded her earthy secrets, gave him girth,
Armoured the skull and braced the heavy limb—
Who frowned above him, proud and grim,
While he sucked from her salty dugs the lore
Of fire and steel and stone and war:
She taught brute facts, brute might, but not the worth

Of spirit, honour and clean mirth . . . .
His shape is Man, his mood is Dinosaur.

Up from the wild red Welter of the past
Foaming he comes: let this rush be his last.

Too patient we have been, thou knowest, God, thou knowest.
We have been slow as doom. Our dead
Of yesteryear lie on the ocean's bed—
We have denied each pleading ghost—
We have been slow: God, make us sure.
We have been slow. Grant we endure
Unto the uttermost, the uttermost.

Did our slow mood, O God, with thine accord?
Then weld our diverse millions, Lord,
Into one single swinging sword.

I have been combing over the files of the Sun
Dial, and it is disheartening to see these deposits
of pearl and pie-crust, this sediment of fine mind,
buried full fathom five in the yellowing archives
of a newspaper. I thought of De Quincey's famous utterance about the press:

Worlds of fine thinking lie buried in that vast abyss, never
to be disentombed or restored to human admiration. Like
the sea, it has swallowed treasures without end, that no
diving-bell will bring up again.

Greatly as we cherish the Sun Dial, we are
jealous of it for sapping all its author's time and

calories. No writer in America has greater or more meaty, stalwart gifts. Don, we cry, spend less time stoking that furnace out in Port Washington, and more on your novels!

There is no more convincing proof of the success of the Sun Dial than the roster of its contributors. Some of the most beautiful lyrics of the past few years have been printed there (I think particularly of two or three by Padraic Colum). In this ephemeral column of a daily newspaper some of the rarest singers and keenest wits of the time have been glad to exhibit their wares, without pay of course. It would be impossible to give a complete list, but among them are William Rose Benét, Clinton Scollard, Edith M. Thomas, Benjamin De Casseres, Gelett Burgess, Georgia Pangborn, Charles Hanson Towne, Clement Wood.

But the tragedy of the colyumist's task is that the better he does it the harder it becomes. People simply will not leave him alone. All day long they drop into his office, or call him up on the phone in the hope of getting into the column. Poor Don! he has become an institution down on Nassau Street: whatever hour of the day you call, you will find his queue there chivvying him. He is too gracious to throw them out: his only expedient is to take them over to the gin cathedral across the street and buy them a drink. Lately

the poor wretch has had to write his Dial out in
the pampas of Long Island, bringing it in with him
in the afternoon, in order to get it done undis-
turbed. How many times I have sworn never to
bother him again! And yet, when one is passing
in that neighbourhood, the temptation is irresistible. . . . I dare say Ben Jonson had the
same trouble. Of course someone ought to en-
dow Don and set him permanently at the head
of a chophouse table, presiding over a kind of
Mermaid coterie of robust wits. He is a master
of the tavernacular.

He is a versatile cove. Philosopher, satirist,
burlesquer, poet, critic, and novelist. Perhaps the
three critics in this country whose praise is best
worth having, and least easy to win, would be
Marquis, Strunsky, and O. W. Firkins. And I
think that the three leading poets male in this
country to-day are Marquis, William Rose Benét,
and (perhaps) Vachel Lindsay. Of course Don
Marquis has an immense advantage over Will
Benét in his stoutness. Will had to feed up on
honey and candied apricocks and mares' milk for
months before they would admit him to the army.

Hermione and her little group of "Serious
Thinkers" have attained the dignity of book
publication, and now stand on the shelf beside
"Danny's Own Story" and "The Cruise of the

Jasper B." This satire on the azure-pedalled
coteries of Washington Square has perhaps
received more publicity than any other of Marquis's writings, but of all Don's drolleries I reserve
my chief affection for Archy. The cockroach, en-
dowed by some freak of transmigration with the
shining soul of a vers libre poet, is a thoroughly
Marquisian whimsy. I make no apology for quoting this prince of blattidae at some length. Many
a commuter, opening his evening paper on the
train, looks first of all to see if Archy
is in the Dial. I love Archy because
there seems to me something thoroughly racial
and native and American about him. Can you
imagine him, for instance, in *Punch?* His author
has never told us which one of the vers libre poets
it is whose soul has emigrated into Archy, but I
feel sure it is not Ezra Pound or any of the expatriated eccentrics who lisp in odd numbers in the
King's Road, Chelsea. Could it be Amy Lowell?
Perhaps it should be explained that Archy's
carelessness as to punctuation and capitals is not,
mere ostentation, but arises from the fact that he
is not strong enough to work the shift key of his
typewriter. Ingenious readers of the Sun Dial
have suggested many devices to make this possible, but none that seem feasible to the roach
himself.

The Argument: Archy, the vers libre cockroach, overhears a person with whiskers and dressed in the uniform of a butler in the British Navy, ask a German waiter if the pork pie is built. Ja, Ja, replies the waiter. Archy's suspicions are awakened, and he climbs into the pork pie through an air hole, and prepares his soul for parlous times. The naval butler takes the pie on board a launch, and Archy, watching through one of the portholes of the pastry, sees that they are picked up by a British cruiser "an inch or two outside the three-mile line." (This was in neutral days, remember.) Archy continues the narrative, in lower case agate:

it is cuthbert with the pork pie the captain has been longing for said a voice and on every side
rang shouts of the pie the pie the captains pie has come at last and a salute of nineteen
guns was fired the pie was carried at once to the
captains mess room where the captain a grizzled veteran sat with
knife and fork in hand and serviette tucked
under his chin i knew cried the captain that if there was a
pork pie in america my faithful cuthbert would
find it for me the butler bowed and all the
ships officers pulled up their chairs to the
table with a rasping sound you may serve it honest
cuthbert said the captain impatiently and the butler broke a
hole in the top crust he touched a hidden mechanism for
immediately something right under me began to
go tick tock tick tock tick tock what is that noise captain said the larboard mate only the patent log

clicking off the knots said the butler it
it needs oiling again but
cuthbert said the captain why are you so
nervous and what means that flush upon your face
that flush your honor is chicken pox said cuthbert i am
subject to sudden attacks of it
unhand that pie cried the ships surgeon leaping to his feet
arrest that butler he is a teuton spy
that is not chicken pox at all it is german measles
ha ha cried the false butler the ship is doomed there is a clock work bomb in this pie my name
is not cuthbert it is friedrich and he leaped
through a port into the sea his blonde side whiskers
which were false falling off as he did so
ha ha rang his
mocking laughter from the ocean as he pulled shoreward with
long strokes your ship is doomed my god said the
senior boatswain what shall we do stop the
clock ordered the captain but i had already done so i

braced my head against the hour hand and my feet against the minute hand and stopped the mechanism the captain drew his sword and pried off all the top crust gentlemen he said yonder cockroach has saved the ship let us throw the pie overboard and steam rapidly away from it advised the starboard ensign not so not so cried the captain yon gallant cockroach must not perish so gratitude is a tradition of the british navy i would sooner perish with him than desert him all the time the strain was getting worse on me if my feet slipped the clock would start again and all would be lost beads of sweat rolled down my forehead and almost blinded me something must be done quick said the first assistant captain the insect is losing his rigidity wait said the surgeon and gave me a hypodermic of some powerful east indian drug which stiffened me like a cataleptic but i could still see and hear for days and days a council of war was held about me every afternoon and wireless reports sent to london save the cockroach even if you lose the ship wirelessed the admiralty england must stand by the smaller nations and every hour the surgeon gave me another hypodermic at the end of four weeks the cabin boy who had been thinking deeply all the time suggested that a plug of wood be inserted in my place which was done and i fell to the deck well nigh exhausted the next day i was set on shore in the captains gig and here i am.

archy

So far as I know, America has made just two entirely original contributions to the world's types of literary and dramatic art. These are the humorous colyum and the burlesque show. The saline and robust repartee of the burlicue is ancient enough in essence, but it is compounded into a new and uniquely American mode, joyously flavoured with Broadway garlic. The newspaper colyum, too, is a native product. Whether Ben Franklin or Eugene Field invented it, it bears the image and superscription of America.

And using the word ephemeral in its strict sense, Don Marquis is unquestionably the cleverest of our ephemeral philosophers. This nation suffers a good deal from lack of humour in high places:

our Great Pachyderms have all Won their Way
to the Top by a Resolute Struggle. But Don
has just chuckled and gone on refusing to answer
letters or fill out Mr. Purinton's blasphemous
efficiency charts or join the Poetry Society or
attend community masques. And somehow all
these things seem to melt away, and you look
round the map and see Don Marquis taking up
all the scenery. . . . He has such an œcu-
menical kind of humour. It's just as true in
Brooklyn as it is in the Bronx.

He is at his best when he takes up some philosophic dilemma, or some quaint abstraction (viz.,
Certainty, Predestination, Idleness, Uxoricide, Pro-
hibition, Compromise, or Cornutation) and sets
the idea spinning. Beginning slowly, carelessly, in
a deceptive, offhand manner, he lets the toy revolve
as it will. Gradually the rotation accelerates;
faster and faster he twirls the thought (sometimes
losing a few spectators whose centripetal powers
are not stanch enough) until, chuckling, he holds
up the flashing, shimmering conceit, whirling
at top speed and ejaculating sparks. What is so
beautiful as a rapidly revolving idea? Marquis's
mind is like a gyroscope: the faster it spins, the
steadier it is. There are laws of dynamics in
colyums just as anywhere else.

What is there in the nipping air of Galesburg,

Illinois, that turns the young sciolists of Knox College toward the rarefied ethers of literature? S. S. McClure, John Phillips, Ralph Waldo Trine, Don Marquis—are there other Knox men in the game, too? Marquis was studying at Galesburg about the time of the Spanish War. He has worked on half a dozen newspapers, and assisted Joel Chandler Harris in editing "Uncle Remus's Magazine." But let him tell his biography in his own words:

Born July 29, 1878, at Walnut, Bureau Co., Ill., a member of the Republican party.

My father was a physician, and I had all the diseases of the time and place free of charge.

Nothing further happened to me until, in the summer of 1896, I left the Republican party to follow the Peerless Leader to defeat.

In 1900 I returned to the Republican party to accept a position in the Census Bureau, at Washington, D. C. This position I filled for some months in a way highly satisfactory to the Government in power. It is particularly gratifying to me to remember that one evening, after I had worked unusually hard at the Census Office, the late President McKinley himself nodded and smiled to me as I passed through the White House grounds on my way home from toil. He had heard of my work that day, I had no doubt, and this was his way of showing me how greatly he appreciated it.

Nevertheless, shortly after President McKinley paid this public tribute to the honesty, efficiency and importance of my work in the Census Office, I left the Republican party again, and accepted a position as reporter on a Washington paper.

Upon entering the newspaper business all the troubles of my earlier years disappeared as if by magic, and I have lived the contented, peaceful, unworried life of the average newspaper man ever since.

There is little more to tell. In 1916 I again returned to the Republican party. This time it was for the express purpose of voting against Mr. Wilson. Then Mr. Hughes was nominated, and I left the Republican party again.

This is the outline of my life in its relation to the times in which I live. For the benefit of those whose curiosity extends to more particular details, I add a careful pen-picture of myself.

It seems more modest, somehow, to put it in the third person:

Height, 5 feet 10½ inches; hair, dove-coloured; scar on little finger of left hand; has assured carriage, walking boldly into good-hotels and mixing with patrons on terms of equality; weight, 200 pounds; face slightly asymmetrical, but not definitely criminal in type; loathes Japanese art, but likes beefsteak and onions; wears No. 8 shoe; fond of Francis Thompson's poems; inside seam of trousers, 32 inches; imitates cats, dogs and barnyard animals for the amusement of young children; eyetooth in right side of upper jaw missing; has always been careful to keep thumb prints from possession of police; chest measurement, 42 inches, varying with respiration; sometimes wears glasses, but usually operates undisguised; dislikes the works of Rabindranath Tagore; corn on little toe of right foot; superstitious, especially with regard to psychic phenomena; eyes, blue; does not use drugs nor read his verses to women's clubs; ruddy complexion; no photograph in possession of police; garrulous and argumen-

tative; prominent cheek bones; avoids Bohemian society,
so-called, and has never been in a thieves' kitchen, a broker's
office nor a class of short-story writing; wears 17-inch collar;
waist measurement none of your business; favourite disease,
hypochondria; prefers the society of painters, actors, writers,
architects, preachers, sculptors, publishers, editors, musicians, among whom he often succeeds in insinuating himself, avoiding association with crooks and reformers as
much as possible; walks with rapid gait; mark of old fracture
on right shin; cuffs on trousers, and coat cut loose, with
plenty of room under the arm pits; two hip pockets; dislikes
Rochefort cheese, "Tom Jones," Wordsworth's poetry,
absinthe cocktails, most musical comedy, public banquets,
physical exercise, Billy Sunday, steam heat, toy dogs, poets
who wear their souls outside, organized charity, magazine
covers, and the gas company; prominent callouses on two
fingers of right hand prevent him being expert pistol shot;
belt straps on trousers; long upper lip; clean shaven; shaggy
eyebrows; affects soft hats; smile, one-sided; no gold fillings
in teeth; has served six years of indeterminate sentence in
Brooklyn, with no attempt to escape, but is reported to
have friends outside; voice, husky; scar above the forehead
concealed by hair; commonly wears plain gold ring on little
finger of left hand; dislikes prunes, tramp poets and imita-
tions of Kipling; trousers cut loose over hips and seat ; would
likely come along quietly if arrested.

I would fail utterly in this rambling anatomy
if I did not insist that Don Marquis regards his
column not merely as a soapslide but rather as a
cudgelling ground for sham and hypocrisy. He
has something of the quick Stevensonian instinct

for the moral issue, and the Devil not infrequently winces about the time the noon edition of the *Evening Sun* comes from the press. There is no man quicker to bonnet a fallacy or drop the acid just where it will disinfect. For instance, this comment on some bolshevictory in Russia:

> A kind word was recently seen, on one of the principal streets of Petrograd, attempting to butter a parsnip.

For the plain man who shies at surplice and stole, the Sun Dial is a very real pulpit, whence, amid excellent banter, he hears much that is purging and cathartic in a high degree. The laughter of fat men is a ringing noble music, and Don Marquis, like Friar Tuck, deals texts and fisticuffs impartially. What an archbishop of Canterbury he would have made! He is a burly and bonny dominie, and his congregation rarely miss the point of the sermon. We cannot close better than by quoting part of his Colyumist's Prayer in which he admits us somewhere near the pulse of the machine:

> I pray Thee, make my colyum read,
> And give me thus my daily bread.
> Endow me, if Thou grant me wit,
> Likewise with sense to mellow it.
> Save me from feeling so much hate
> My food will not assimilate;

Open mine eyes that I may see
Thy world with more of charity,
And lesson me in good intents
And make me friend of innocence. . . .
Make me (sometimes at least) discreet;
Help me to hide my self-conceit,
And give me courage now and then
To be as dull as are most men.
And give me readers quick to see
When I am satirizing Me. . . .
Grant that my virtues may atone
For some small vices of mine own.

And it is thoroughly characteristic of Don
Marquis that he follows his prayer with this
comment:

People, when they pray, usually pray not for what they
really want—and intend to have if they can get it—but for
what they think the Creator wants them to want. We made
a certain attempt to be sincere in the above verses; but even
at that no doubt a lot of affectation crept in.

THE ART OF WALKING

Away with the stupid adage about a man being as old as his
    arteries!
He is as old as his calves—his garteries. . . .
                        —*Meditations of Andrew McGill.*

T HERE was fine walking on the hills in the
        direction of the sea."
        This heart-stirring statement, which I
find in an account of the life of William and
Dorothy Wordsworth when they inhabited a
quiet cottage near Crewkerne in Dorset, reminds
me how often the word "walking" occurs in any
description of Wordsworth's existence. De
Quincey assures us that the poet's props were very
ill shapen—"they were pointedly condemned by
all female connoisseurs in legs"—but none the less
he was *princeps arte ambulandi.* Even had he
lived to-day, when all our roads are barbarized by
exploding gasoline vapours, I do not think Wordsworth would have flivvered. Of him the Opium
Eater made the classic pronouncement: "I cal-
culate that with these identical legs W. must have
traversed a distance of 175,000 to 180,000 English

miles—a mode of exertion which, to him, stood
in the stead of alcohol and all other stimulants
whatsoever to the animal spirits; to which,
indeed, he was indebted for a life of unclouded
happiness, and we for much of what is most excellent in his writings."

A book that says anything about walking has
a ready passage to my inmost heart. The best
books are always those that set down with "amor-
ous precision" the satisfying details of human
pilgrimage. How one sympathizes with poor
Pepys in his outburst (April 30, 1663) about a
gentleman who seems to have been "Always
Taking the Joy Out of Life":

Lord! what a stir Stankes makes, with his being crowded
in the streets, and wearied in walking in London, and would
not be wooed to go to a play, nor to Whitehall, or to see the
lions, though he was carried in a coach. I never could have
thought there had been upon earth a man so little curious in
the world as he is.

Now your true walker is mightily "curious in
the world," and he goes upon his way zealous to
sate himself with a thousand quaintnesses. When
he writes a book he fills it full of food, drink,
tobacco, the scent of sawmills on sunny afternoons, and arrivals at inns late at night. He
writes what Mr. Mosher calls a book-a-bosom.

Diaries and letters are often best of all because
they abound in these matters. And because walking can never again be what it was—the motor-
cars will see to that—it is our duty to pay it
greater reverence and honour.

Wordsworth and Coleridge come first to mind
in any talk about walking. The first time they
met was in 1797 when Coleridge tramped from
Nether Stowey to Racedown (thirty miles in an
air-line, and full forty by road) to make the
acquaintance of William and Dorothy. That is
practically from the Bristol Channel to the English ditto, a rousing stretch. It was Wordsworth's pamphlet describing a walk across France
to the Alps that spurred Coleridge on to this
expedition. The trio became fast friends, and
William and Dorothy moved to Alfoxden (near
Nether Stowey) to enjoy the companionship.
What one would give for some adequate account
of their walks and talks together over the
Quantocks. They planned a little walking trip
into Devonshire that autumn (1797) and "The
Ancient Mariner" was written in the hope of de-
fraying the expenses of the adventure.

De Quincey himself, who tells us so much
jovial gossip about Wordsworth and Coleridge,
was no mean pedestrian. He describes a forty-
mile all-night walk from Bridgewater to Bristol,

on the evening after first meeting Coleridge. He
could not sleep after the intellectual excitement
of the day, and through a summer night "divinely
calm" he busied himself with meditation on the
sad spectacle he had witnessed: a great mind
hastening to decay.

I have always fancied that walking as a fine
art was not much practised before the eighteenth
century. We know from Ambassador Jusserand's
famous book how many wayfarers were on the
roads in the fourteenth century, but none of these
were abroad for the pleasures of moving meditation and scenery. We can gather from Mr.
Tristram's "Coaching Days and Coaching Ways"
that the highroads were by no means safe for
solitary travellers even so late as 1750. In
"Joseph Andrews" (1742) whenever any of the
characters proceed afoot they are almost certain
to be held up. Mr. Isaac Walton, it is true, was a
considerable rambler a century earlier than this,
and in his Derbyshire hills must have passed many
lonely gullies; but footpads were more likely to
ambush the main roads. It would be a hard-
hearted bandit who would despoil the gentle
angler of his basket of trouts. Goldsmith, too,
was a lusty walker, and tramped it over the Continent for two years (1754-6) with little more
baggage than a flute: he might have written "The

Handy Guide for Beggars" long before Vachel Lindsay. But generally speaking, it is true that cross-country walks for the pure delight of rhythmically placing one foot before the other were rare before Wordsworth. I always think of him as one of the first to employ his legs as an instrument of philosophy.

After Wordsworth they come thick and fast. Hazlitt, of course—have you paid the tax that R.L.S. imposes on all who have not read Hazlitt's "On Going A Journey?" Then Keats: never was there more fruitful walk than the early morning stroll from Clerkenwell to the Poultry in October, 1816, that produced "Much have I travelled in the realms of gold." He must have set out early enough, for the manuscript of the sonnet was on Cowden Clarke's table by breakfast time. And by the way, did you know that the copy of Chapman's Homer which inspired it belonged to the financial editor of the *Times?* Never did financial editor live to better purpose!

There are many words of Keats that are a joyful viaticum for the walker: get these by rote in some membrane of memory:

The great Elements we know of are no mean comforters: the open sky sits upon our senses like a sapphire crown—the Air is our robe of state—the Earth is our throne, and the sea a mighty minstrel playing before it.

The Victorians were great walkers. Railways were but striplings; inns were at their prime. Hark to the great names in the walker's Hall of Fame: Tennyson, FitzGerald, Matthew Arnold, Carlyle, Kingsley, Meredith, Richard Jefferies. What walker can ever forget the day when he first read "The Story of My Heart?" In my case it was the 24th of August, 1912, on a train from London to Cambridge. Then there were George Borrow, Emily Brontë on her Yorkshire moors, and Leslie Stephen, one of the princes of the clan and founder of the famous Sunday Tramps of whom Meredith was one. Walt Whitman would have made a notable addition to that posse of philosophic walkers, save that I fear the garrulous half-baked old barbarian would have been disappointed that he could not dominate the conversation.

There have been stout walkers in our own day. Mr. W. H. Davies (the Super-Tramp), G. M. Trevelyan, Hilaire Belloc, Edward Thomas who died on the field of honour in April, 1917, and Francis Ledwidge, who was killed in Flanders. Who can forget his noble words, "I have taken up arms for the fields along the Boyne, for the birds and the blue sky over them." There is Walter Prichard Eaton, the Jefferies of our own Berkshires. One could extend the list almost without end. Sometimes it seems as though literature were a co-product of legs and head.

Charles Lamb and Leigh Hunt were great city ramblers, followed in due course by Dickens, R.L.S., Edward Lucas, Holbrook Jackson, and Pearsall Smith. Mr. Thomas Burke is another, whose "Nights in Town" will delight the lover of the greatest of all cities. But urban wanderings, delicious as they are, are not quite what we mean by walking. On pavements one goes by fit and start, halting to see, to hear, and to speculate. In the country one captures the true ecstasy of the long, unbroken swing, the harmonious glow of mind and body, eyes fed, soul feasted, brain and muscle exercised alike.

Meredith is perhaps the Supreme Pontiff of modern country walkers: no soft lover of drowsy golden weather, but master of the stiffer breed who salute frost and lashing rain and roaring southwest wind, who leap to grapple with the dissolving riddles of destiny. February and March are his months:

> For love we Earth, then serve we all;
>   Her mystic secret then is ours:
> We fall, or view our treasures fall,
>   Unclouded, as beholds her flowers.

> Earth, from a night of frosty wreck,
>   Enrobed in morning's mounted fire,

When lowly, with a broken neck,
The crocus lays her cheek to mire.

I suppose every walker collects a few precious
books which form the bible of his chosen art. I
have long been collecting a Walker's Breviary
of my own. It includes Stevenson's "Walking
Tours," G. M. Trevelyan's "Walking," Leslie
Stephen's "In Praise of Walking," shards and
crystals from all the others I have mentioned.
Michael Fairless, Vachel Lindsay, and Frank
Sidgwick have place in it. On my private shelf
stands "Journeys to Bagdad" by Mr. Charles
Brooks, who has good pleasantry to utter on this
topic; and a manly little volume, "Walking as
Education," by the Rev. A. N. Cooper, "the
walking parson," published in England in 1910.
On that same shelf there will soon stand a volume
of delicious essays by one of the most accomplished
of American walkers, Mr. Robert Cortes Holliday,
the American Belloc, whose "Walking Stick
Papers" has beckoned to the eye of a far-seeing
publisher. Mr. Holliday it is who has bravely
stated why so few of the fair sex are able to
participate in walking tours:

No one, though (this is the first article to be observed),
should ever go a journey with any other than him with whom
one walks arm in arm, in the evening, the twilight, and, talk-

ing (let us suppose) of men's given names, agrees that if either should have a son he shall be named after the other. Walking in the gathering dusk, two and two, since the world began, there have always been young men who have thus to one another plighted their troth. If one is not still one of these, then, in the sense here used, journeys are over for him. What is left to him of life he may enjoy, but not journeys. Mention should be made in passing that some have been found so ignorant of the nature of journeys as to suppose that they might be taken in company with members, or a member, of the other sex. Now, one who writes of journeys would cheerfully be burned at the stake before he would knowingly underestimate women. But it must be confessed that it is another season in the life of man that they fill.

They are too personal for the high enjoyment of going a journey. They must forever be thinking about you or about themselves; with them everything in the world is somehow tangled up in these matters; and when you are with them (you cannot help it, or if you could they would not allow it) you must forever be thinking about them or yourself. Nothing on either side can be seen detached. They cannot rise to that philosophic plane of mind which is the very marrow of going a journey. One reason for this is that they can never escape from the idea of society: You are in their society, they are in yours; and the multitudinous personal ties which connect you all to that great order called society that you have for a period got away from physically are present. Like the business man who goes on a vacation from his business and takes his business habits along with him, so on a journey they would bring society along, and all sort of etiquette.

He that goes a journey shakes off the trammels of the world; he has fled all impediments and inconveniences; he belongs, for the moment, to no time or place. He is neither rich nor poor, but in that which he thinks and sees. There is not such another Arcadia for this on earth as in going a journey. He that goes a journey escapes, for a breath of air, from all conventions; without which, though, of course, society would go to pot; and which are the very natural instinct of women.

Mr. Holliday has other goodly matter upon the philosophy and art of locomotion, and those who are wise and have a lively faith may be admitted to great and surpassing delights if they will here and now make memorandum to buy his book, which will soon be published.

Speaking of Vachel Lindsay, his "Handy Guide for Beggars" will bring an itch along the shanks of those who love shoe-leather and a knobbed stick. Vachel sets out for a walk in no mean and pettifogging spirit: he proceeds as an army with banners: he intends that the world shall know he is afoot: the Great Khan of Springfield is unleashed—let alewives and deacons tremble!

Ungenerous hosts have cozened Vachel by begging him to recite his poems at the beginning of each course, in the meantime getting on with their eating; but despite the naïveté of his eagerness to sing, there is a plain and manly simplicity about Vachel that delights us all. We like to know that here is a poet who has wrestled with poverty, who never wrote a Class Day poem at

Harvard, who has worn frayed collars or none at all, and who lets the barber shave the back of his neck. We like to know that he has tramped the ties in Georgia, harvested in Kansas, been fumigated in New Jersey, and lives contented in Illinois. Four weeks a year he lives as the darling of the cisalleghany Browning Societies, but he is always glad to get back to Springfield and resume his robes as the local Rabindranath. If he ever buys an automobile I am positive it will be a Ford. Here is *homo americanus*, one of ourselves, who never wore spats in his life.

But even the plain man may see visions. Walking on crowded city streets at night, watching the lighted windows, delicatessen shops, peanut carts, bakeries, fish stalls, free lunch counters piled with crackers and saloon cheese, and minor poets struggling home with the Saturday night marketing—he feels the thrill of being one, or at least two-thirds, with this various, grotesque, pathetic, and surprising humanity. The sense of fellowship with every other walking biped, the full-blooded understanding that Whitman and O. Henry knew in brimming measure, comes by gulps and twinges to almost all. That is the essence of Lindsay's feeling about life. He loves crowds, companionship, plenty of sirloin and onions, and seeing his name in print. He sings

and celebrates the great symbols of our hodge-
podge democracy: ice cream soda, electrical sky-
signs, Sunday School picnics, the movies, Mark
Twain.   In the teeming ooze and ocean bottoms
of our atlantic humanity he finds rich corals and
rainbow shells, hospitality, reverence, love, and
beauty.

This is the sentiment that makes a merry
pedestrian, and Vachel has scrutineered and scuf-
fled through a dozen states, lightening larders
and puzzling the worldly. Afoot and penniless
is his technique—"stopping when he had a mind
to, singing when he felt inclined to"—and begging his meals and bed. I suppose he has had
as many free meals as any American citizen; and
this is how he does it, copied from his little pamphlet used on many a road:

RHYMES TO BE TRADED FOR BREAD

Being new verses by Nicholas Vachel Lindsay, Springfield,
Illinois, June, 1912, printed expressly as a substitute for money.

This book is to be used in exchange for the necessities of
life on a tramp-journey from the author's home town, through
the West and back, during which he will observe the following
rules:

(1) Keep away from the cities.
(2) Keep away from the railroads.
(3) Have nothing to do with money.   Carry no baggage.
(4) Ask for dinner about quarter after eleven.

(5) Ask for supper, lodging, and breakfast about quarter of five.

(6) Travel alone.

(7) Be neat, truthful, civil, and on the square.

(8) Preach the Gospel of Beauty.

In order to carry out the last rule there will be three exceptions to the rule against baggage. (1) The author will carry a brief printed statement, called "The Gospel of Beauty." (2) He will carry this book of rhymes for distribution. (3) Also he will carry a small portfolio with pictures, etc., chosen to give an outline of his view of the history of art, especially as it applies to America.

Perhaps I have tarried too long over Vachel; but I have set down his theories of vagabonding because many walkers will find them interesting. "The Handy Guide for Beggars" will leave you footsore but better for the exercise. And when the fascinating story of American literature in this decade (1910-20) is finally written, there will be a happy and well-merited corner in it for a dusty but "neat, truthful, and civil" figure from Springfield, Illinois.

A good pipeful of prose to solace yourself withal, about sunset on a lonely road, is that passage on "Lying Awake at Night" to be found in "The Forest," by Stewart Edward White. Major White is one of the best friends the open-air walker has, and don't forget it!

The motors have done this for us at least, that

as they have made the highways their own beyond dispute, walking will remain the mystic
and private pleasure of the secret and humble few.
For us the byways, the footpaths, and the pas-
tures will be sanctified and sweet. Thank
heaven there are still gentle souls uncorrupted
by the victrola and the limousine. In our old
trousers and our easy shoes, with pipe and stick,
we can do our fifteen miles between lunch and
dinner, and glorify the ways of God to man.

And sometimes, about two o'clock of an afternoon (these spells come most often about half an
hour after lunch), the old angel of peregrination
lifts himself up in me, and I yearn and wamble for
a season afoot. When a blue air is moving
keenly through bare boughs this angel is most
vociferous. I gape wanly round the lofty citadel
where I am pretending to earn the Monday
afternoon envelope. The filing case, thermostat,
card index, typewriter, automatic telephone:
these ingenious anodynes avail me not. Even
the visits of golden nymphs, sweet ambassadors
of commerce, who rustle in and out of my room
with memoranda, mail, manuscripts, aye, even
these lightfoot figures fail to charm. And the
mind goes out to the endless vistas of streets,
roads, fields, and rivers that summon the wanderer
with laughing voice. Somewhere a great wind is

scouring the hillsides; and once upon a time a man set out along the Great North Road to walk to Royston in the rain. . . .

Grant us, O Zeus! the tingling tremour of thigh and shank that comes of a dozen sturdy miles laid underheel. Grant us "fine walking on the hills in the direction of the sea"; or a winding road that tumbles down to some Cotswold village. Let an inn parlour lie behind red curtains, and a table be drawn toward the fire. Let there be a loin of cold beef, an elbow of yellow cheese, a tankard of dog's nose. Then may we prop our Bacon's Essays against the pewter and study those mellow words: "Certainly it is heaven upon earth to have a man's mind move in charity, rest in providence, and turn upon the poles of truth." *Haec studia per-noctant nobiscum, peregrinantur, rusticantur.*

RUPERT BROOKE

RUPERT Brooke had the oldest pith of England in his fibre. He was born of East Anglia, the original vein of English blood. Ruddy skin, golden-brown hair, blue eyes, are the stamp of the Angles. Walsingham, in Norfolk, was the home of the family. His father was a master at Rugby; his grandfather a canon in the church.

In 1913 Heffer, the well-known bookseller and publisher of Cambridge, England, issued a little anthology called *Cambridge Poems 1900-1913*. This volume was my first introduction to Brooke. As an undergraduate at Oxford during the years 1910-13 I had heard of his work from time to time; but I think we youngsters at Oxford were too absorbed in our own small versemakings to watch very carefully what the "Tabs" were doing. His poem *The Old Vicarage, Grantchester*, reprinted in Heffer's *Cambridge Poems*, first fell under my eye during the winter of 1913-14.

Grantchester is a tiny hamlet just outside Cambridge; set in the meadows along the Cam or Granta (the earlier name), and next door to the Trump-

ington of Chaucer's "The Reeve's Tale." All
that Cambridge country is flat and comparatively
uninteresting; patchworked with chalky fields
bright with poppies; slow, shallow streams drifting
between pollard willows; it is the beginning of the
fen district, and from the brow of the Royston
downs (thirteen miles away) it lies as level as a
table-top with the great chapel of King's clear
against the sky. It is the favourite lament of
Cambridge men that their *"Umgebung"* is so dull
and monotonous compared with the rolling witch-
ery of Oxfordshire.

But to the young Cantab sitting over his beer at
the Café des Westens in Berlin, the Cambridge
villages seemed precious and fair indeed. Balanc-
ing between genuine homesickness for the green
pools of the Cam, and a humorous whim in his
rhymed comment on the outlying villages, Brooke
wrote the Grantchester poem; and probably
when the fleeting pang of nostalgia was over
enjoyed the evening in Berlin hugely. But the
verses are more than of merely passing interest.
To one who knows that neighbourhood the picture
is cannily vivid. To me it brings back with painful intensity the white winding road from Cambridge to Royston which I have bicycled hundreds
of times. One sees the little inns along the way
—the *Waggon and Horses*, the *Plough*, the *King's*

Arms—and the recurring blue signboard *Fine Royston Ales* (the Royston brewery being famous in
those parts). Behind the fun there shines
Brooke's passionate devotion to the soil and soul
of England which was to reach its final expression
so tragically soon. And even behind this the
immortal questions of youth which have no
country and no clime—

> Say, is there Beauty yet to find?
> And Certainty? and Quiet kind?

No lover of England, certainly no lover of
Cambridge, is likely to forget the Grantchester
poem. But knowing Brooke only by that, one
may perhaps be excused for having merely ticketed
him as one of the score of young varsity poets
whom Oxford and Cambridge had graduated in
the past decade and who are all doing fine and
promising work. Even though he tarried here
in the United States ("El Cuspidorado," as he
wittily observed) and many hold precious the
memory of his vivid mind and flashing face, to
most of us he was totally unknown. Then came
the War; he took part in the unsuccessful Antwerp
Expedition; and while in training for the Ægean
campaign he wrote the five sonnets entitled
"1914." I do not know exactly when they were
written or where first published. Their great
popularity began when the Dean of St. Paul's

quoted from them in a sermon on Easter Day,
1915, alluding to them as the finest expression of
the English spirit that the War had called forth.
They came to New York in the shape of clippings
from the London *Times*. No one could read the
matchless sonnet:

> "If I should die, think only this of me:
>> That there's some corner of a foreign field
> That is for ever England."

and not be thrilled to the quick. A country doctor in Ohio to whom I sent a copy of the sonnet
wrote "I cannot read it without tears." This was
poetry indeed; like the Scotchman and his house,
we kent it by the biggin o't. I suppose many
another stranger must have done as I did: wrote
to Brooke to express gratitude for the perfect
words. But he had sailed for the Mediterranean
long before. Presently came a letter from London
saying that he had died on the very day of my
letter—April 23, 1915. He died on board the
French hospital ship *Duguay-Trouin*, on Shakespeare's birthday, in his 28th year. One gathers
from the log of the hospital-ship that the cause of
his death was a malignant ulcer, due to the sting
of some venomous fly. He had been weakened
by a previous touch of sunstroke.

A description of the burial is given in "Me-
morials of Old Rugbeians Who Fell in the Great

War." It vividly recalls Stevenson's last journey
to the Samoan mountain top which Brooke himself had so recently visited. The account was
written by one of Brooke's comrades, who has
since been killed in action:

We found a most lovely place for his grave, about a mile
up the valley from the sea, an olive grove above a watercourse,
dry now, but torrential in winter. Two mountains flank it
on either side, and Mount Khokilas is at its head. We chose
a place in the most lovely grove I have ever seen, or imagined,
a little glade of about a dozen trees, carpeted with mauve-
flowering sage. Over its head droops an olive tree, and round
it is a little space clear of all undergrowth.

About a quarter past nine the funeral party arrived and
made their way up the steep, narrow, and rocky path that
leads to the grave. The way was so rough and uncertain that
we had to have men with lamps every twenty yards to guide
the bearers. He was borne by petty officers of his own company, and so slowly did they go that it was not till nearly
eleven that they reached the grave.

We buried him by cloudy moonlight. He wore his uniform,
and on the coffin were his helmet, belt, and pistol (he had no
sword). We lined the grave with flowers and olive, and
Colonel Quilter laid an olive wreath on the coffin. The
chaplain who saw him in the afternoon read the service very
simply. The firing party fired three volleys and the bugles
sounded the "Last Post."

And so we laid him to rest in that lovely valley, his head
towards those mountains that he would have loved to know,
and his feet towards the sea. He once said in chance talk
that he would like to be buried in a Greek island. He could

have no lovelier one than Skyros, and no quieter resting place.

On his grave we heaped great blocks of white marble; the men of his company made a great wooden cross for his head, with his name upon it, and his platoon put a smaller one at his feet. On the back of the large cross our interpreter wrote in Greek. . . . "Here lies the servant of God, sub-lieutenant in the English navy, who died for the deliverance of Constantinople from the Turks."

The next morning we sailed, and had no chance of revisiting his grave.

It is no mere flippancy to say that the War did much for Rupert Brooke. The boy who had written many hot, morbid, immature verses and a handful of perfect poetry, stands now by one swift translation in the golden cloudland of English letters. There will never, can never, be any laggard note in the praise of his work. And of a young poet dead one may say things that would be too fulsome for life. Professor Gilbert Murray is quoted:

"Among all who have been poets and died young, it is hard to think of one who, both in life and death, has so typified the ideal radiance of youth and poetry."

In the grave among the olive trees on the island of Skyros, Brooke found at least one Certainty— that of being "among the English poets." He would probably be the last to ask a more high-sounding epitaph.

His "Collected Poems" as published consist of eighty-two pieces, fifty of which were published in his first book, issued (in England only) in 1911. That is to say fifty of the poems were written before the age of 24, and seventeen of the fifty before 21. These last are thoroughly youthful in formula. We all go through the old familiar cycle, and Brooke did not take his youth at second hand. Socialism, vegetarianism, bathing by moonlight in the Cam, sleeping out of doors, walking barefoot on the crisp English turf, channel crossings and what not—it is all a part of the grand game. We can only ask that the man really see what he says he sees, and report it with what grace he can muster.

And so of the seventeen earliest poems there need not be fulsome praise. Few of us are immortal poets by twenty-one. But even Brooke's undergraduate verses refused to fall entirely into the usual grooves of sophomore song. So unerring a critic as Professor Woodberry (his introduction to the "Collected Poems" is so good that lesser hands may well pause) finds in them "more of the intoxication of the god" than in the later rounder work. They include the dreaming tenderness of *Day That I Have Loved;* they include such neat little pictures of the gross and sordid as the two poems *Wagner* and *Dawn,* written on a trip in Germany. (It is curious that the only note of exasperation in Brooke's poems occurs when he writes from Germany. One finds it again, wittily put, in *Grantchester*.)

This vein of brutality and resolute ugliness that one finds here and there in Brooke's work is not wholly amiss nor unintelligible. Like all young men of quick blood he seized gaily upon the earthy basis of our humanity and found in it food for purging laughter. There was never a young poet worth bread and salt who did not scrawl ribald verses in his day; we may surmise that Brooke's peers at King's would recall many vigorous stanzas that are not included in the volume at hand. The few touches that we have in this vein show a masculine fear on Brooke's part of being merely pretty in his verse. In his young thirst for reality he did not boggle at coarse figures or loathsome metaphors. Just as his poems of 1905-08 are of the cliché period where all lips are "scarlet," and lamps are "relumed," so the section dated 1908-11 shows Brooke in the *Shropshire Lad* stage, at the mercy of extravagant sex images, and yet developing into the dramatic felicity of his sonnet *The Hill*:

Breathless, we flung us on the windy hill,
Laughed in the sun, and kissed the lovely grass,
You said, "Through glory and ecstasy we pass;

Wind, sun, and earth remain, the birds sing still,
When we are old, are old. . . ." "And when we die
  All's over that is ours; and life burns on
Through other lovers, other lips," said I,
—"Heart of my heart, our heaven is now, is won!"

"We are Earth's best, that learnt her lesson here.
  Life is our cry.   We have kept the faith!" we said:
  "We shall go down with unreluctant tread
Rose-crowned into the darkness!"   . . .   Proud we were
And laughed, that had such brave true things to say.
—And then you suddenly cried, and turned away.

The true lover of poetry, it seems to me, cannot
but wish that the "1914" sonnets and the most
perfect of the later poems had been separately
issued.   The best of Brooke forms a thin sheaf of
consummate beauty, and I imagine that the little
edition of "1914 and Other Poems," containing the
thirty-two later poems, which was published in England and issued in Garden City by Doubleday, Page
& Company in July, 1915, to save the American copy
right, will always be more precious than the complete
edition.   As there were only twenty-five copies
of this first American edition, it is extremely rare
and will undoubtedly be sought after by collectors.
But for one who is interested to trace the growth
of Brooke's power, the steadying of his poetic
orbit and the mounting flame of his joy in life,
the poems of 1908-11 are an instructive study.

From the perfected brutality of *Jealousy* or *Mene-laus and Helen* or *A Channel Passage* (these bite like Meredith) we see him passing to sonnets that taste of Shakespeare and foretell his utter mastery of the form. What could better the wit and beauty of this song:

"Oh! Love," they said, "is King of Kings,
    And Triumph is his crown.
Earth fades in flame before his wings,
    And Sun and Moon bow down."
But that, I knew, would never do;
    And Heaven is all too high.
So whenever I meet a Queen, I said,
    I will not catch her eye.

"Oh! Love," they said, and "Love," they said,
    "The Gift of Love is this;
A crown of thorns about thy head,
    And vinegar to thy kiss!"—
But Tragedy is not for me;
    And I'm content to be gay.
So whenever I spied a Tragic Lady,
    I went another way.

And so I never feared to see
    You wander down the street,
Or come across the fields to me
    On ordinary feet.
For what they'd never told me of,
    And what I never knew;
It was that all the time, my love,
    Love would be merely you.

We come then to the five sonnets inspired by
the War. Let us be sparing of clumsy comment.
They are the living heart of young England; the
throbbing soul of all that gracious manhood torn
from its happy quest of Beauty and Certainty,
flung unheated into the absurdities of War, and
yet finding in this supreme sacrifice an answer to
all its pangs of doubt. All the hot yearnings of
"1905-08" and "1908-11" are gone; here is no
Shropshire Lad enlisting for spite, but a joyous
surrender to England of all that she had given.
See his favourite metaphor (that of the swimmer)
recur—what pictures it brings of "Parson's
Pleasure" on the Cher and the willowy bathing
pool on the Cam. How one recalls those white
Greek bodies against the green!

> Now, God be thanked who has matched us with His hour,
>   And caught our youth, and wakened us from sleeping,
> With hand made sure, clear eye, and sharpened power,
>   To turn, as swimmers into cleanness leaping.

To those who tell us England is grown old and
fat and soft, there is the answer. It is no hymn
of hate that England's youth has sung, but the
farewell of those who, loving life with infinite
zest, have yet found in surrendering it to her the
Beauty, the Certainty, yes and the Quiet, which
they had sought. On those five pages are packed

in simple words all the love of life, the love of
woman, the love of England that make Brooke's
memory sweet. Never did the sonnet speak to
finer purpose. "In his hands the thing became
a trumpet"—

THE DEAD

Blow out, you bugles, over the rich Dead!
 There's none of these so lonely and poor of old,
 But, dying, has made us rarer gifts than gold.
These laid the world away; poured out the red
Sweet wine of youth; gave up the years to be
 Of work and joy, and that unhoped serene,
 That men call age; and those who would have been,
Their sons, they gave, their immortality.

Blow, bugles, blow! They brought us, for our dearth
 Holiness, lacked so long, and Love, and Pain.
Honour has come back, as a King, to earth,
 And paid his subjects with a royal wage;
And Nobleness walks in our ways again;
 And we have come into our heritage.

It would be misleading, perhaps, to leave
Brooke's poetry with the echo of this solemn note.
No understanding of the man would be complete
without mentioning the vehement gladness and
merriment he found in all the commonplaces of life.
Poignant to all cherishers of the precious details
of existence must be his poem *The Great Lover*

where he catalogues a sort of trade order list of his
stock in life. The lines speak with the very
accent of Keats. These are some of the things
he holds dear—

> White plates and cups, clean-gleaming,
> Ringed with blue lines; and feathery, faery dust;
> Wet roofs, beneath the lamp-light; the strong crust
> Of friendly bread; and many tasting food;
> Rainbows; and the blue bitter smoke of wood;
> And radiant raindrops couching in cool flowers;
> And flowers themselves, that sway through sunny hours,
> Dreaming of moths that drink them under the moon;
> Then, the cool kindliness of sheets, that soon
> Smoothe away trouble; and the rough male kiss
> Of blankets; grainy wood; live hair that is
> Shining and free; blue-massing clouds; the keen
> Unpassioned beauty of a great machine;
> The benison of hot water; furs to touch;
> The good smell of old clothes; and other such——
> . . . . All these have been my loves.

Of his humour only those who knew him per-
sonally have a right to speak; but where does one
find a more perfect bit of gentle satire than *Heaven*
where he gives us a Tennysonian fish pondering
the problem of a future life.

> This life cannot be All, they swear,
> For how unpleasant, if it were!
> One may not doubt that, somehow, Good
> Shall come of Water and of Mud;

And, sure, the reverent eye must see
A Purpose in Liquidity.
We darkly know, by Faith we cry
The future is not Wholly Dry.   .   .   .
But somewhere, beyond Space and Time,
Is wetter water, slimier slime!

No future anthology of English wit can be complete without that exquisite bit of fooling.

Of such a sort, to use Mr. Mosher's phrase, was Rupert Chawner Brooke, "the latest and greatest of young Englishmen."

THE MAN

THE big room was very still. Outside, beneath a thin, cold drizzle, the first tinge of green showed on the broad lawn. The crocuses were beginning to thrust their spears through the sodden mold. One of the long French windows stood ajar, and in the air that slipped through was a clean, moist whiff of coming spring. It was the end of March.

In the leather armchair by the wide, flat desk sat a man. His chin was on his chest; the lowered head and the droop of the broad, spare shoulders showed the impact of some heavy burden. His clothes were gray—a trim, neatly cut business suit; his hair was gray; his gray-blue eyes were sombre. In the gathering dusk he seemed only a darker shadow in the padded chair. His right hand—the long, firm, nervous hand of a scholar—rested on the blotting pad. A silver pen had slipped from his fingers as he sat in thought. On the desk lay some typed sheets which he was revising.

Sitting there, his mind had been traversing the memories of the past two and a half years. Every

line of his lean, strong figure showed some trace of
the responsibilities he had borne. In the greatest
crisis of modern times he had steadfastly pursued
an ideal, regardless of the bitterness of criticism and
the sting of ridicule. The difficulties had been
tremendous. Every kind of influence had been
brought upon him to do certain things, none of
which he had done. A scholar, a dreamer, a life-
long student of history, he had surprised his associates by the clearness of his vision, the tenacity of
his will. Never, perhaps, in the history of the
nation had a man been more brutally reviled than
he—save one! And his eyes turned to the wall
where, over the chimney piece, hung the portrait
of one of his predecessors who had stood for his
ideals in a time of fiery trial. It was too dark now
to see the picture but he knew well the rugged,
homely face, the tender, pain-wrenched mouth.

This man had dreamed a dream. Climbing
from the humble youth of a poor student, nour-
ished in classroom and library with the burning
visions of great teachers, he had hoped in this highest of positions to guide his country in the difficult
path of a higher patriotism. Philosopher, idealist,
keen student of men, he had been able to keep his
eyes steadfast on his goal despite the intolerable
cloud of unjust criticism that had rolled round
him. Venomous and shameful attacks had hurt

him, but had never abated his purpose. In a world reeling and smoking with the insane fury of war, one nation should stand unshaken for the message of the spirit, for the glory of humanity, for the settlement of disputes by other means than gunpowder and women's tears. That was his dream. To that he had clung.

He shifted grimly in his chair, and took up the pen.

What a long, heart-rending strain it had been! His mind went back to the golden August day when the telegram was laid on his desk announcing that the old civilization of Europe had fallen into fragments. He remembered the first meeting thereafter, when his associates, with grave, anxious faces, debated the proper stand for them to take. He remembered how, in the swinging relaxation of an afternoon of golf, he had thoughtfully planned the wording of his first neutrality proclamation.

In those dim, far-off days, who had dreamed what would come? Who could have believed that great nations would discard without compunction all the carefully built-up conventions of international law? That murder in the air, on land, on the sea, under the sea, would be rewarded by the highest military honours? That a supposedly friendly nation would fill another land

with spies—even among the accredited envoys of
diplomacy?

Sadly this man thought of the long painful fight
he had made to keep one nation at least out of the
tragic, barbaric struggle. Giving due honour to
convinced militarist and sincere pacifist, his own
course was still different. That his country, disregarding the old fetishes of honour and insult,
should stand solidly for humanity; should endure
all things, suffer all things, for humanity's sake;
should seek to bind up the wounds and fill the starving mouths. That one nation—not because she
was weak, but because she was strong—should, with
God's help, make a firm stand for peace and show
to all mankind that force can never conquer force.

"A nation can be so right that it should be too
proud to fight." Magnificent words, true words,
which one day would re-echo in history as the
utterance of a man years in advance of his time—
but what rolling thunders of vituperation they
had cost him! *Too proud to fight!* . . . If
only it had been possible to carry through to the
end this message from Judea!

But, little by little, and with growing anguish,
he had seen that the nation must take another
step. Little by little, as the inhuman frenzies of
warfare had grown in savagery, inflicting unspeakable horror on non-combatants, women and chil-

dren, he had realized that his cherished dream
must be laid aside. For the first time in human
history a great nation had dared to waive pride,
honour, and—with bleeding heart—even the lives
of its own for the hope of humanity and civilization. With face buried in his hands he reviewed
the long catalogue of atrocities on the seas. He
could feel his cheeks grow hot against his palms.
*Arabic, Lusitania, Persia, Laconia, Falaba, Gul-
flight, Sussex, California*—the names were etched
in his brain in letters of grief. And now, since
the "barred-zone" decree . . .

He straightened in his chair. Like a garment
the mood of anguish slipped from him. He snap-
ped on the green desk light and turned to his personal typewriter. As he did so, from some old
student day a phrase flashed into his mind—the
words of Martin Luther, the Thuringian peasant
and university professor, who four hundred years
before had nailed his theses on the church door
at Wittenberg:

"*Gott helfe mir, ich kann nicht anders.*"

They chimed a solemn refrain in his heart as he
inserted a fresh sheet of paper behind the roller
and resumed his writing. . . .

"*With a profound sense of the solemn and even
tragical character of the step I am taking and of the*

*grave responsibilities which it involves. I
advise that the Congress declare the recent course of
the Imperial German Government to be in fact nothing less than war against the Government and people
of the United States. . . ."*

The typewriter clicked industriously. The face
bent intently over the keys was grave and quiet,
but as the paper unrolled before him some of his
sadness seemed to pass away. A vision of his
country, no longer divided in petty schisms,
engrossed in material pursuits, but massed in one
by the force and fury of a valiant ideal, came into
his mind.

"It is for humanity," he whispered to himself.
"*Ich kann nicht anders. . . .*"

*"We have no quarrel with the German people. We
have no feeling toward them but one of sympathy and
friendship. It was not upon their impulse that their
government acted in entering this war. It was not
with their previous knowledge or approval. . . .
Self-governed nations do not fill their neighbour states
with spies, or set the course of intrigue to bring about
some critical posture of affairs which will give them
an opportunity to strike and make conquest. . . .
A steadfast concert for peace can never be maintained
except by a partnership of democratic nations. . . .*

Only free peoples can hold their purpose and their honour steady to a common end and prefer the interests of mankind to any narrow interest of their own."

With the gathering of the dusk the rain had stopped. He rose from his chair and walked to the window. The sky had cleared; in the west shone a faint band of clear apple green in which burned one lucent star. Distantly he could hear the murmur of the city like the pulsing heartbeat of the nation. As often, in moments of tension, he seemed to feel the whole vast stretch of the continent throbbing; the yearning breast of the land trembling with energy; the great arch of sky, spanning from coast to coast, quiver with power unused. The murmur of little children in their cradles, the tender words of mothers, the footbeat of men on the pavements of ten thousand cities, the flags leaping in air from high buildings, ships putting out to sea with gunners at their sterns—in one aching synthesis the vastness and dearness and might of his land came to him. A mingled nation, indeed, of various and clashing breeds; but oh, with what a tradition to uphold!

Words were forming in his mind as he watched the fading sky, and he returned quietly to the typewriter:

"*We are glad to fight thus for the ultimate peace of the world and for the liberation of its peoples, the German peoples included. . . . The world must be made safe for democracy.*"

The world must be made safe for democracy! As the wires leaped and the little typewriter spoke under the pressure of his strong fingers, scenes passed in his mind of the happy, happy Europe he had known in old wander days, years before.

He could see the sun setting down dark aisles of the Black Forest; the German peasants at work in the fields; the simple, cordial friendliness of that lovely land. He remembered French villages beside slow-moving rivers; white roads in a hot shimmer of sun; apple orchards of the Moselle. And England—dear green England, fairest of all —the rich blue line of the Chiltern Hills, and Buckinghamshire beech woods bronze and yellow in the autumn. He remembered thatched cottages where he had bicycled for tea, and the naïve rustic folk who had made him welcome.

What deviltry had taken all these peaceful people, gripped them and maddened them, set them at one another's throats? Millions of children, millions of mothers, millions of humble workers, happy in the richness of life—where were they now? Life, innocent human life—the most

precious thing we know or dream of, freedom to
work for a living and win our own joys of home
and love and food—what Black Death had maddened the world with its damnable seeds of hate?
Would life ever be free and sweet again?

The detestable sultry horror of it all broke
upon him anew in a tide of anguish. No, the
world could never be the same again in the lives
of men now living. But for the sake of the generations to come—he thought of his own tiny
grandchildren—for the love of God and the mercy
of mankind, let this madness be crushed. If his
country must enter the war let it be only for the
love and service of humanity. "It is a fearful
thing," he thought, "but the right is more precious
than peace."

Sad at heart he turned again to the typewriter,
and the keys clicked off the closing words:

*"To such a task we can dedicate our lives and our
fortunes, everything that we are and everything that
we have, with the pride of those who know that the
day has come when America is privileged to spend
her blood and her might for the principles that gave
her birth and happiness and the peace which she has
treasured."*

He leaned back in his chair, stiff and weary.
His head ached hotly. With elbows on the desk

he covered his forehead and eyes with his hands.
All the agony, the bitterness, the burden of preceding days swept over him, but behind it was a
cool and cleansing current of peace. "*Ich kann
nicht anders,*" he whispered.

Then, turning swiftly to the machine, he typed
rapidly:

"*God helping her, she can do no other.*"

THE HEAD OF THE FIRM

HE ALWAYS lost his temper when the foreign mail came in. Sitting in his private room, which overlooked a space of gardens where bright red and yellow flowers were planted in rhomboids, triangles, parallelograms, and other stiff and ugly figures, he would glance hastily through the papers and magazines. He was familiar with several foreign languages, and would skim through the text. Then he would pound the table with his fist, walk angrily about the floor, and tear the offensive journals into strips. For very often he found in these papers from abroad articles or cartoons that were most annoying to him, and very detrimental to the business of his firm.

His assistants tried to keep foreign publications away from him, but he was plucky in his own harsh way. He insisted on seeing them. Always the same thing happened. His face would grow grim, the seam-worn forehead would corrugate, the muscles of his jaw throb nervously. His gray eyes would flash—and the fist come down heavily on the mahogany desk.

When a man is nearly sixty and of a full-blooded

physique, it is not well for him to have these frequent pulsations of rage. But he had always found it hard to control his temper. He sometimes remembered what a schoolmaster had said to him at Cassel, forty-five years before: "He who loses his temper will lose everything."

But he must be granted great provocation. He had always had difficulties to contend with. His father was an invalid, and he himself was puny in childhood; infantile paralysis withered his left arm when he was an infant; but in spite of these handicaps he had made himself a vigorous swimmer, rider, and yachtsman; he could shoot better with one arm than most sportsmen with two. After leaving the university he served in the army, but at his father's death the management of the vast family business came into his hands. He was then twenty-eight.

No one can question the energy with which he set himself to carry on the affairs of the firm. Generous, impetuous, indiscreet, stubborn, pugnacious, his blend of qualities held many of the elements of a successful man of business. His first act was to dismiss the confidential and honoured assistant who had guided both his father and grandfather in the difficult years of the firm's growth. But the new executive was determined to run the business his own way. Disregarding criticism, ridicule, or flattery, he declared it his mission to spread the influence of the business to the ends of the earth. "We must have our place in the sun," he said; and announced himself as the divine instrument through whom this would be accomplished. He made it perfectly plain that no man's opposition would balk him in the management of the firm's affairs. One of his most famous remarks was: "Considering myself as the instrument of the Lord, without heeding the views and opinions of the day, I go my way." The board of directors censured him for this, but he paid little heed.

The growth of the business was enormous; nothing like it had been seen in the world's history. Branch offices were opened all over the globe. Vessels bearing the insignia of the company were seen on every ocean. He himself with his accustomed energy travelled everywhere to advance the interests of trade. In England, Russia, Denmark, Italy, Austria, Turkey, the Holy Land, he made personal visits to the firm's best customers. He sent his brother to America to spread the goodwill of the business; and other members of the firm to France, Holland, China, and Japan. Telegram after telegram kept the world's cables busy as he distributed congratulations, condolences, messages of one kind and another to foreign merchants. His publicity department never rested. He employed famous scientists and inventors to improve the products of his factories. He reared six sons to carry on the business after him.

This is no place to record minutely the million activities of thirty years that made his business one of the greatest on earth. It is all written down in history. Suffice it to say that those years did not go by without sorrows. He was afflicted with an incurable disease. His temperament, like high tension steel, was of a brittle quality; it had the tendency to snap under great strains. Living always at fever pitch, sparing himself no fatigue of body or soul, the whirring dynamo of energy in him often showed signs of overstress.

It is hard to conceive what he must have gone through in those last months. You must remember the extraordinary conditions in his line of business caused by the events of recent years. He had lived to see his old friends, merchants with whom he had dealt for decades, some of them the foreign representatives of his own firm, out of a job and hunted from their homes by creditors. He had lived to realize that the commodity he and his family had been manufacturing for generations was out of date, a thing no longer needed or wanted by the modern world. The strain which

his mind was enduring is shown by the febrile
and unbalanced tone of one of his letters, sent
to a member of his own family who ran one of the
company's branch offices but was forced to resign
by bankruptcy:

"I have heard with wrath of the infamous
outrage committed by our common enemies upon
you and upon your business. I assure you that
your deprivation can be only temporary. The
mailed fist, with further aid from Almighty God,
will restore you to your office, of which no man by
right can rob you. The company will wreak
vengeance on those who have dared so insolently
to lay their criminal hands on you. We hope to
welcome you at the earliest opportunity."

The failure of his business was the great drama
of the century; and it is worth while to remember
what it was that killed it—and him. While the
struggle was still on there were many arguments
as to what would bring matters to an end; some
cunning invention, some new patent that would
outwit the methods of his firm. But after all it
was nothing more startling than the printing press
and the moral of the whole matter may be put in
those fine old words, "But above all things, truth
beareth away the victory." Little by little, the
immense power of the printed word became too
strong for him. Rave and fume as he might, and

hammer the mahogany desk, the rolling thunders of a world massed against him cracked even his stiff will. Little by little the plain truth sifted into the minds and hearts of the thousands working in his huge organization. In Russia, in Greece, in Spain, in Austria, in China, in Mexico, he saw men bursting the shells of age and custom that had cramped them. One by one his competitors adopted the new ideas, or had them forced upon them; profit-sharing, workmen's insurance, the right of free communities to live their own lives.

Deep in his heart he must have known he was doomed to fail, but that perverse demon of strong-headed pugnacity was trenched deep within him. He was always a fighter, but his face, though angry, obstinate, proud, was still not an evil face. He broke down while there was still some of the business to save and some of the goodwill intact.

It was the printing press that decided it: the greatest engine in the world, to which submarines and howitzers and airplanes are but wasteful toys. For when the printing presses are united the planet may buck and yaw, but she comes into line at last. A million inky cylinders, roaring in chorus, were telling him the truth. When his assistants found him, on his desk lay a half-ripped magazine where he had tried to tear up a mocking cartoon.

I think that as he sat at his table in those last days, staring with embittered eyes at the savage words and pictures that came to him from over the seven seas, he must have had some vision of the shadowy might of the press, of the vast irresistible urge of public opinion, that hung like dark wings above his head. For little by little the printed word incarnates itself in power, and in ways undreamed of makes itself felt. Little by little the wills of common men, coalescing, running together like beads of mercury on a plate, quivering into rhythm and concord, become a mighty force that may be ever so impalpable, but grinds empires to powder. Mankind suffers hideous wrongs and cruel setbacks, but when once the collective purpose of humanity is summoned to a righteous end, it moves onward like the tide up a harbour.

The struggle was long and bitter. His superb organization, with such colossal resources for human good, lavished in the fight every energy known to man. For a time it seemed as though he would pull through. His managers had foreseen every phase of this unprecedented competition, and his warehouses were stocked. But slowly the forces of his opponents began to focus themselves.

Then even his own employees suspected the

truth. His agents, solicitors, and salesmen, scattered all over the globe, realized that one company cannot twist the destiny of mankind. He felt the huge fabric of his power quiver and creak.

The business is now in the hands of the executors, pending a reorganization.

17 HERIOT ROW

THERE is a small black notebook into which I look once or twice a year to refresh my memory of a carnal and spiritual pilgrimage to Edinburgh, made with Mifflin McGill (upon whose head be peace) in the summer of 1911. It is a testament of light-hearted youth, savoury with the unindentured joys of twenty-one and the grand literary passion. Would that one might again steer *Shotover* (dearest of pushbikes) along the Banbury Road, and see Mifflin's lean shanks twirl up the dust on the way to Stratford! Never was more innocent merriment spread upon English landscape. When I die, bury the black notebook with me.

That notebook is memorable also in a statistical way, and perchance may serve future historians as a document proving the moderate cost of wayfaring in those halcyon days. Nothing in Mr. Pepys' diary is more interesting than his meticulous record of what his amusements cost him. Mayhap some future economist will pore upon these guileless confessions. For in the black memorandum book I succeeded, for almost the only time in my life, in keeping an accurate record of the lapse of coin during nine whole days. I shall deposit the document with the Congressional Library in Washington for future annalists; in the meantime I make no excuse for recounting the items of the first sixty hours. Let no one take amiss the frequent entries marked "cider." July, 1911, was a hot month and a dusty, and we were biking fifty miles the day. Please reckon exchange at two cents per penny.

		£	s.	d
July 16	pint cider			4
	½ pint cider			1½
	lunch at Banbury . . .		2	2
	pint cider at Ettington . . .			3
	supper at Stratford		1	3
	stamp and postcard			2
			4	3½
July 17	Postcards and stamps . . .			9
	pencil			1
	Warwick Castle		2	–
	cider at the *Bear and Baculus* (which Mifflin *would* call the *Bear and Bacillus*)		.	2½
	Bowling Green Inn, bed and breakfast		3	2
	Puncture		1	–
	Lunch, Kenilworth		1	6
	Kenilworth Castle			6

Postcards	**4**
Lemonade, Coventry . . .	**4**
Cider	2½
Supper, Tamworth, *The Castle Hotel*	2 1
	16 5½
July 18 Johnson house, Lichfield . .	3
cider at *The Three Crowns* . .	4
postcard and shave	4
The King's Head, bed and breakfast	3 7
cider	2
tip on road*	1½
lunch, Uttoxeter	1 3
cider, Ashbourne, *The Green Man*	3
landlord's drink, Ashbourne † .	1
supper, *Newhaven House,* . .	1 –
lemonade, Buxton	3
TOTAL	£1–4–1
	($5.78)

That is to say, 24 bob for two and a half days. We used to reckon that ten shillings a day would do us very nicely, barring luxuries and emergen-

---

*As far as I can remember, this was a gratuity to a rather tarnished subject who directed us at a fork in the road, near a railway crossing.

†This was a copper well lavished; for the publican, a ventripotent person with a liquid and glamorous brown eye, told us excellent gossip about Dr. Johnson and George Eliot, both heroes in that neighbourhood. "Yes," we said, "that man Eliot was a great writer," and he agreed.

cies. We attained a zealous proficiency in reckoning shillings and pence, and our fervour in posting our ledgers would have gladdened a firm of auditors. I remember lying on the coping of a stone bridge over the water of Teviot near Hawick, admiring the green-brown tint of the swift stream bickering over the stones. Mifflin was writing busily in his notebook on the other side of the bridge. I thought to myself, "Bless the lad, he's jotting down some picturesque notes of something that has struck his romantic eye." And just then he spoke—"Four and eleven pence half-penny so far to-day!"

Would I could retrogress over the devious and enchanting itinerary. The McGill route from Oxford to Auld Reekie is 417 miles; it was the afternoon of the ninth day when with thumping hearts we saw Arthur's Seat from a dozen miles away. Our goal was in sight!

There was a reason for all this pedalling madness. Ever since the days when we had wandered by Darby Creek, reading R. L. S. aloud to one another, we had planned this trip to the gray metropolis of the north. A score of sacred names had beckoned us, the haunts of the master. We knew them better than any other syllables in the world. Heriot Row, Princes Street, the Calton Hill, Duddingston Loch, Antigua Street, the

Water of Leith, Colinton, Swanston, the Pentland
Hills—O my friends, do those names mean to
you what they did to us? Then you are one of
the brotherhood—what was to us then the sweetest
brotherhood in the world!

In a quiet little hotel in Rutland Square we
found decent lodging, in a large chamber which
was really the smoking room of the house. The
city was crowded with tourists on account of an
expected visit of the King and Queen; every other
room in the hotel was occupied. Greatly to our
satisfaction we were known as "the smoking-
room gentlemen" throughout our stay. Our
windows opened upon ranks of corridor-cars
lying on the Caledonian Railway sidings, and the
clink and jar of buffers and coupling irons were
heard all night long. I seem to remember that
somewhere in his letters R. L. S. speaks of that
same sound. He knew Rutland Square well, for
his boyhood friend Charles Baxter lived there.
Writing from Samoa in later years he says that
one memory stands out above all others of his
youth—Rutland Square. And while that was of
course only the imaginative fervour of the moment, yet we were glad to know that in that quiet
little cul de sac behind the railway terminal we
were on ground well loved by Tusitala.

The first evening, and almost every twilight

while we were in Auld Reekie, we found our way
to 17 Heriot Row—famous address, which had
long been as familiar to us as our own. I think
we expected to find a tablet on the house com-
memorating the beloved occupant; but no; to our
surprise it was dark, dusty, and tenantless. A
sign TO SELL was prominent. To take the name
of the agent was easy. A great thought struck
us. Could we not go over the house in the character of prospective purchasers? Mifflin and I
went back to our smoking room and concocted a
genteel letter to Messrs. Guild and Shepherd,
Writers to the Signet.

Promptly came a reply (Scots business men
answer at once).

> 16 Charlotte Square
> Edinburgh
> 26th July, 1911

DEAR SIR,
17 HERIOT ROW
We have received your letter regarding this house. The
house can be seen at any time, and if you will let us know
when you wish to view it we shall arrange to have it opened.
> We are,
> Yours faithfully,
> GUILD AND SHEPHERD.

Our hearts were uplifted, but now we were
mightily embarrassed as to the figure we would cut

before the Writers to the Signet. You must remember that we were two young vagabonds in the earliest twenties, travelling with slim knapsacks, and much soiled by a fortnight on the road. I was in knickerbockers and khaki shirt; Mifflin in greasy gray flannels and subfusc Norfolk. Our only claims to gentility were our monocles. Always take a monocle on a vagabond tour: it is a never-failing source of amusement and passport of gentility. No matter how ragged you are, if you can screw a pane in your eye you can awe the yokel or the tradesman.

The private records of the firm of Guild and Shepherd doubtless show that on Friday, July 28, 1911, one of their polite young attachés, appearing as per appointment at 17 Heriot Row, was met by two eccentric young gentlemen, clad in dirty white flannel hats, waterproof capes, each with an impressive monocle. Let it be said to the honour of the attaché in question that he showed no symptoms of surprise or alarm. We explained, I think, that we were scouting for my father, who (it was alleged) greatly desired to settle down in Edinburgh. And we had presence of mind enough to enquire about plumbing, stationary wash-tubs, and the condition of the flues. I wish I could remember what rent was quoted.

He showed us all through the house; and you may imagine that we stepped softly and with beating hearts. Here we were on the very track of the Magician himself: his spirit whispered in the lonely rooms. We imagined R. L. S. as a little child, peering from the windows at dusk to see Leerie light the street-lamps outside—a quaint, thin, elvish face with shining brown eyes; or held up in illness by Cummie to see the gracious dawn heralded by oblongs of light in the windows across the Queen Street gardens. We saw the college lad, tall, with tweed coat and cigarette, returning to Heriot Row with an armful of books, in sad or sparkling mood. The house was dim and dusty: a fine entrance hall, large dining room facing the street—and we imagined Louis and his parents at breakfast. Above this, the drawing room, floored with parquet oak, a spacious and attractive chamber. Above this again, the nursery, and opening off it the little room where faithful Cummie slept. But in vain we looked for some sign or souvenir of the entrancing spirit. The room that echoed to his childish glee, that heard his smothered sobs in the endless nights of childish pain, the room where he scribbled and brooded and burst into gusts of youth's passionate outcry, is now silent and forlorn.

With what subtly mingled feelings we peered

from room to room, seeing everything, and yet not daring to give ourselves away to the courteous young agent. And what was it he said?—"This was the house of Lord So-and-so" (I forget the name)— "and incidentally, Robert Louis Stevenson lived here once. His signature occurs once or twice in the deeds."

Incidentally! . . .

Like many houses in Auld Reekie, 17 Heriot Row is built on a steep slant of ground, so that the rear of the house is a storey or more higher than the face. We explored the kitchens, laundries, store-rooms, and other "offices" with care, imagining that little "Smoutie" may have run here and there in search of tid-bits from the cook. Visions of that childhood, fifty years before, were almost as real as our own. We seemed to hear the young treble of his voice. That house was the home of the Stevensons for thirty years (1857-1887)—surely even the thirty years that have gone by since Thomas Stevenson died cannot have laid all those dear ghosts we conjured up!

We thanked our guide and took leave of him. If the firm of Guild and Shepherd should ever see this, surely they will forgive our innocent deception, for the honour of R. L. S. I wonder if any one has yet put a tablet on the house? If not, Mifflin and I will do so, some day.

In the evenings we used to wander up to Heriot
Row in the long Northern dusk, to sit on the front
steps of number 17 waiting for Leerie to come and
light the famous lamp which still stands on the
pavement in front of the dining-room windows:

For we are very lucky, with a lamp before the door,
And Leerie stops to light it as he lights so many more;
And O! before you hurry by with ladder and with light,
O Leerie, see a little child and nod to him to-night!

But no longer does Leerie "with lantern and
with ladder come posting up the street." Nowadays he carries a long pole bearing a flame cunningly sheltered in a brass socket. But the
Leerie of 1911 ("Leerie-light-the-lamps" is a
generic nickname for all lamplighters in Scotland)
was a pleasant fellow even if ladderless, and we
used to have a cigar ready for him when he
reached 17. We told him of R. L. S., of whom
he had vaguely heard, and explained the sanctity
of that particular lamp. He in turn talked freely
of his craft, and learning that we were Americans
he told us of his two sisters "in Pennsylvania, at
21 Thorn Street." He seemed to think Pennsylvania a town, but finally we learned that the
Misses Leerie lived in Sewickley where they were
doing well, and sending back money to the "kid-
dies." Good Leerie, I wonder do you still light the

lamps on Heriot Row, or have you too seen redder
beacons on Flanders fields?

One evening I remember we fell into discussion
whether the lamp-post was still the same one that
R. L. S. had known.   We were down on hands and
knees on the pavement, examining the base of the
pillar by match-light in search of possible dates.
A very seedy and disreputable looking man
passed, evidently regarding us with apprehension
as detectives.   Mifflin, never at a loss, remarked
loudly "No, I see no footprints here," and as the
ragged one passed hastily on with head twisted
over his shoulder, we followed him.   At the corner
of Howe Street he broke into an uneasy shuffle,
and Mifflin turned a great laugh into a Scotland
Yard sneeze.

Howe Street crosses Heriot Row at right angles,
only a few paces from No. 17.   It dips sharply
downhill toward the Water of Leith, and Mifflin
and I used to stand at the corner and wonder
just where took place the adventure with the lame
boy which R. L. S. once described when setting
down some recollections of childhood·

In Howe street, round the corner from our house, I often
saw a lame boy of rather a rough and poor appearance.   He
had one leg much shorter than the other, and wallowed in his
walk, in consequence, like a ship in a seaway.   I had read
more than enough, in tracts and goody story books, of the

isolation of the infirm; and after many days of bashfulness
and hours of consideration, I finally accosted him, sheepishly
enough I daresay, in these words: "Would you like to
play with me?" I remember the expression, which
sounds exactly like a speech from one of the goody books
that had nerved me to the venture. But the answer
was not he one I had anticipated, for it was a blast of oaths.
I need not say how fast I fled. This incident was the more
to my credit as I had, when I was young, a desperate
aversion to addressing strangers, though when once we had
got into talk I was pretty certain to assume the lead. The
last particular may still be recognized. About four years
ago I saw my lame lad, and knew him again at once. He
was then a man of great strength, rolling along, with an inch
of cutty in his mouth and a butcher's basket on his arm.
Our meeting had been nothing to him, but it was a great
affair to me.

We strolled up the esplanade below the Castle,
pausing in Ramsay's Gardens to admire the
lighted city from above. In the valley between
the Castle and Princes Street the pale blue mist
rises at night like an exhalation from the old gray
stones. The lamps shining through it blend in
a delicate opalescent sheen, shot here and there
with brighter flares. As the sky darkens the
castle looms in silhouette, with one yellow square
below the Half Moon Battery. "There are no
stars like the Edinburgh street lamps," says R.
L. S. Aye, and the brightest of them all shines
on Heriot Row.

The vision of that child face still comes to me, peering down from the dining-room window. R. L. S. may never have gratified his boyish wish to go round with Leerie and light the lamps, but he lit many and more enduring flames even in the hearts of those who never saw him.

FRANK CONFESSIONS OF A PUBLISHER'S READER

[*Denis Dulcet, brother of the well-known poet Dunraven Dulcet and the extremely well-known literary agent Dove Dulcet, was for many years the head reader for a large publishing house. It was my good fortune to know him intimately, and when he could be severed from his innumerable manuscripts, which accompanied him everywhere, even in bed, he was very good company. His premature death from reader's cramp and mental hernia was a sad loss to the world of polite letters. Thousands of mediocre books would have been loaded upon the public but for his incisive and unerring judgment. When he lay on his deathbed, surrounded by half-read MSS., he sent for me, and with an air of extreme solemnity laid a packet in my hand. It contained the following confession, and it was his last wish that it should be published without alteration. I include it here in memory of my very dear friend.*]

IN MY youth I was wont to forecast various occupations for myself. Engine driver, tugboat captain, actor, statesman, and wild

animal trainer—such were the visions with which
I put myself to sleep. Never did the merry life
of a manuscript reader swim into my ken. But
here I am, buried elbow deep in the literary output
of a commercial democracy. My only excuse for
setting down these paragraphs is the hope that
other more worthy members of the ancient and
honorable craft may be induced to speak out in
meeting. In these days when every type of man
is interviewed, his modes of thinking conned
and commented upon, why not a symposium of
manuscript readers? Also I realized the other
day, while reading a manuscript by Harold Bell
Wright, that my powers are failing. My old
trouble is gaining on me, and I may not be long
for this world. Before I go to face the greatest
of all Rejection Slips, I want to utter my message
without fear or favour.

As a class, publishers' readers are not vocal.
They spend their days and nights assiduously (in
the literal sense) bent over mediocre stuff, poking
and poring in the unending hope of finding something rich and strange. A gradual *stultitia* seizes
them. They take to drink; they beat their wives;
they despair of literature. Worst, and most
preposterous, they one and all nourish secret
hopes of successful authorship. You might think
that the interminable flow of turgid blockish

fiction that passes beneath their weary eyes would justly sicken them of the abominable gymnastic of writing. But no: the venom is in the blood.

Great men have graced the job—and got out of it as soon as possible. George Meredith was a reader once; so was Frank Norris; also E. V. Lucas and Gilbert Chesterton. One of the latter's comments on a manuscript is still preserved. Writing of a novel by a lady who was the author of many unpublished stories, all marked by perseverance rather than talent, he said, "Age cannot wither nor custom stale her infinite lack of variety." But alas, we hear too little of these gentlemen in their capacity as publishers' pursuivants. Patrolling the porches of literature, why did they not bequeath us some pandect of their experience, some rich garniture of commentary on the adventures that befell? But they, and younger men such as Coningsby Dawson and Sinclair Lewis, have gone on into the sunny hayfields of popular authorship and said nothing.

But these brilliant swallow-tailed migrants are not typical. Your true specimen of manuscript reader is the faithful old percheron who is content to go on, year after year, sorting over the literary pemmican that comes before him, inexhaustible in his love for the delicacies of good writing, happy if once or twice a twelve-month he chance upon

some winged thing. He is not the pettifogging
pilgarlic of popular conception: he is a devoted
servant of letters, willing to take his thirty or
forty dollars a week, willing to suffer the *peine
forte et dure* of his profession in the knowledge of
honest duty done, writing terse and marrowy
little essays on manuscripts, which are buried in
the publishers' files. This man is an honour to
the profession, and I believe there are many such.
Certainly there are many who sigh wistfully when
they must lay aside some cherished writing of their
own to devote an evening to illiterate twaddle.
Five book manuscripts a day, thirty a week,
close to fifteen hundred a year—that is a fair
showing for the head reader of a large publishing
house.

One can hardly blame him if he sometimes grow
skeptic or acid about the profession of letters.
Of each hundred manuscripts turned in there
will rarely be more than three or four that merit
any serious consideration; only about one in a
hundred will be acceptable for publication. And
the others—alas that human beings should have
invented ink to steal away their brains! "Only
a Lady Barber" is the title of a novel in manuscript which I read the other day. Written in the
most atrocious dialect, it betrayed an ignorance
of composition that would have been discreditable

to a polyp. It described the experiences of a
female tonsor somewhere in Idaho, and closed
with her Machiavellian manoeuvres to entice
into her shaving chair a man who had bilked her,
so that she might slice his ear. No need to harrow
you with more of the same kind. I read almost
a score every week. Often I think of a poem
which was submitted to me once, containing this
immortal couplet:

She damped a pen in the ooze of her brain and wrote a verse
  on the air,
A verse that had shone on the disc of the sun, had she chosen
  to set it there.

Let me beg you, my dears, leave the pen un-
damped unless your cerebral ooze really has something to impart. And then, once a year or so,
when one is thinking that the hooves of Pegasus
have turned into pigs' trotters, comes some
Joseph Conrad, some Walter de la Mare, some
Rupert Brooke or Pearsall Smith, to restore one's
sanity.

Or else—what is indeed more frequent—the
reader's fainting spirits are repaired not by the
excellence of the manuscript before him, but by
its absolute literary nonentity, a kind of intellectual Absolute Zero. Lack of merit may be so
complete, so grotesque, that the composition

affords to the sophistic eye a high order of comedy.
A lady submits a poem in many cantos, beginning

> Our heart is but a bundle of muscle
> In which our passions tumble and tussle.

Another lady begins her novel with the following
psychanalysis:

"Thus doth the ever-changing course of things run a perpetual circle." . . . She read the phrase and then
reflected, the cause being a continued prognostication, beginning and ending as it had done the day before, to-morrow
and forever, maybe, of her own ailment, a paradoxical malady, being nothing more nor less than a pronounced case of
malnutrition of the soul, a broken heart-cord, aggravated by a
total collapse of that portion of the mentalities which had
been bolstered up by undue pride, fallacious arguments,
modern foibles and follies peculiar to the human species,
both male and female, under favorable social conditions,
found in provincial towns as well as in large cities and fash-
ionable watering places.

But as a fitting anodyne to this regrettable case
of soul malnutrition, let me append a description
of a robuster female, taken verbatim from a manuscript (penned by masculine hand) which became a by-word in one publisher's office.

She was a beautiful young lady. She was a medium-
sized, elegant figure, wearing a neatly-fitted travelling dress of
black alpaca. Her raven-black hair, copious both in length

and volume and figured like a deep river, rippled by the wind, was parted in the centre and combed smoothly down, ornamenting her pink temples with a flowing tracery that passed round to its modillion windings on a graceful crown. Her mouth was set with pearls adorned with elastic rubies and tuned with minstrel lays, while her nose gracefully concealed its own umbrage, and her eyes imparted a radiant glow to the azure of the sky. Jewels of plain gold were about her ears and her tapering strawberry hands, and a golden chain, attached to a time-keeper of the same material, sparkled on an elegantly-rounded bosom that was destined to be pushed forward by sighs.'

Let it not be thought that only the gracious sex can inspire such plenitude of meticulous portraiture! Here is a description of the hero in a novel by a man which appeared on my desk recently:

For some time past there had been appearing at the home of Sarah Ellenton, a man not over fifty years of age, well groomed and of the appearances of being on good terms with prosperity in many phases. His complexion was reddish. His hazel eyes deepset and close together were small and shifting. His nose ran down to a point in many lines, and from the point back to where it joined above his lip, the course was seen to swerve slightly to one side. His upper lip assumed almost any form and at all times. His mouth ran across his face in a thin line, curved by waves according to the smiles and expressions he employed. Below those features was a chin of fine proportions, showing nothing to require study, but in his jaw hinges there was a device

that worked splendidly, when he wished to show unction
and charity, by sending out his chin on such occasions in
the kindest advances one would wish to see.

It was not long before Sarah became Mrs. John R. Quinley.

I hear that the authors are going to unionize
themselves and join the A. F. of L.   The word
"author" carries no sanctity with me: I have
read too many of them.   If their forming a trade
union will better the output of American literature
I am keen for it.   I know that the professional
reader has a jaundiced eye; insensibly he acquires
a parallax which distorts his vision.   Reading in-
cessantly, now fiction, now history, poetry, essays,
philosophy, science, exegetics, and what not, he
becomes a kind of pantechnicon of slovenly knowledge; a knower of thousands of things that aren't
so.   Every crank's whim, every cretin's philosophy, is fired at him first of all.   Every six months
comes in the inevitable treatise on the fourth
dimension or on making gold from sea-water, or on
using moonlight to run dynamos, or on Pope
Joan or Prester John.   And with it all he must
retain his simple-hearted faith in the great art of
writing and in the beneficence of Gutenberg.

Manuscript readers need a trade union far
worse than authors.   There is all too little clan-
nishness among us.   We who are the helpless target for the slings and arrows of every writer who

chooses to put pen on foolscap—might we not meet now and then for the humour of exchanging anecdotes? No class of beings is more in need of the consolations of intercourse. Perpend, brothers! Let us order a tierce of malmsey and talk it over! Perchance, too, a trade union among readers might be of substantial advantage. Is it not sad that a man should read manuscripts all the sweet years of his maturity, and be paid forty dollars a week? Let us make sixty the minimum—or let there be a pogrom among the authors!

WILLIAM McFEE

M'Phee is the most tidy of chief engineers. If the leg of a cockroach gets into one of his slide-valves the whole ship knows it, and half the ship has to clean up the mess.

—RUDYARD KIPLING.

THE next time the Cunard Company commissions a new liner I wish they would sign on Joseph Conrad as captain, Rudyard Kipling as purser, and William McFee as chief engineer. They might add Don Marquis as deck steward and Hall Caine as chief-stewardess. Then I would like to be at Raymond and Whitcomb's and watch the clerks booking passages!

William McFee does not spell his name quite as does the Scotch engineer in Mr. Kipling's *Brugglesmith*, but I feel sure that his attitude toward cockroaches in the slide-valve is the same. Unhappily I do not know Mr. McFee in his capacity as engineer; but I know and respect his feelings as a writer, his love of honourable and honest work, his disdain for blurb and blat. And by an author's attitude toward the purveyors of publicity, you may know him.

One evening about the beginning of December,
1915, I was sitting by the open fire in Hempstead,
Long Island, a comparatively inoffensive young
man, reading the new edition of Flecker's "The
Golden Journey to Samarkand" issued that
October by Martin Secker in London. Mr.
Secker, like many other wise publishers, inserts
in the back of his books the titles of other volumes
issued by him. Little did I think, as I turned to
look over Mr. Secker's announcements, that a train
of events was about to begin which would render
me, during the succeeding twelve months, a
monomaniac in the eyes of my associates; so
much so that when I was blessed with a son and
heir just a year later I received a telegram signed
by a dozen of them: *"Congratulations. Name
him Casuals!"*

It was in that list of Mr. Secker's titles for the
winter of 1915-16 that my eyes first rested, with a
premonitory lust, upon the not-to-be-forgotten
words.

MCFEE, WILLIAM: CASUALS OF THE SEA.
Who could fail to be stirred by so brave a title?
At once I wrote for a copy.

My pocket memorandum book for Sunday,
January 9, 1916, contains this note:

"Finished reading *Casuals of the Sea*, a good
book. H——still laid up with bad ankle. In the

P. M. we sat and read Bible aloud to Celia before the open fire."

My first impressions of *"Casuals of the Sea, a good book"* are interwoven with memories of Celia, a pious Polish serving maid from Pike County, Pennsylvania, who could only be kept in the house by nightly readings of another Good Book. She was horribly homesick (that was her first voyage away from home) and in spite of persistent Bible readings she fled after two weeks, back to her home in Parker's Glen, Pa. She was our first servant, and we had prepared a beautiful room in the attic for her. However, that has nothing to do with Mr. McFee.

Casuals of the Sea is a novel whose sale of ten thousand copies in America is more important as a forecast of literary weather than many a popular distribution of a quarter million. Be it known by these presents that there are at least ten thousand librivora in this country who regard literature not merely as an emulsion. This remarkable novel, the seven years' study of a busy engineer occupied with boiler inspections, indicator cards and other responsibilities of the Lord of Below, was the first really public appearance of a pen that will henceforth be listened to with respect.

Mr. McFee had written two books before "Casuals" was published, but at that time it was not easy to find any one who had read them. They were *Letters from an Ocean Tramp* (1908) and *Aliens* (1914); the latter has been rewritten since then and issued in a revised edition. It is a very singular experiment in the art of narrative, and a rich commentary on human folly by a man who has made it his hobby to think things out for himself. And the new version is headlighted by a preface which may well take its place among the most interesting literary confessions of this generation, where Mr. McFee shows himself as that happiest of men, the artist who also has other and more urgent concerns than the whittling of a paragraph:—

Of art I never grow weary, but she calls me over the world. I suspect the sedentary art worker. Most of all I suspect the sedentary writer. I divide authors into two classes— genuine artists, and educated men who wish to earn enough to let them live like country gentlemen. With the latter I have no concern. But the artist knows when his time has come. In the same way I turned with irresistible longing to the sea, whereon I had been wont to earn my living. It is a good life and I love it. I love the men and their ships. I find in them a never-ending panorama which illustrates my theme, the problem of human folly.

Mr. McFee, you see, has some excuse for being a good writer because he has never had to write for a living. He has been writing for the fun of it

ever since he was an apprentice in a big engineering
shop in London twenty years ago.   His profession
deals with exacting and beautiful machinery, and
he could no more do hack writing than hack
engineering.   And unlike the other English real-
ists of his generation who have cultivated a cheap
flippancy, McFee finds no exhilaration in easy
sneers at middle-class morality.   He has a dirk
up his sleeve for Gentility (how delightfully he
flays it in *Aliens*) but he loves the middle classes
for just what they are: the great fly-wheel of the
world.   His attitude toward his creations is that
of a "benevolent marbleheart" (his own phrase).
He has seen some of the seams of life, and like
McAndrew he has hammered his own philosophy.
It is a manly, just, and gentle creed, but not a soft
one.   Since the war began he has been on sea service, first on a beef-ship and transport in the
Mediterranean, now as sub-lieutenant in the
British Navy.   When the war is over, and if he
feels the call of the desk, Mr. McFee's brawny
shoulder will sit in at the literary feast and a big
handful of scribblers will have to drop down the
dumb-waiter shaft to make room for him.   It is a
disconcerting figure in Grub Street, the man who
really has something to say.

Publishers are always busy casting horoscopes
for their new finds.   How the benign planets must

have twirled in happy curves when Harold Bell Wright was born, if one may credit his familiar mage, Elsbury W. Reynolds! But the fame that is built merely on publishers' press sheets does not dig very deep in the iron soil of time. We are all only raft-builders, as Lord Dunsany tells us in his little parable; even the raft that Homer made for Helen must break up some day. Who in these States knows the works of Nat Gould? Twelve million of his dashing paddock novels have been sold in England, but he is as unknown here as is Preacher Wright in England. What is so dead as a dead best seller? Sometimes it is the worst sellers that come to life, roll away the stone, and an angel is found sitting laughing in the sepulchre. Let me quote Mr. McFee once more: "I have no taste for blurb, but I cannot refuse facts."

William M. P. McFee was born at sea in 1881. His father, an English skipper, was bringing his vessel toward the English coast after a long voyage. His mother was a native of Nova Scotia. They settled in New Southgate, a northern middle-class suburb of London, and here McFee was educated in the city schools of which the first pages of *Casuals of the Sea* give a pleasant description. Then he went to a well-known grammar school at Bury St. Edmunds in Suffolk—what we would call over

here a high school. He was a quiet, sturdy boy,
and a first-rate cricketer.

At sixteen he was apprenticed to a big engineering firm in Aldersgate. This is one of the oldest
streets in London, near the Charterhouse, Smith-
field Market, and the famous "Bart's" Hospital.
In fact, the office of the firm was built over one
of the old plague pits of 1665. His father had died
several years before; and for the boy to become an
apprentice in this well-known firm Mrs. McFee
had to pay three hundred pounds sterling. McFee
has often wondered just what he got for the
money. However, the privilege of paying to be
better than someone else is an established way of
working out one's destiny in England, and at the
time the mother and son knew no better than to
conform. You will find this problem, and the
whole matter of gentility, cuttingly set out in
Aliens.

After three years as an apprentice, McFee was
sent out by the firm on various important engineering jobs, notably a pumping installation at Tring,
which he celebrated in a pamphlet of very credit-
able juvenile verses, for which he borrowed Mr.
Kipling's mantle. This was at the time of the
Boer War, when everybody in trousers who wrote
verses was either imitating Kipling or reacting
from him.

His engineering work gave young McFee a powerful interest in the lives and thoughts of the working classes. He was strongly influenced by socialism, and all his spare moments were spent with books. He came to live in Chelsea with an artist friend, but he had already tasted life at first hand, and the rather hazy atmosphere of that literary and artistic utopia made him uneasy. His afternoons were spent at the British Museum reading room, his evenings at the Northampton Institute, where he attended classes, and even did a little lecturing of his own. Competent engineer as he was, that was never sufficient to occupy his mind. As early as 1902 he was writing short stories and trying to sell them.

In 1905 his uncle, a shipmaster, offered him a berth in the engine room of one of his steamers, bound for Trieste. He jumped at the chance. Since then he has been at sea almost continuously, save for one year (1912-13) when he settled down in Nutley, New Jersey, to write. The reader of *Aliens* will be pretty familiar with Nutley by the time he reaches page 416. "Netley" is but a thin disguise. I suspect a certain liveliness in the ozone of Nutley. Did not Frank Stockton write some of his best tales there? Some day some literary meteorologist will explain how these intellectual anticyclones originate in such places as

Nutley (N. J), Galesburg (Ill.), Port Washington (N. Y.), and Bryn Mawr (Pa.)

The life of a merchantman engineer would not seem to open a fair prospect into literature. The work is gruelling and at the same time monotonous. Constant change of scene and absence of home ties are (I speak subject to correction) demoralizing; after the coveted chief's certificate is won, ambition has little further to look forward to. A small and stuffy cabin in the belly of the ship is not an inviting study. The works of Miss Corelli and Messrs. Haig and Haig are the only diversions of most of the profession. Art, literature, and politics do not interest them. Picture postcards, waterside saloons, and the ladies of the port are the glamour of life that they delight to honour.

I imagine that Mr. Carville's remarkable account (in *Aliens*) of his induction into the profession of marine engineering has no faint colour of reminiscence in Mr. McFee's mind. The filth, the intolerable weariness, the instant necessity of the tasks, stagger the easygoing suburban reader. And only the other day, speaking of his work on a seaplane ship in the British Navy, Mr. McFee said some illuminating things about the life of an engineer:

It is Sunday, and I have been working. Oh, yes, there is plenty of work to do in the world, I find, wherever I go.

But I cannot help wondering why Fate so often offers me the dirty end of the stick. Here I am, awaiting my commission as an engineer-officer of the R.N.R., and I am in the thick of it day after day. I don't mean, when I say "work," what you mean by work. I don't mean work such as my friend the Censor does, or my friend the N.E.O. does, nor my friends and shipmates, the navigating officer, the flying men, or the officers of the watch. I mean *work*, hard, sweating, nasty toil, coupled with responsibility. I am not alone. Most ships of the naval auxiliary are the same.

I am anxious for you, a landsman, to grasp this particular fragment of the sorry scheme of things entire, that in no other profession have the officers responsible for the carrying out of the work to toil as do the engineers in merchantmen, in transports, in fleet auxiliaries. You do not expect the major to clear the waste-pipe of his regimental latrines. You do not expect the surgeon to superintend the purging of his bandages. You do not expect the navigators of a ship to paint her hull. You do not expect an architect to make bricks (sometimes without straw). You do not expect the barrister to go and repair the lock on the law courts door, or oil the fans that ventilate the halls of justice. Yet you do, collectively, tolerate a tradition by which the marine engineer has to assist, overlook, and very often perform work corresponding precisely to the irrelevant chores mentioned above, which are in other professions relegated to the humblest and roughest of mankind. I blame no one. It is tradition, a most terrible windmill at which to tilt; but I conceive it my duty to set down once at least the peculiar nature of an engineer's destiny. I have had some years of it, and I know what I am talking about.

The point to distinguish is that the engineer not only has the responsibility, but he has, in nine cases out of ten, to do it.

He, the officer, must befoul his person and derange his hours of rest and recreation, that others may enjoy. He must be available twenty-four hours a day, seven days a week, at sea or in port. Whether chief or the lowest junior, he must be ready to plunge instantly to the succour of the vilest piece of mechanism on board. When coaling, his lot is easier imagined than described.

The remarkable thing to note is that Mr. McFee imposed upon these laborious years of physical toil a strenuous discipline of intellect as well. He is a born worker: patient, dogged, purposeful. His years at sea have been to him a more fruitful curriculum than that of any university. The patient sarcasm with which he speaks of certain Oxford youths of his acquaintance does not escape me. His sarcasm is just and on the target. He has stood as Senior Wrangler in a far more exacting *viva voce*—the University of the Seven Seas.

If I were a college president, out hunting for a faculty, I would deem that no salary would be too big to pay for the privilege of getting a man like McFee on my staff. He would not come, of course! But how he has worked for his mastery of the art of life and the theory thereof! When his colleagues at sea were dozing in their deck chairs or rattling the bones along the mahogany, he was sweating in his bunk, writing or reading.

He has always been deeply interested in painting,
and no gallery in any port he visited ever escaped
him. These extracts from some of his letters will
show whether his avocations were those of most
engineers:

As I crossed the swing-bridge of the docks at Garston
(Liverpool) the other day, and saw the tapering spars sil-
houetted against the pale sky, and the zinc-coloured river
with its vague Cheshire shores dissolving in mist, it occurred
to me that if an indulgent genie were to appear and make me
an offer I would cheerfully give up writing for painting.
As it is, I see things in pictures and I spend more time in the
Walker Gallery than in the library next door.

I've got about all I *can* get out of books, and now I don't
relish them save as memories. The reason for my wish, I
suppose, is that character, not incident, is my *metier*. And
you can *draw* character, *paint* character, but you can't very
well blat about it, can you?

I am afraid Balzac's job is too big for anybody nowadays.
The worst of writing men nowadays is their horrible ignorance of how people live, of ordinary human possibilities.

A——. is always pitching into me for my insane ideas about
"cheap stuff." He says I'm on the wrong tack and I'll be a
failure if I don't do what the public wants. I said I didn't
care a blue curse what the public wanted, nor did I worry
much if I never made a big name. All I want is to do some
fine and honourable work, to do it as well as I possibly could,
and there my responsibility ended. . . . To hell with
writing, I want to *feel* and *see!*

I am laying in a gallon of ink and a couple of cwt. of paper,
to the amusement of the others, who imagine I am a mer-

chant of some sort who has to transact business at sea because
Scotland yard are after him!

His kit for every voyage, besides the gallon of ink
and the hundredweight of foolscap, always included a score of books, ranging from Livy or
Chaucer to Gorky and histories of Italian art.
Happening to be in New York at the time of the
first exhibition in this country of "futurist" pictures, he entered eagerly into the current discussion in the newspaper correspondence columns.
He wrote for a leading London journal an article
on "The Conditions of Labour at Sea." He
finds time to contribute to the *Atlantic Monthly*
pieces of styptic prose that make zigzags on the
sphygmograph of the editor. His letters written
weekly to the artist friend he once lived with in
Chelsea show a humorous and ironical mind ranging over all topics that concern cultivated men.
I fancy he could out-argue many a university
professor on Russian fiction, or Michelangelo, or
steam turbines.

When one says that McFee found little intel-
lectually in common with his engineering col-
leagues- that is not to say that he was a prig.
He was interested in everything that they were,
but in a great deal more, too. And after obtaining
his extra chief's certificate from the London

Board of Trade, with a grade of ninety-eight per cent., he was not inclined to rest on his gauges.

In 1912 he took a walking trip from Glasgow to London, to gather local colour for a book he had long meditated; then he took ship for the United States, where he lived for over a year writing hard. Neither *Aliens* nor *Casuals of the Sea*, which he had been at work on for years, met with the favour of New York publishers. He carried his manuscripts around the town until weary of that amusement; and when the United Fruit Company asked him to do some engineering work for them he was not loath to get back into the old harness. And then came the war.

Alas, it is too much to hope that the Cunard Company will ever officer a vessel as I have suggested at the outset of these remarks. But I made my proposal not wholly at random, for in Conrad, Kipling, and McFee, all three, there is something of the same artistic creed. In those two magnificent prefaces—to *A Personal Record* and to *The Nigger of the Narcissus*— Conrad has set down, in words that should be memorable to every trafficker in ink, his conception of the duty of the man of letters. They can never be quoted too often:

"All ambitions are lawful except those which climb upward on the miseries or credulities of mankind. . . . The sight of human affairs deserves admiration and pity. And he is not insensible who pays them the undemonstrative tribute of a sigh which is not a sob, and of a smile which is not a grin."

That is the kind of tribute that Mr. McFee has paid to the Gooderich family in *Casuals of the Sea*. Somewhere in that book he has uttered the immortal remark that "The world belongs to the Enthusiast who keeps cool." I think there is much of himself in that aphorism, and that the cool enthusiast, the benevolent marbleheart, has many fine things in store for us.

And there is one other sentence in *Casuals of the Sea* that lingers with me, and gives a just trace of the author's mind. It is worth remembering, and I leave it with you:

"She considered a trouble was a trouble and to be treated as such, instead of snatching the knotted cord from the hand of God and dealing murderous blows."

RHUBARB

WE USED to call him Rhubarb, by reason of his long russet beard, which we imagined trailing in the prescriptions as he compounded them, imparting a special potency. He was a little German druggist—*Deutsche Apotheker*—and his real name was Friedrich Wilhelm Maximilian Schulz.

The village of Kings is tucked away in Long Island, in the Debatable Land where the generous boundary of New York City zigzags in a sporting way just to permit horse racing at Belmont Park. It is the most rustic corner of the City. To most New Yorkers it is as remote as Helgoland and as little known. It has no movie theatre, no news-stand, no cigar store, no village atheist. The railroad station, where one hundred and fifty trains a day do not stop, might well be mistaken for a Buddhist shrine, so steeped in discreet melancholy is it. The Fire Department consists of an old hose wagon first used to extinguish fires kindled by the Republicans when Rutherford B. Hayes was elected. In the weather-beaten Kings Lyceum "East Lynne" is still per-

formed once a year. People who find Quogue
and Cohasset too exciting, move to Kings to cool
off. The only way one can keep servants out
there is by having the works of Harold Bell
Wright in the kitchen for the cook to read.

Stout-hearted Mr. Schulz came to Kings long
ago. There is quite a little German colony there.
With a delicatessen store on one side of him and
a man who played the flute on the other, he felt
hardly at all expatriated. The public house on
the corner serves excellent *Rheingold,* and on winter evenings Friedrich and Minna would sit by the
stove at the back of the drugstore with a jug of
amber on the table and dream of Stuttgart.

It did not take me long to find out that apothe-
cary Schulz was an educated man. At the rear
of the store hung two diplomas of which he was
very proud. One was a certificate from the Stuttgart Oberrealschule; the other his license to
practise homicidal pharmacy in the German
Empire, dated 1880. He had read the "Kritik der
reinen Vernunft", and found it more interesting
than Henry James, he told me. Julia and I used
to drop into his shop of an evening for a mug of hot
chocolate, and always fell into talk. His Minna, a
frail little woman with a shawl round her shoulders,
would come out into the store and talk to us, too,
and their pet dachshund would frolic at our feet.

They were a quaint couple, she so white and shy and fragile; he ruddy, sturdy, and positive.

It was not till I told him of my years spent at a German University that he really showed me the life that lay behind his shopman activity. We sometimes talked German together, and he took me into their little sitting room to see his photographs of home scenes at Stuttgart. It was over thirty years since he had seen German soil, but still his eyes would sparkle at the thought. He and Minna, being childless, dreamed of a return to the Fatherland as their great end in life.

What an alluring place the little drugstore was! I was fascinated by the rows and rows of gleaming bottles labelled with mysterious Latin abbreviations. There were cases of patent remedies—Mexican Mustang Liniment, Swamp Root, Danderine, Conway's Cobalt Pills, Father Finch's Febrifuge, Spencer's Spanish Specific. Soap, talcum, cold cream, marshmallows, tobacco, jars of rock candy, what a medley of paternostrums! And old Rhubarb himself, in his enormous baggy trousers—infinite breeches in a little room, as Julia used to say.

I wish I could set him down in all his rich human flavour. The first impression he gave was one of cleanness and good humour. He was always in shirtsleeves, with suspenders forming an

X across his broad back; his shirt was fresh
laundered, his glowing beard served as cravat.
He had a slow, rather ponderous speech,
with deep gurgling gutturals and a decrescendo
laugh, slipping farther and farther down into
his larynx. Once, when we got to know each
other fairly well, I ventured some harmless jest
about Barbarossa. He chuckled; then his face
grew grave. "I wish Minna could have the
beard," he said. "Her chest is not strong. It
would be a fine breast-protector for her. But
me, because I am strong like a horse, I have it
all!" He thumped his chest ruefully with his
broad, thick hand.

Despite his thirty years in America, good
Schulz was still the Deutsche Apotheker and not
at all the American druggist. He had installed
a soda fountain as a concession, but it puzzled him
sorely, and if he was asked for anything more complex than chocolate ice cream soda he would
shake his head solemnly and say: "That I have not
got." Motorists sometimes turned off the Jericho
turnpike and stopped at his shop asking for banana
splits or grape juice highballs, or frosted pineapple
fizz. But they had to take chocolate ice cream
soda or nothing. Sometimes in a fit of absent-
mindedness he would turn his taps too hard and
the charged water would spout across the imita-

tion marble counter. He would wag his beard deprecatingly and mutter a shamefaced apology, smiling again when the little black dachshund came trotting to sniff at the spilt soda and rasp the wet floor with her bright tongue.

At the end of September he shut up the soda fountain gladly, piling it high with bars of castile soap or cartons of cod liver oil. Then Minna entered into her glory as the dispenser of hot chocolate which seethed and sang in a tall silvery tank with a blue gas burner underneath. This she served in thick china mugs with a clot of whipped cream swimming on top. Julia would buy a box of the cheese crackers that Schulz kept in stock specially for her, and give several to the sleek little black bitch that stood pleading with her quaint turned-out fore-feet placed on Julia's slippers. Schulz, beaming serenely behind a pyramid of "intense carnation" bottles on his per-fume counter, would chuckle at the antics of his pet. "Ah, he is a wise little dog!" he would exclaim with naïve pride. "He knows who is friendly!" He always called the little dog "he," which amused us.

On Sunday afternoon the drugstore was closed from one to five, and during those hours Schulz took his weekly walk, accompanied by the dog which plodded desperately after him on her short legs. Sometimes we met him swinging along the by-roads, flourishing a cudgel and humming to himself. Whenever he saw a motor coming he halted, the little black dachshund would look up at him, and he would stoop ponderously down, pick her up and carry her in his arms until all danger was past.

As the time went on he and I used to talk a good deal about the war. Minna, pale and weary, would stand behind her steaming urn, keeping the shawl tight round her shoulders; Rhubarb and I would argue without heat upon the latest news from the war zone. I had no zeal for converting the old fellow from his views; I understood his sympathies and respected them. Reports of atrocities troubled him as much as they did me; but the spine of his contention was that the German army was unbeatable. He got out his faded discharge ticket from the Würtemberger Landsturm to show the perfect system of the Imperial military organization. In his desk at the back of the shop he kept a war map cut from a Sunday supplement and over this we would argue, Schulz breathing hard and holding his beard aside in one hand as he bent over the paper. When other customers came in, he would put the map away with a twinkle, and the topic was dropped. But often the glass top of the perfume

counter was requisitioned as a large-scale battle-
ground, and the pink bottle of rose water set to
represent Von Hindenburg while the green phial
of smelling salts was Joffre or Brussilov. We
fought out the battle of the Marne pretty com-
pletely on the perfume counter. *"Warte doch!"*
he would cry. "Just wait! You will see! All
the world is against her, but Germany will win!"

Poor Minna was always afraid her husband and
I would quarrel. She knew well how opposite
our sympathies were; she could not understand
that our arguments were wholly lacking in personal animus. When I told him of the Allies'
growing superiority in aircraft Rhubarb would
retort by showing me clippings about the German
trench fortifications, the "pill boxes" made of
solid cement. I would speak of the deadly curtain
fire of the British; he would counter with mysterious allusions to Krupp. And his conclusions
were always the same. "Just wait! Germany
will win!" And he would stroke his beard placidly. "But, Fritz!" Minna used to cry in a
panic, "The gentleman might think differently!"
Rhubarb and I would grin at each other, I would
buy a tin of tobacco, and we would say good
night.

How dear is the plain, unvarnished human
being when one sees him in a true light! Schulz's

honest, kindly face seemed to me to typify all
that I knew of the finer qualities of the Germans;
the frugal simplicity, the tenderness, the proud,
stiff rectitude.   He and I felt for each other, I
think, something of the humorous friendliness of
the men in the opposing trenches.   Chance had
cast us on different sides of the matter.   But
when I felt tempted to see red, to condemn the
Germans *en masse*, to chant litanies of hate, I used
to go down to the drugstore for tobacco or a mug
of chocolate.   Rhubarb and I would argue it out.

But that was a hard winter for him.   The growing anti-German sentiment in the neighbourhood reduced his business considerably.   Then
he was worried over Minna.   Often she did not
appear in the evenings, and he would explain
that she had gone to bed.   I was all the more surprised to meet her one very snowy Sunday afternoon, sloshing along the road in the liquid mire,
the little dog squattering sadly behind, her small
black paws sliding on the ice-crusted paving.
"What on earth are you doing outdoors on a day
like this?" I said.

"Fritz had to go to Brooklyn, and I thought he
would be angry if Lischen didn't get her airing."

"You take my advice and go home and get into
some dry clothes," I said severely.

Soon after that I had to go away for three

weeks. I was snowbound in Massachusetts for
several days; then I had to go to Montreal on
urgent business. Julia went to the city to visit
her mother while I was away, so we had no news
from Kings.

We got back late one Sunday evening. The
plumbing had frozen in our absence; when I lit the
furnace again, pipes began to thaw and for an
hour or so we had a lively time. In the course of
a battle with a pipe and a monkey wrench I
sprained a thumb, and the next morning I stopped
at the drug-store on my way to the train to get
some iodine.

Rhubarb was at his prescription counter weigh-
ing a little cone of white powder in his apothe-
cary's scales. He looked far from well. There
were great pouches under his eyes; his beard was
unkempt; his waistcoat spotted with food stains.
The lady waiting received her package, and went
out. Rhubarb and I grasped hands.

"Well," I said, "what do you think now about
the war? Did you see that the Canadians took a
mile of trenches five hundred yards deep last
week? Do you still think Germany will win?"
To my surprise he turned on his heel and began
apparently rummaging along a row of glass jars.
His gaze seemed to be fastened upon a tall bottle
containing ethyl alcohol. At last he turned

round.　His broad, naïve face was quivering like blanc-mange.

"What do I care who wins?" he said.　"What does it matter to me any more?　Minna is dead. She died two weeks ago of pneumonia."

As I stood, not knowing what to say, there was a patter along the floor.　The little dachshund came scampering into the shop and frisked about my feet.

THE HAUNTING BEAUTY OF
STRYCHNINE

A LITTLE-KNOWN TOWN OF UNEARTHLY BEAUTY

SLOWLY, reluctantly (rather like a *vers libre* poem) the quaint little train comes to a stand. Along the station platform each of the *fiacre* drivers seizes a large dinner-bell and tries to outring the others. You step from the railway carriage—and instantly the hellish din of those droschky bells faints into a dim, far-away tolling. Your eye has caught the superb sweep of the Casa Grande beetling on its crag. Over the sapphire canal where the old men are fishing for sprats, above the rugged scarp where the blue-bloused *ouvriers* are quarrying the famous champagne cheese, you see the Gothic transept of the Palazzio Ginricci, dour against a nacre sky. An involuntary tremolo eddies down your spinal marrow. The Gin Palace, you murmur. . . . At last you are in Strychnine.

Unnoted by Baedeker, unsung by poets, unrhapsodied by press agents—there lurks the little town of Strychnine in that far and untravelled

corner where France, Russia, and Liberia meet
in an unedifying Zollverein. The strychnine
baths have long been famous among physicians,
but the usual ruddy tourist knows them not. The
sorrowful ennui of a ten-hour journey on the
B. V. D. *Chemise de fer* (with innumerable ex-
aminations of luggage), while it has kept out the
contraband Swiss cheese which is so strictly inter-
dicted, has also kept away the rich and garrulous
tourist. But he who will endure to the end that
tortuous journey among flat fields of rye and
parsimony, will find himself well rewarded. The
long tunnel through Mondragone ends at length,
and you find yourself on the platform with the
droschky bells clanging in your ears and the ineff-
able majesty of the Casa Grande crag soaring behind the jade canal.

The air was chill, and I buttoned my surtout
tightly as I stepped into the curious seven-wheeled
sforza lettered *Hôtel Decameron*. We rumbled
andante espressivo over the hexagonal cobbles of
the Chaussée d'Arsenic, crossed the mauve canal
and bent under the hanging cliffs of the cheese
quarries. I could see the fishwives carrying great
trays of lampreys and lambrequins toward the fish
market. It is curious what quaintly assorted impressions one receives in the first few minutes in a
strange place. I remember noticing a sausage

kiosk in the *markt-platz* where a man in a white
coat was busily selling hot icons. They are de-
livered fresh every hour from the Casa Grande
(the great cheese cathedral) on the cliff.

The Hôtel Decameron is named after Boccaccio,
who was once a bartender there. It stands in a
commanding position on the Place Nouveau Riche
overlooking the Casino and the odalisk erected by
Edward VII in memory of his cure. After two
weeks of the strychnine baths the merry monarch
is said to have called for a corncob pipe and a
plate of onions, after which he made his escape
by walking over the forest track to the French
frontier, although previous to this he had not
walked a kilometer without a cane since John Bull
won the Cowes regatta. The *haut ton* of the section in which the Hôtel Decameron finds itself
can readily be seen by the fact that the campa-
nile of the Duke of Marmalade fronts on the rue
Sauterne, just across from the barroom of the
Hôtel. The antiquaries say there is an underground corridor between the two.

The fascinations of a stay in Strychnine are
manifold. I have a weak heart, so I did not try
the baths, although I used to linger on the terrace
of the Casino about sunset to hear Tinpanni's band
and eat a bronze bowl of Kerosini's gooseberry
fool. I spent a great deal of my time exploring

the chief glory of the town, the Casa Grande,
which stands on the colossal crag honeycombed
underneath with the shafts and vaults of the
cheese mine. There is nothing in the world more
entrancing than to stand (with a vinaigrette at
one's nose) on the ramp of the Casa, looking down
over the ochre canal, listening to the hoarse
shouts of the workmen as they toil with pick and
shovel, laying bare some particularly rich lode of
the pale, citron-coloured cheese which will some
day make Strychnine a place of *pélérinage* for all
the world. *Pay homage to the fromage* is a rough
translation of the motto of the town, which is car-
ved in old Gothic letters on the apse of the Casa
itself. Limberg, Gruyère, Alkmaar, Neufchâtel,
Camembert and Hoboken—all these famous
cheeses will some day pale into whey before the
puissance of the Strychnine curd. I was signally
honoured by an express invitation of the bur-
gomaster to be present at a meeting of the Cheese-
mongers' Guild at the Rathaus. The Kurdmeister, who is elected annually by the town council, spoke most eloquently on the future of the
cheese industry, and a curious rite was performed.
Before the entrance of the ceremonial cheese,
which is cut by the Kurdmeister himself, all those
present donned oxygen masks similar to those
devised by the English to combat the German

poison-gas. And I learned that oxygen helmets are worn by the workmen in the quarries to prevent prostration.

It was with unfeigned regret that I found my fortnight over. I would gladly have lingered in the medieval cloisters of the Gin Palace, and sat for many mornings under the pistachio trees on the terrace sipping my *verre* of native wine. But duties recalled me to the beaten paths of travel, and once more I drove in the old-fashioned ambulance to catch my even more old-fashioned train. The B. V. D. trains only leave Strychnine when there is a stern wind, as otherwise the pungent fumes of the cheese carried in the luggage van are very obnoxious to the passengers. Some day some American efficiency expert will visit the town and teach them to couple their luggage van on to the rear of the train. But till then Strychnine will be to me, and to every other traveller who may chance that way, a fragrant memory.

And as you enter the tunnel, the last thing you see is the onyx canal and the old women fishing for lambrequins and palfreys.

INGO

"ZUM ANDENKEN"

THE first night we sat down at the inn table for supper I lost my heart to Ingo! Ingo was just ten years old. He wore a little sailor suit of blue and white striped linen; his short trousers showed chubby brown calves above his white socks; his round golden head cropped close in the German fashion. His blue eyes were grave and thoughtful. By great good fortune we sat next each other at table, and in my rather grotesque German I began a conversation. How careful Ingo was not to laugh at the absurdities of my syntax! How very courteous he was!

Looking back into the mysterious panorama of pictures that we call memory, I can see the long dining room of the old gasthaus in the Black Forest, where two Americans on bicycles appeared out of nowhere and asked for lodging. They were the first Americans who had ever been seen in that remote valley, and the Gasthaus zur Krone ("the Crown Inn") found them very

142

amusing. Perhaps you have never seen a country tavern in the Schwarzwald? Then you have something to live for. A long, low building with a moss-grown roof and tremendous broad eaves sheltering little galleries; and the barn under the same roof for greater warmth in winter. One side of the house was always strong with an excellent homely aroma of cow and horse; one had only to open a door in the upper hall, a door that looked just like a bedroom entrance, to find oneself in the haymow. There I used to lie for hours reading, and listening to the summer rain thudding on the shingles. Sitting in the little gallery under the eaves, looking happily down the white road where the yellow coach brought the mail twice a day, one could see the long vista of the valley, the women with bright red jackets working in the fields, and the dark masses of forest on the hillside opposite. There was much rain that summer; the mountains were often veiled all day long in misty shreds of cloud, and the two Americans sat with pipes and books at the long dining table, greeted by gales of laughter on the part of the robust landlord's niece when they essayed the native idiom. "*Sie arbeiten immer!*" she used to say; "*Sie werden krank!*" ("You're always working; you'll be ill!")

There is a particular poignance in looking

back now on those happy days two years before the war. Nowhere in all the world, I suppose, are there more cordial, warmhearted, simple, human people than the South Germans. On the front of the inn there was a big yellow metal sign, giving the military number of the district, and the mobilization points for the Landsturm and the Landwehr, and we realized that even here the careful organization of the military power had numbered and ticketed every village. But what did it mean to us? War was a thing unthinkable in those days. We bicycled everywhere, climbed mountains, bathed in waterfalls, chatted fluent and unorthodox German with everyone we met, and played games with Ingo.

Dear little Ingo! At the age when so many small boys are pert, impudent, self-conscious, he was the simplest, happiest, gravest little creature. His hobby was astronomy, and often I would find him sitting quietly in a corner with a book about the stars. On clear evenings we would walk along the road together, in the mountain hush that was only broken by the brook tumbling down the valley, and he would name the constellations for me. His little round head was thrilled through and through by the immense mysteries of space; sometimes at meal times he would fall into a muse, forgetting his beef and gravy. Once I asked him at dinner what he was thinking of. He looked up with his clear gray-blue eyes and flashing smile: *"Von den Sternen!"*   ("Of the stars.")

The time after supper was reserved for games, in which Wolfgang, Ingo's smaller brother (aged seven), also took part. Our favourite pastimes were "Irrgarten" and "Galgenspiel," in which we found enormous amusement. Galgenspiel was Ingo's translation of "Hangman," a simple pastime which had sometimes entertained my own small brother on rainy days; apparently it was new in Germany. One player thinks of a word, and sets down on paper a dash for each letter in this word. It is the task of the other to guess the word, and he names the letters of the alphabet one by one.   Every time he mentions a letter that is contained in the word you must set it down in its proper place in the word, but every time he mentions a letter that is not in the word you draw a portion of a person depending from a gallows; the object of course being for him to guess the word before you finish drawing the effigy. We played the game entirely in German, and I can still see Ingo's intent little face bent over my preposterous drawings, cudgelling his quick and happy little brain to spot the word before the hangman could finish his grim task. "Quick, Ingo!" I would cry. "You will get yourself

hung!" and he would laugh in his own lovable
way. There was never a jollier way of learning a
foreign language than by playing games with
Ingo.

The other favourite pastime was drawing mazes
on paper, labyrinths of winding paths which must
be traversed by a pencil point. The task was to
construct a maze so complicated that the other
could not find his way out, starting at the middle.
We would sit down at opposite ends of the room
to construct our mysteries of blind alleys and
misleading passages, then each one would be
turned loose in the "irrgarten" drawn by the other.
Ingo would stand at my side while I tried in
obstinate stupidity to find my way through his
little puzzle; his eager heart inside his sailor
blouse would pound like a drum when I was near-
ing the dangerous places where an exit might be
won. He would hold his breath so audibly, and
his blue eyes would grow so anxious, that I always
knew when not to make the right turning, and
my pencil would wander on in hopeless despair
until he had mercy on me and led me to freedom.

After lunch every day, while waiting for the
mail-coach to come trundling up the valley, Ingo
and I used to sit in the little balcony under the
eaves, reading. He introduced me to his
favourite book *Till Eulenspiegel*, and we sped

joyously through the adventures of that immortal buffoon of German folk-lore. We took turns reading aloud: every paragraph or so I would appeal for an explanation of something. Generally I understood well enough, but it was such a delight to hear Ingo strive to make the meaning plain. What a puckering of his bright boyish forehead, what a grave determination to elucidate the fable! What a mingling of ecstatic pride in having a grown man as pupil, with deference due to an elder. Ingo was a born gentleman and in his fiercest transports of glee never forgot his manners! I would make some purposely ludicrous shot at the sense, and he would double up with innocent mirth. His clear laughter would ring out, and his mother, pacing a digestive stroll on the highway below us, would look up crying in the German way, *"Gott! wie er freut sich!"* The progress of our reading was held up by these interludes, but I could never resist the temptation to start Ingo explaining.

Ingo having made me free of his dearest book, it was only fair to reciprocate. So one day Lloyd and I bicycled down to Freiburg, and there, at a heavenly "bookhandler's," I found a copy of 'Treasure Island' in German. Then there was revelry in the balcony! I read the tale aloud, and I wish R. L. S. might have seen the

shining of Ingo's eyes! Alas, the vividness of
the story interfered with the little lad's sleep, and
his mother was a good deal disturbed about this
violent yarn we were reading together. How
close he used to sit beside me as we read of the
dark doings at the *Admiral Benbow;* and how his
face would fall when, clear and hollow from the
sounding-board of the hills, came the quick *clop,
clop* of the mail-man's horses.

I don't know anything that has ever gone
deeper in my memory than those hours spent
with Ingo. I have a little snapshot of him I
took the misty, sorrowful morning when I bicycled
away to Basel and left the Gasthaus zur Krone
in its mountain valley. The blessed little lad
stands up erect and stiff in the formal German
way, and I can see his blue eyes alight with friendliness, and a little bit unhappy because his eccentric American comrade was going away and there
would be no more afternoons with *Till Eulenspiegel* on the balcony. I wonder if he thinks of
me as often as I do of him? He gave me a glimpse
into the innocent heaven of a child's heart that I
can never forget. By now he is approaching sixteen, and I pray that whatever the war may take
away from me it will spare me my Ingo. It is
strange and sad to recall that his parting present
to me was a drawing of a Zeppelin, upon which he

toiled manfully all one afternoon. I still have it in my scrap-book.

And I wonder if he ever looks in the old copy of "Hauff's Märchen" that I bought for him in Freiburg, and sees the English words that he was to learn how to translate when he should grow older! As I remember them, they ran like this:

For Ingo to learn English will very easy be
If someone is as kind to him as he has been to me;
Plays games with him, reads fairy tales, corrects all his mistakes,
And never laughs too loudly at the blunders that he makes—
Then he will find, as I did, how well two pleasures blend:
To learn a foreign language, and to make a foreign friend.

If I love anybody in the world, I love Ingo. And that is why I cannot get up much enthusiasm for hymns of hate.

HOUSEBROKEN

AFTER Simmons had been married two years he began to feel as though he needed a night off. But he hesitated to mention the fact, for he knew his wife would feel hurt to think that he could dream of an evening spent elsewhere than in their cosy sitting room. However, there were no two ways about it: the old unregenerate male in Simmons yearned for something more exciting than the fireside armchair, the slippers and smoking jacket, and the quiet game of cards. Visions of the old riotous evenings with the boys ran through his mind; a billiard table and the click of balls; the jolly conversation at the club, and glass after glass of that cold amber beer. The large freedom of the city streets at night, the warm saloons on every corner, the barrooms with their pyramids of bottles flashing in the gaslight—these were the things that made a man's life amusing. And here he was cooped up in a little cage in the suburbs like a tame cat!

Thoughts of this kind had agitated Simmons for a long time, and at last he said something to Ethel. He had keyed himself up to meet a sharp retort,

some sarcastic comment about his preferring a
beer garden to his own home, even an outburst
of tears. But to his amazement Ethel took it
quite calmly.

"Why, yes, of course, dear," she said. "It'll
do you good to have an evening with your friends."

A little taken aback, he asked whether she would
rather he didn't go.

"Why, no," she answered. "I shall have a
lovely time. I won't be lonely."

This was on Monday. Simmons planned to go
out on Friday night, meeting the boys for dinner
at the club, and after that they would spend the
evening at Boelke's bowling alley. All the week
he went about in a glow of anticipation. At the
office he spoke in an offhand way of the pleasant
evenings a man can have in town, and pitied the
prosaic beggars who never stir from the house at
night.

On Friday evening he came home hurriedly,
staying just long enough to shave and change his
collar. Ethel had on a pretty dress and seemed
very cheerful. A strange sinking came over him
as he saw the familiar room shining with firelight
and the shabby armchair.

"Would you rather I stayed at home?" he
asked.

"Not a bit," she said, quite as though she meant

it.   "Diana has a steak in the oven, and I've got
a new book to read.   I won't wait up for you."

He kissed her and went off.

When he got on the trolley a sudden revulsion
struck him.   He was tired and wanted to go
home.   Why on earth spend the evening with a
lot of drunken rowdies when he might be at his
own hearth watching Ethel's face bent over her
sewing?   He saw little enough of her anyway.

At the door of the club he halted.   Inside, the
crowd was laughing, shouting jests, dicing for
cocktails.   Suddenly he turned and ran.

He cursed himself for a fool, but none the less
an irresistible force seemed to draw him home.
On the car he sat glum and silent, wondering how
all the other men could read their papers so
contentedly.

At last he reached the modest little suburb.   He
hurried along the street and had almost entered
his gate when he paused.

Through the half-drawn curtains he could see
Ethel sitting comfortably by the lamp.   She was
reading, and the cat was in her lap.   His heart
leaped with a great throb.   But how could he go
in now?   It was barely eight o'clock.   After all
his talk about a man's need of relaxation and
masculine comradeship—why, she would never
stop laughing!   He turned and tiptoed away.

That evening was a nightmare for Simmons. Opposite his house was a little suburban park, and thither he took himself. For a long while he sat on a bench cursing. Twice he started for the trolley, and again returned. It was a damp autumn night; little by little the chill pierced his light coat and he sneezed. Up and down the little park he tramped, biting a dead cigar. Once he went as far as the drugstore and bought a box of crackers.

At last—it seemed years—the church chimes struck ten and he saw the lights go out in his house. He forced himself to make twenty-five more trips around the gravel walk and then he could wait no longer. Shivering with weariness and cold, he went home.

He let himself in with his latch key and tiptoed upstairs. He leaned over the bed and Ethel stirred sleepily.

"What time is it, dear?" she murmured. "You're early, aren't you?"

"One o'clock," he lied bravely—and just then the dining-room clock struck half-past ten and supported him.

"Did you have a good time?"

"Bully—perfectly bully," he said. "There's nothing like a night with the boys now and then."

THE HILARITY OF HILAIRE

I REMEMBER some friends of mine telling me how they went down to Horsham, in Sussex, to see Hilaire Belloc. They found him in the cellar, seated astraddle of a gigantic wine-cask just arrived from France, about to proceed upon the delicate (and congenial) task of bottling the wine. He greeted them like jovial Silenus, and with competitive shouts of laughter the fun went forward. The wine was strained, bottled, sealed, labelled, and binned, the master of the vintage initiating his young visitors into the rite with bubbling and infectious gaiety—improvising verses, shouting with merriment, full of an energy and vivacity almost inconceivable to Saxon phlegm. My friends have always remembered it as one of the most diverting afternoons of their lives; and after the bottling was done and all hands thoroughly tired, he took them a swinging tramp across the Sussex Downs, talking hard all the way.

I

That is the Belloc we all know and love: vigorous, Gallic, bursting with energy, hospitality, and

154

wit: the *enfant terrible* of English letters for the
past fifteen years.   Mr. Joyce Kilmer's edition of
Belloc's verses is very welcome.*   His introduction is charming: the tribute of an understanding
lover. Perhaps he labours a little in proving
that Belloc is essentially a poet rather than a
master of prose; perhaps too some of his judgments of Pater, Hardy, Scott, and others of whom
one has heard, are precipitate and smack a little
of the lecture circuit: but there is much to be grate-
ful for in his affectionate and thoughtful tribute.
Perhaps we do not enough realize how outstand-
ing and how engaging a figure Mr. Belloc is.

Hilaire Belloc is of soldierly, artistic, and lettered blood.   Four of his great-uncles were gen-
erals under Napoleon.   The father of his grandmother fought under Soult at Corunna. A
brother of his grandmother was wounded at
Waterloo.

His grandmother, Louise Marie Swanton, who
died in 1890, lived both in France and England,
and was famous as the translator into French
of Moore's "Life of Byron," "Uncle Tom's
Cabin," and works by Dickens and Mrs. Gaskell.
She married Hilaire Belloc, an artist, whose pictures are in the Louvre and many French mu-

*Verses by Hilaire Belloc; with an introduction by Joyce Kilmer. New York:
Laurence J. Gomme, 1916.

seums; his tomb may be seen in Père la Chaise.
Their son was Louis Swanton Belloc, a lawyer,
who married an English wife.

The only son of this couple was the present
Hilaire Belloc, born at Lacelle St. Cloud, July
27, 1870—the "Terrible Year" it was called—
until 1914.

Louis Belloc died in 1872, and as a very small
child Hilaire went to live in Sussex, the gracious
shire which both he and Rudyard Kipling have
so often and so thrillingly commemorated. Slin-
don, near Arundel, became his home, the rolling
hills, clean little rivers, and picturesque villages
of the South Downs moulded his boyish thoughts.

In 1883 he went to the famous Catholic school
at Edgbaston. Mr. Thomas Seccombe, in a
recent article on Belloc (from which I dip a number of biographical facts), quotes a description
of him at this period:

"I remember very well Belloc coming to the
Oratory School— some time in '83, I suppose.
He was a small, squat person, of the shaggy
kind, with a clever face and sharp, bright eyes.
Being amongst English boys, his instinctive com-
bativeness made him assume a decidedly French
pose, and this no doubt brought on him many a
gibe, which, we may be equally sure, he was well
able to return. I was amongst the older boys,

and saw little of him. But I recollect finding him one day studying a high wall (of the old Oratory Church, since pulled down). It turned out that he was calculating its exact height by some cryptic mathematical process which he proceeded to explain. I concealed my awe, and did not tell him that I understood nothing of his terms, his explanations, or deductions; it would have been unsuitable for a big fellow to be taught by a 'brat.' In those days the boys used to act Latin plays of Terence, which enjoyed a certain celebrity, and from his first year Belloc was remarkable. His rendering of the impudent servant maid was the inauguration of a series of triumphs during his whole school career."

In '89 Hilaire left school, and served for a year in the French field artillery, in a regiment stationed at Toul. Here he revived the Gallic heritage which was naturally his, learned to talk continually in French, and to drink wine. You will remember that in "The Path to Rome" he starts from Toul; but I cannot quote the passage; someone (who the devil is it?) has borrowed my copy. It is the perpetual fate of that book—everyone should have six copies.

After the rough and saline company of French gunners it is a comical contrast to find him winning a scholarship at Balliol College, Oxford—

admittedly the most rarefied and azure-pedalled precinct in England. He matriculated at Balliol in January, 1895, and was soon known as one of the "characters" of the college. There was little of the lean and pallid clerk of Oxenford in his bearing: he was the Roman candle of the Junior Common Room, where the vivacious and robust humour of the barracks at Toul at first horrified and then captivated the men from the public schools. Alternately blasphemous and idolatrous he may have seemed to Winchester and Eton: a devil for work and a genius at play. He swam, wrestled, shouted, rode, drank, and debated, says Mr. Seccombe. He read strange books, swore strange oaths, and amazed his tutors by the fire and fury of his historical study. His rooms were a continual focus of noise: troops of friends, song, loud laughter, and night-long readings from Rabelais. And probably his battels, if they are still recorded in the Balliol buttery, would show a larger quantity of ale and wine consumed than by any other man who ever made drinking a fine art at Balliol. Some day perhaps some scholar will look the matter up.

Balliol is not beautiful: more than any other of the older colleges in Oxford, she has suffered from the "restorations" of the 70's and 80's. It is a favourite jest to pretend to confuse her with the

Great Western Railway Station, which never fails to bring a flush to a Balliol cheek. But whatever the merciless hand of the architect has done to turn her into a jumble of sham Gothic spikes and corners, no one can doubt her wholesome democracy of intellect, her passion for sound scholarship, and the unsurpassable gift of her undergraduates for the delicately obscene. This may be the wake of a tradition inaugurated by Belloc; but I think it goes farther back than that. At any rate, in Oxford the young energumen found himself happy and merry beyond words: he worked brilliantly, was a notable figure in the Union debates, argued passionately against every conventional English tradition, and attacked authority, complacence, and fetichism of every kind. Never were dons of the donnish sort more brilliantly twitted than by young Belloc. And, partly because of his failure to capture an All Souls fellowship (the most coveted prize of intellectual Oxford) the word "don" has retained a tinge of acid in Belloc's mind ever since. (Who can read without assentive chuckles his delicious "Lines to a Don!" It was the favourite of all worthy dons at Oxford when I was there.) He has never had any reverence for a man merely because he held a post of authority.

Of the Balliol years Mr. Seccombe says:

"He was a few years older and more experienced than most of his college friends, but had lost little of the intoxication, the contagion and the ringing laughter of earliest manhood. He dazzled and infected everyone with his mockery and his laughter. There never was such an undergraduate, so merry, so learned in medieval trifling and terminology, so perfectly spontaneous in rhapsody and extravaganza, so positive and final in his judgments—who spoke French, too, like a Frenchman, in a manner unintelligible to our public-school-French-attuned ears."

No one can leave those Balliol years behind without some hope to quote the ringing song in which Belloc recalled them at the time of the Boer War. It is the perfect expression of joyful masculine life and overflowing fellowship. It echoes unforgettably in the mind.

TO THE BALLIOL MEN STILL IN AFRICA

Years ago when I was at Balliol,
  Balliol men—and I was one—
Swam together in winter rivers,
  Wrestled together under the sun.
And still in the heart of us, Balliol, Balliol,
  Loved already, but hardly known,
Welded us each of us into the others:
  Called a levy and chose her own.

Here is a House that armours a man
　　With the eyes of a boy and the heart of a ranger,
And a laughing way in the teeth of the world
　　And a holy hunger and thirst for danger:
Balliol made me, Balliol fed me,
　　Whatever I had she gave me again:
And the best of Balliol loved and led me,
　　God be with you, Balliol men.

I have said it before, and I say it again,
　　There was treason done, and a false word spoken,
And England under the dregs of men,
　　And bribes about, and a treaty broken:
But angry, lonely, hating it still,
　　I wished to be there in spite of the wrong.
My heart was heavy for Cumnor Hill
　　And the hammer of galloping all day long.

Galloping outward into the weather,
　　Hands a-ready and battle in all:
Words together and wine together
　　And song together in Balliol Hall.
Rare and single!　Noble and few!　. . .
　　Oh! they have wasted you over the sea!
The only brothers ever I knew,
　　The men that laughed and quarrelled with me.

.　　.　　.　　.　　.　　.　　.

Balliol made me, Balliol fed me,
　　Whatever I had she gave me again;
And the best of Balliol loved and led me,
　　God be with you, Balliol men.

Belloc took a First in the Modern History
School in 1895. No one ever experienced more
keenly the tingling thrill of the eager student who
finds himself cast into the heart of Oxford's
abundant life: the thousands of books so gener-
ously alive; the hundreds of acute and worthy
rivals crossing steel on steel in play, work, and
debate; the endless throb of passionate speculation into all the crowding problems of human
history. The zest and fervour of those younger
days he has never outgrown, and there are few
writers of our time who have appealed so imperiously to the young. In the Oxford before
the war all the undergraduates were reading
Belloc: you would hardly find a college room that
did not shelve one or two of his volumes.

II

There is no space to chronicle the life in detail.
The romantic voyage to California, and marriage
at twenty-six (Mrs. Belloc died in 1914); his life
in Chelsea and then in Sussex; the books on
Revolutionary France, on military history, biography and topography; the flashing essays,
political satires, and whimsical burlesques that
ran so swiftly from his pen—it did not take England long to learn that this man was very much
alive. In 1903 he was naturalized as a British

subject, and humorously contemplated changing
his name to "Hilary Bullock." In 1906 he joined
the Liberal benches in the House of Commons,
but the insurgent spirit that had cried out in
college debates against the lumbering shams of
British political life was soon stabbing at the
party system. Here was a ringing voice indeed:
one can hear that clear, scornful tenor startling
the House with its acid arraignment of parliamen-
tary stratagems and spoils. As Mr. Kilmer
says, "British politicians will not soon forget
the motion which Hilaire Belloc introduced one
day in the early Spring of 1908, that the Party
funds, hitherto secretly administered, be pub-
licly audited. His vigorous and persistent
campaign against the party system has placed
him, with Cecil Chesterton, in the very front ranks
of those to whom the democrats of Great Britain
must look for leadership and inspiration."

Perhaps we can take issue with Mr. Kilmer in
his estimate of Belloc's importance as a poet. He
is a born singer, of course; his heart rises to a lyric
just as his tongue to wine and argument and his
legs to walking or saddle leather. But he writes
poetry as every honest man should: in an imper-
ative necessity to express a passing squall of
laughter, anger, or reverence; and in earnest
hope of being condemned by Mr. W. S. Braith-

waite, which happens to so few. His "The South Country" will make splendid many an anthology. But who shall say that his handful of verses, witty, debonair, bacchanalian, and tender, is his most important contribution?

What needs to be said is that Belloc is an authentic child gotten of Rabelais. I can never forget a lecture I heard him give in the famous Examination Schools at Oxford—that noble building consecrated to human suffering, formerly housing the pangs of students and now by sad necessity a military hospital. Ruddy of cheek, a burly figure in his academic gown, without a scrap of notes and armed only with an old volume of Rabelais in the medieval French, he held us spellbound for an hour and a half—or was it three hours?—with flashing extempore talk about this greatest figure of the Renaissance.

Rabelais, he told us, was the symbolic figure of the incoming tide of Europe's rebirth in the sixteenth century. Rabelais, the priest, physician, and compounder of a new fish sauce, held that life is its own justification, and need not be lived in doleful self-abasement. Do what you wish, enjoy life, be interested in a thousand things, feel a perpetual inquisitive delight in all the details of human affairs! *The gospel of exuberance*—that is Rabelais. Is it not Belloc, too?

Rabelais came from Touraine—the heart of Gaul, the island of light in which the tradition of civilization remained unbroken. One understands Rabelais better if one knows the Chinon wine, Belloc added. His writing is married to the soil and landscape from which he sprang. His extraordinary volatility proceeds from a mind packed full of curiosity and speculation. For an instance of his exuberance see his famous list of fools, in which all fools whatsoever that ever walked on earth are included.

Now no one who loves Belloc can paddle in Rabelais without seeing that he, too, was sired from Chinon. Dip into Gargantua: there you will find the oinolatrous and gastrolatrous catalogues that Belloc daily delights in; the infectious droll patter of speech, piling quip on quip. Then look again into "The Path to Rome." How well does Mr. John Macy tell us "literature is not born spontaneously out of life. Every book has its literary parentage, and criticism reads like an Old Testament chapter of 'begats.' Every novel was suckled at the breasts of older novels."

III

In Belloc we find the perfect union of the French and English minds. Rabelaisian in fecundity, wit, and irrepressible sparkle, he is also of

English blood and sinew, wedded to the sweet
Sussex weald. History, politics, economics, military topography, poetry, novels, satires, nonsense
rhymes—all these we may set aside as the hundred
curiosities of an eager mind. (The dons, by the
way, say that in his historical work he generalizes
too hastily; but was ever history more crisply
written?) It is in the essays, the thousand little
inquirendoes into the nature of anything, everything or nothing, that one comes closest to the real
man. His prose leaps and sparks from the pen.
It is whimsical, tender, biting, garrulous. It is
familiar and unfettered as open-air talk. His
passion for places—roads, rivers, hills, and inns;
his dancing persiflage and buoyancy; his Borrovian love of vagabondage—these are the glories
of a style that is quick, close-knit, virile, and vibrant. Here Belloc ranks with Bunyan, Swift,
and Defoe.

Whoso dotes upon fine prose, prose interlaced
with humour, pathos, and whim, orchestrated to a
steady rhythm, coruscated with an exquisite
tenderness for all that is lovable and high spirited
on this dancing earth, go you now to some bookseller and procure for yourself a little volume
called "A Picked Company" where Mr. E. V.
Lucas has gathered some of the best of Mr.
Belloc's pieces. Therein will you find love of

food, companionship, cider and light wines;
love of children, artillery, and inns in the out-
lands; love of salt water, great winds, and brown
hills at twilight—in short, passionate devotion to
all the dear devices that make life so sweet. Hear
him on "A Great Wind":

A great wind is every man's friend, and its strength is the
strength of good fellowship; and even doing battle with it is
something worthy and well chosen. It is health in us, I say,
to be full of heartiness and of the joy of the world, and of
whether we have such health our comfort in a great wind is a
good test indeed. No man spends his day upon the mountains when the wind is out, riding against it or pushing forward
on foot through the gale, but at the end of his day feels that
he has had a great host about him. It is as though he had
experienced armies. The days of high winds are days of
innumerable sounds, innumerable in variation of tone and of
intensity, playing upon and awakening innumerable powers
in man. And the days of high wind are days in which a
physical compulsion has been about us and we have met pressure and blows, resisted and turned them; it enlivens us with
the simulacrum of war by which nations live, and in the just
pursuit of which men in companionship are at their noblest.

IV

And lest all this disjointed talk about Belloc's
prose seem but ungracious recognition of Mr.
Kilmer's service in reminding us of the poems,
let us thank him warmly for his essay. Let us
thank him for impressing upon us that there are

living to-day men who write as nobly and simply
as Belloc on Sussex, with his sweet broken music:

I never get between the pines
    But I smell the Sussex air;
Nor I never come on a belt of sand
    But my home is there.
And along the sky the line of the Downs
    So noble and so bare.

A lost thing could I never find,
    Nor a broken thing mend:
And I fear I shall be all alone
    When I get towards the end.
Who will there be to comfort me
    Or who will be my friend?

I will gather and carefully make my friends
    Of the men of the Sussex Weald,
They watch the stars from silent folds,
    They stiffly plough the field.
By them and the God of the South Country
    My poor soul shall be healed.

If I ever become a rich man,
    Or if ever I grow to be old,
I will build a house with deep thatch
    To shelter me from the cold,
And there shall the Sussex songs be sung
    And the story of Sussex told.

I will hold my house in the high wood
    Within a walk of the sea,
And the men that were boys when I was a boy
    Shall sit and drink with me.

A CASUAL OF THE SEA

He that will learn to pray, let him go to sea.
—GEORGE HERBERT.

BOOKS sometimes make surprising connections with life. Fifteen-year-old Tommy Jonkers, shipping as O. S. (ordinary seaman) on the S. S. *Fernfield* in Glasgow in 1911, could hardly have suspected that the second engineer would write a novel and put him in it; or that that same novel would one day lift him out of focsle and galley and set him working for a publishing house on far-away Long Island. Is it not one more proof of the surprising power of the written word?

For Tommy is not one of those who expect to find their names in print. The mere sight of his name on a newspaper page, in an article I wrote about him, brought (so he naïvely told me) tears to his eyes. Excellent, simple-hearted Tommy! How little did you think, when you signed on to help the *Fernfield* carry coal from Glasgow to Alexandria, that the long arm of the Miehle press was already waiting for you; that thousands of

169

good people reading a certain novel would be
familiar with your "round rosy face and clear
sea-blue eyes."

"Tommy" (whose real name is Drevis) was born
in Amsterdam in 1896. His father was a fireman
at sea, and contributed next to nothing to the
support of Tommy and his pretty little sister
Greta. They lived with their grandmother, near
the quays in Amsterdam, where the masts of
ships and the smell of tar interfered with their
lessons. Bread and treacle for breakfast, black
beans for lunch, a fine thick stew and plenty more
bread for supper—that and the Dutch school
where he stood near the top of his class are what
Tommy remembers best of his boyhood. His
grandmother took in washing, and had a hard
time keeping the little family going. She was a
fine, brusque old lady and as Tommy went off
to school in the mornings she used to frown at
him from the upstairs window because his hands
were in his pockets. For as everybody knows,
only slouchy good-for-nothings walk to school
with pocketed hands.

Tommy did so well in his lessons that he was
one of the star pupils given the privilege of learning an extra language in the evenings. He chose
English because most of the sailors he met
talked English, and his great ambition was to be a

seaman. His uncle was a quartermaster in the Dutch navy, and his father was at sea; and Tommy's chance soon came.

After school hours he used to sell postcards, cologne, soap, chocolates, and other knicknacks to the sailors, to earn a little cash to help his grandmother. One afternoon in the spring of 1909 he was down on the docks with his little packet of wares, when a school friend came running to him.

"Drevis, Drevis!" he shouted, "they want a mess-room boy on the *Queen Eleanor!*"

It didn't take Drevis long to get aboard the *Queen Eleanor*, a British tramp out of Glasgow, bound for Hamburg and Vladivostok. He accosted the chief engineer, his blue eyes shining eagerly.

"Yes," says the chief, "I need a mess-room steward right away—we sail at four o'clock."

"Try me!" pipes Drevis. (Bless us, the boy was barely thirteen!)

The chief roars with laughter.

"Too small!" he says.

Drevis insisted that he was just the boy for mess-room steward.

"Well," says the chief, "go home and put on a pair of long pants and come back again. Then we'll see how you look!"

Tommy ran home rejoicing. His Uncle Hen-

drick was a small man, and Tommy grabbed a
pair of his trousers. Thus fortified, he hastened
back to the *Queen Eleanor*. The chief cackled,
but he took him on at two pounds five a month.

Tommy didn't last long as mess-room boy.
He broke so many cups the engineers had to
drink out of dippers, and they degraded him to
cabin boy at a pound a month. Even as cabin
boy he was no instant success. He used to forget
to empty the chief's slop-pail, and the water
would overflow the cabin. He felt the force of a
stout sea boot not a few times in learning the
golden rubric of the tramp steamer's cabin boy.

"Drevis" was a strange name to the English
seamen, and they christened him "Tommy,"
and that handle turns him still.

Tommy's blue eyes and honest Netherland grin
and easy temper kept him friendly with all the
world. The winds of chance sent him scudding
about the globe, a true casual of the seas. His
first voyage as A. B. was on the *Fernfield* in 1911,
and there he met a certain Scotch engineer. This
engineer had a habit of being interested in human
problems, and Tommy's guileless phiz attracted
him. Under his tutelage Tommy acquired a
thirst for promotion, and soon climbed to the rank
of quartermaster.

One thing that always struck Tommy was the

number of books the engineer had in his cabin.
A volume of Nat Gould, Ouida or "The Duchess" would be the largest library Tommy would
have found in the other bunks; but here, before
his wondering gaze, were Macaulay, Gibbon,
Gorki, Conrad, Dickens, Zola, Shakespeare, Mon-
taigne, Chaucer, Shaw, and what not. And
what would Master Tommy have said had he
known that his friend, even then, was working
on a novel in which he, Tommy, would play an
important rôle!

The years went by. On sailing ships, on steam
tramps, on private yachts, as seaman, as quartermaster, as cook's helper, Tommy drifted about
the world. One day when he was twenty years
old he was rambling about New York just before
sailing for Liverpool on the steam yacht *Alvina*.
He was one of a strictly neutral crew (the United
States was still neutral in those days) signed on to
take a millionaire's pet plaything across the
wintry ocean. She had been sold to the Russian
Government (there still was one then!)

Tommy was passing through the arcade of the
Pennsylvania Station when his eye fell upon the
book shop there. He was startled to see in the
window a picture of the Scotch engineer—his best
friend, the only man in the world who had ever
been like a father to him. He knew that the

engineer was far away in the Mediterranean, working on an English transport. He scanned the poster with amazement.

Apparently his friend had written a book. Tommy, like a practical seaman, went to the heart of the matter. He went into the shop and bought the book. He fell into talk with the bookseller, who had read the book. He told the bookseller that he had known the author, and that for years they had served together on the same vessels at sea. He told how the writer, who was the former second engineer of the *Fernfield*, had done many things for the little Dutch lad whose own father had died at sea. Then came another surprise.

"I believe you're one of the characters in the story," said the bookseller.

It was so. The book was "Casuals of the Sea," the author, William McFee, who had been a steamship engineer for a dozen years; and Drevis Jonkers found himself described in full in the novel as "Drevis Noordhof," and playing a leading part in the story. Can you imagine the simple sailor's surprise and delight? Pleased beyond measure, in his soft Dutch accent liberally flavoured with cockney he told the bookseller how Mr. McFee had befriended him, had urged him to go on studying navigation so that he might become an officer; and that though they had not met for several years he still receives letters from his friend, full of good advice about saving his money, where to get cheap lodgings in Brooklyn, and not to fall into the common error of sailors in thinking that Hoboken and Passyunk Avenue are all America. And Tommy went back to his yacht chuckling with delight, with a copy of "Casuals of the Sea" under his arm.

Here my share in the adventure begins. The bookseller, knowing my interest in the book, hastened to tell me the next time I saw him that one of the characters in the story was in New York. I wrote to Tommy asking him to come to see me. He wrote that the *Alvina* was to sail the next day, and he could not get away. I supposed the incident was closed.

Then I saw in the papers that the *Alvina* had been halted in the Narrows by a United States destroyer, the Government having suspected that her errand was not wholly neutral. Rumour had it that she was on her way to the Azores, there to take on armament for the house of Romanoff. She was halted at the Quarantine Station at Staten Island, pending an investigation.

Then enters the elbow of coincidence. Looking over some books in the very same bookshop where Tommy had bought his friend's novel, I overheard another member of the *Alvina's* crew asking about "Casuals of the Sea." His chum Tommy had told him about his adventure, and he, too, was there to buy one. (Not every day does one meet one's friends walking in a 500-page novel!) By the never-to-be-sufficiently-admired hand of chance I was standing at Joe Hogan's very elbow when he began explaining to the book clerk that he was a friend of the Dutch sailor who had been there a few days before.

So a few days later, behold me on the Staten Island ferry, on my way to see Tommy and the *Alvina.*

I'm afraid I would always desert the office if there's a plausible excuse to bum about the water-front. Is there any passion in the breast of mankind more absorbing than the love of ships? A tall Cunarder putting out to sea gives me a keener thrill than anything the Polo Grounds or the Metropolitan Opera can show. Of what avail a meeting of the Authors' League when one can know the sights, sounds, and smells of West or South Street? I used to lug volumes of Joseph Conrad down to the West-Street piers to give them to captains and first mates of liners, and get them to talk about the ways of the sea. That was how I met Captain Claret of the *Minnehaha,* that prince of seamen; and Mr. Pape of the *Orduña,*

Mr. Jones of the *Lusitania* and many another. They knew all about Conrad, too. There were five volumes of Conrad in the officers' cabins on the *Lusitania* when she went down, God rest her. I know, because I put them there.

And the Staten Island ferry is a voyage on the Seven Seas for the landlubber. After months of office work, how one's heart leaps to greet our old mother the sea! How drab, flat, and humdrum seem the ways of earth in comparison to the hardy and austere life of ships! There on every hand go the gallant shapes of vessels—the *James L. Morgan*, dour little tug, shoving two barges; *Themistocles*, at anchor, with the blue and white Greek colours painted on her rusty flank; the *Comanche* outward bound for Galveston (I think); the *Ascalon*, full-rigged ship, with blue-jerseyed sailormen out on her bowsprit snugging the canvas. And who is so true a lover of the sea as one who can suffer the ultimate indignities—and love her still! I am queasy as soon as I sight Sandy Hook. . . .

At the quarantine station I had a surprise. The *Alvina* was not there. One old roustabout told me he thought she had gone to sea. I was duly taken aback. Had I made the two-hour trip for nothing? Then another came to my aid.

"There she is, up in the bight," he said. I followed his gesture, and saw her—a long, slim white hull, a cream-coloured funnel with a graceful rake; the Stars and Stripes fresh painted in two places on her shining side. I hailed a motor boat to take me out. The boatman wanted three dollars, and I offered one. He protested that the yacht was interned and he had no right to take visitors out anyway. He'd get into trouble with "39"— "39" being a United States destroyer lying in the Narrows a few hundred yards away. After some bickering we compromised on a dollar and a quarter.

That was a startling adventure for the humble publisher's reader! Wallowing in an ice-glazed motor boat, in the lumpy water of a "bight"— surrounded by ships and the men who sail them—I might almost have been a hardy newspaper man! But Long Island commuters are nurtured to a tough and perilous life, and I clambered the *Alvina's* side without dropping hat, stick, or any of my pocketful of manuscripts.

Joe Hogan, the steward, was there in his white jacket. He introduced me to the cook, the bosun, the "chief," the wireless, and the "second." The first officer was too heavy with liquor to notice the arrival of a stranger. Messrs. Haig and Haig, those *Dioscuri* of seamen, had been at work. The skipper was ashore. He owns a saloon.

The *Alvina* is a lovely little vessel, 215 feet long, they told me, and about 525 tons. She is fitted with mahogany throughout; the staterooms all have brass double beds and private bathrooms attached; she has her own wireless telegraph and telephone, refrigerating apparatus, and everything to make the owner and his guests comfortable. But her beautiful furnishings were tumbled this way and that in preparation for the sterner duties that lay before her. The lower deck was cumbered with sacks of coal lashed down. A transatlantic voyage in January is likely to be a lively one for a yacht of 500 tons.

I found Tommy below in his bunk, cleaning up. He is a typical Dutch lad—round, open face, fair hair, and guileless blue eyes. He showed me all his treasures—his certificates of good conduct from all the ships (both sail and steam) on which he has served; a picture of his mother, who died when he was six; and of his sister Greta—a very pretty girl —who is also mentioned in *Casuals of the Sea.* The drunken fireman in the story who dies after a debauch was Tommy's father who died in the same way. And with these other treasures Tommy showed me a packet of letters from Mr. McFee. I do not want to offend Mr. McFee by describing his letters to this Dutch sailor-boy as "sen-

sible," but that is just what they were. Tommy
is one of his own "casuals"—

> —those frail craft upon the restless Sea
> Of Human Life, who strike the rocks uncharted,
> Who loom, sad phantoms, near us, drearily,
> Storm-driven, rudderless, with timbers started—

and these sailormen who drift from port to port on
the winds of chance are most in need of sound
Ben Franklin advice. Save your money; put
it in the bank; read books; go to see the museums,
libraries, and art galleries; get to know something
about this great America if you intend to settle
down there—that is the kind of word Tommy gets
from his friend.

Gradually, as I talked with him, I began to see
into the laboratory of life where "Casuals of the
Sea" originated. This book is valuable because
it is a triumphant expression of the haphazard,
strangely woven chances that govern the lives of
the humble. In Tommy's honest, gentle face, and
in the talk of his shipmates when we sat down to
dinner together, I saw a microcosm of the strange
barren life of the sea where men float about for
years like driftwood. And out of all this ebbing
tide of aimless, happy-go-lucky humanity McFee
had chanced upon this boy from Amsterdam and
had tried to pound into him some good sound
common sense.

When I left her that afternoon, the *Alvina* was getting up steam, and she sailed within a few hours. I had eaten and talked with her crew, and for a short space had a glimpse of the lives and thoughts of the simple, childlike men who live on ships. I realized for the first time the truth of that background of aimless hazard that makes "Casuals of the Sea" a book of more than passing merit.

As for Tommy, the printed word had him in thrall though he knew it not. When he got back from Liverpool, two months later, I found him a job in the engine room of a big printing press. He was set to work oiling the dynamos, and at ten dollars a week he had a fine chance to work his way up. Indeed, he enrolled in a Scranton correspondence course on steam engineering and enchanted his Hempstead landlady by his simple ways. That lasted just two weeks. The level ground made Tommy's feet uneasy. The last I heard he was on a steam yacht on Long Island Sound.

But wherever steam and tide may carry him, Tommy cherishes in his heart his own private badge of honour: his friend the engineer has put him in a book! And there, in one of the noblest and most honest novels of our day, you will find him—a casual of the sea!

THE LAST PIPE

The last smoker I recollect among those of the old school was a clergyman. He had seen the best society, and was a man of the most polished behaviour. This did not hinder him from taking his pipe every evening before he went to bed. He sat in his armchair, his back gently bending, his knees a little apart, his eyes placidly inclined toward the fire. The end of his recreation was announced by the tapping of the bowl of his pipe upon the hob, for the purpose of emptying it of its ashes. Ashes to ashes; head to bed.

—LEIGH HUNT.

THE sensible man smokes (say) sixteen pipefuls a day, and all differ in value and satisfaction. In smoking there is, thank heaven, no law of diminishing returns. I may puff all day long until I nigresce with the fumes and soot, but the joy loses no savour by repetition. It is true that there is a peculiar blithe rich taste in the first morning puffs, inhaled after breakfast. (Let me posit here the ideal conditions for a morning pipe as I know them.) After your bath, breakfast must be spread in a chamber of eastern exposure; let there be hominy and cream, and if possible, brown sugar. There follow scrambled

182

eggs, shirred to a lemon-yellow, with toast sliced in triangles, fresh, unsalted butter, and Scotch bitter marmalade. Let there be without fail a platter of hot bacon, curly, juicy, fried to the debatable point where softness is overlaid with the faintest crepitation of crackle, of crispyness. If hot Virginia corn pone is handy, so much the better. And coffee, two-thirds hot milk, also with brown sugar. It must be permissible to call for a second serving of the scrambled eggs; or, if this is beyond the budget, let there be a round of judiciously grilled kidneys, with mayhap a sprinkle of mushrooms, grown in chalky soil. That is the kind of breakfast they used to serve in Eden before the fall of man and the invention of innkeepers with their crass formulae.

After such a breakfast, if one may descend into a garden of plain turf, mured about by an occluding wall, with an alley of lime trees for sober pacing: then and there is the fit time and place for the first pipe of the day. Pack your mixture in the bowl; press it lovingly down with the cushion of the thumb; see that the draught is free—and then for your *säckerhets tändstickor!* A day so begun is well begun, and sin will flee your precinct. Shog, vile care! The smoke is cool and blue and tasty on the tongue; the arch of the palate is receptive to the fume; the curling

vapour ascends the chimneys of the nose. Fill
your cheeks with the excellent cloudy reek, blow
it forth in twists and twirls. The first pipe!

But, as I was saying, joy ends not here.
Granted that the after-breakfast smoke excels
in savour, succeeding fumations grow in mental
reaction. The first pipe is animal, physical, a
matter of pure sensation. With later kindlings of
the weed the brain quickens, begins to throw out
tendrils of speculation, leaps to welcome problems
for thought, burrows tingling into the unknowable. As the smoke drifts and shreds about your
neb, your mind is surcharged with that impon-
derable energy of thought, which cannot be seen
or measured, yet is the most potent force in
existence. All the hot sunlight of Virginia that
stirred the growing leaf in its odorous plantation
now crackles in that glowing dottel in your briar
bowl. The venomous juices of the stalk seep
down the stem. The most precious things in the
world are also vivid with poison.

Was Kant a smoker? I think he must have
been. How else could he have written "The Criti-
que of Pure Reason"? Tobacco is the handmaid of
science, philosophy, and literature. Carlyle eased
his indigestion and snappish temper by perpetual
pipes. The generous use of the weed makes the
enforced retirement of Sing Sing less irksome to

forgers, second-story men, and fire bugs. Samuel Butler, who had little enough truck with church-men, was once invited to stay a week-end by the Bishop of London. Distrusting the entertaining qualities of bishops, and rightly, his first impulse was to decline. But before answering the Bishop's letter he passed it to his manservant for advice. The latter (the immortal Alfred Emery Cathie) said: "There is a crumb of tobacco in the fold of the paper, sir: I think you may safely go." He went, and hugely enjoyed himself.

There is a Bible for smokers, a book of delight-ful information for all acolytes of this genial ritual, crammed with wit and wisdom upon the art and mystery we cherish. It is called "The Social History of Smoking," by G. L. Apperson. Alas, a friend of mine, John Marshall (he lives some-where in Montreal or Quebec), borrowed it from me, and obstinately declines to return it. If he should ever see this, may his heart be loosened and relent. Dear John, I wish you would return that book. (*Canadian journals please copy!*)

I was contending that the joy of smoking in-creases harmonically with the weight of tobacco consumed, within reasonable limits. Of course the incessant smoker who is puffing all day long sears his tongue and grows callous to the true

delicacy of the flavour.   For that reason it is best
not to smoke during office hours.   This may be a
hard saying to some, but a proper respect for the
art impels it.   Not even the highest ecclesiast
can be at his devotions always.   It is not those
who are horny with genuflection who are nearest
the Throne of Grace.   Even the Pope (I speak in
all reverence) must play billiards or trip a coranto
now and then!

    This is the schedule I vouch for:

> After breakfast: 2 pipes
> At luncheon: 2 pipes
> Before dinner: 2 pipes
> Between dinner and bed: 10 to 12 pipes
> (Cigars and cigarettes as occasion may require.)

    The matter of smoking after dinner requires con-
sideration.   If your meal is a heavy, stupefying
anodyne, retracting all the humane energies from
the skull in a forced abdominal mobilization to
quell a plethora of food into subjection and
assimilation, there is no power of speculation left
in the top storeys.   You sink brutishly into an
armchair, warm your legs at the fire, and let the
leucocytes and phagocytes fight it out.   At such
times smoking becomes purely mechanical.   You
imbibe and exhale the fumes automatically.   The
choicest aromatic blends are mere fuel.   Your

eyes see, but your brain responds not. The vital juices, generous currents, or whatever they are that animate the intelligence, are down below hatches fighting furiously to annex and drill into submission the alien and distracting mass of food that you have taken on board. They are like stevedores, stowing the cargo for portability. A little later, however, when this excellent work is accomplished, the bosun may trill his whistle, and the deck hands can be summoned back to the navigating bridge. The mind casts off its corporeal hawsers and puts out to sea. You begin once more to live as a rational composition of reason, emotion, and will. The heavy dinner postpones and stultifies this desirable state. Let it then be said that light dining is best: a little fish or cutlets, white wine, macaroni and cheese, ice cream and coffee. Such a régime restores the animal health, and puts you in vein for a continuance of intellect.

Smoking is properly an intellectual exercise. It calls forth the choicest qualities of mind and soul. It can only be properly conducted by a being in full possession of the five wits. For those who are in pain, sorrow, or grievous perplexity it operates as a sovereign consoler, a balm and balsam to the harassed spirit; it calms the fretful, makes jovial the peevish. Better than

any ginseng in the herbal, does it combat fatigue
and old age. Well did Stevenson exhort virgins not
to marry men who do not smoke.

Now we approach the crux and pinnacle of this
inquirendo into the art and mystery of smoking.
That is to say, the last pipe of all before the so-
long indomitable intellect abdicates, and the body
succumbs to weariness.

No man of my acquaintance has ever given me
a satisfactory definition of *living*. An alternating
systole and diastole, says physiology. Chlor-
ophyl becoming xanthophyl, says botany. These
stir me not. I define life as a process of the Will-
to-Smoke: recurring periods of consciousness in
which the enjoyability of smoking is manifest, in-
terrupted by intervals of recuperation.

Now if I represent the course of this process by
a graph (the co-ordinates being Time and the
Sense-of-by-the-Smoker-enjoyed-Satisfaction) the
curve ascends from its origin in a steep slant,
then drops away abruptly at the recuperation in-
terval. This is merely a teutonic and pedantic
mode of saying that the best pipe of all is the last
one smoked at night. It is the penultimate moment that is always the happiest. The sweetest
pipe ever enjoyed by the skipper of the *Hesperus*
was the one he whiffed just before he was tirpitzed
by the poet on that angry reef.

The best smoking I ever do is about half past
midnight, just before "my eyelids drop their
shade," to remind you again of your primary
school poets. After the toils, rebuffs, and exhilarations of the day, after piaffing busily on the
lethal typewriter or *schreibmaschine* for some
hours, a drowsy languor begins to numb the
sense. In dressing gown and slippers I seek my
couch; Ho, Lucius, a taper! and some solid, invig-
orating book for consideration. My favourite is
the General Catalogue of the Oxford University
Press: a work so excellently full of learning; printed
and bound with such eminence of skill; so noble a
repository or Thesaurus of the accumulated
treasures of human learning, that it sets the
mind in a glow of wonder. This is the choicest
garland for the brain fatigued with the insignificant and trifling tricks by which we earn our
daily bread. There is no recreation so lovely as
that afforded by books rich in wisdom and ribbed
with ripe and sober research. This catalogue
(nearly 600 pages) is a marvellous précis of the
works of the human spirit. And here and there,
buried in a scholarly paragraph, one meets a
topical echo: "THE OXFORD SHAKESPEARE GLOS-
SARY: by C. T. ONIONS: Mr. Onions' glossary,
offered at an insignificant price, relieves English
scholarship of the necessity of recourse to the lexi-

con of Schmidt." Lo, how do even professors and privat-docents belabour one another!

With due care I fill, pack, and light the last pipe of the day, to be smoked reverently and solemnly in bed. The thousand brain-murdering interruptions are over. The gentle sibilance of air drawn through the glowing nest of tobacco is the only sound. With reposeful heart I turn to some favourite entry in my well-loved catalogue.

"HENRY PEACHAM'S COMPLEAT GENTLEMAN. Fashioning him absolut in the most necessary and Commendable Qualities concerning Minde, or Body, that may be required in a Noble Gentleman. Wherunto is annexed a Description of the order of a Maine Battaile or Pitched Field, eight severall wayes, with the Art of Limming and other Additions newly Enlarged. Printed from the edition of 1634; first edition, 1622, with an introduction by G. S. Gordon. 1906. Pp xxiv + 16 unpaged + 262. 7s. 6d. net. *At the Clarendon Press.*"

Or this:

"H. HIS DEVISES, for his owne exercise, and his Friends pleasure. Printed from the edition of 1581, with an introduction. 1906. Pp xviii + 104. 5s. net."

O excellent H! Little did he dream that his devises (with an introduction by Professor Sir

Walter Raleigh) would be still giving his Friends pleasure over three hundred years later. The compiler of the catalogue says here with modest and pardonable pride "strongly bound in exceptionally tough paper and more than once described by reviewers as leather. Some of the books are here printed for the first time, the rest are reproductions of the original editions, many having prefaces by good hands."

One o'clock is about to chime in the near-by steeple, but my pipe and curiosity are now both going strong.

"THE CURES OF THE DISEASED in remote Regions, preventing Mortalitie incident in Forraine Attempts of the English Nation. 1598. The earliest English treatise on tropical diseases. 1915. 1s. 6d. net."

Is that not the most interesting comment on the English colonial enterprises in Elizabeth's reign? And there is no limit to the joys of this marvellous catalogue. How one dreams of the unknown delights of "Two Fifteenth-Century Cookery Books," or "Dan Michel's Ayenbite of Inwyt, 1340" (which means, as I figure it, the "Backbite of Conscience"), or "Origenis Hexaplorum quae supersunt sive Veterum Interpretum Graecorum in totum Vetus Testamentum Fragmenta, edidit F. Field. 1865. Two volumes

£6 6s. net" or "Shuckford's Sacred and Profane
History of the World, from the Creation of the
World to the Dissolution of the Assyrian Empire
at the death of Sardanapalus, and to the Declen-
sion of The Kingdom of Judah and Israel under the
Reigns of Ahaz and Pekah, with the Creation
and Fall of Man.   1728, reprinted 1848.   Pp 550.
10s. net."

But I dare not force my hobbies on you further.
One man's meat is another's caviar.   I dare not
even tell you what my favourite tobaccos are, for
recently when I sold to a magazine a very worthy
and excellent poem entitled "My Pipe," mentioning the brands I delight to honour, the editor made
me substitute fictitious names for my dearly loved
blends.   He said that sound editorial policy for-
bids mentioning commercial products in the text
of the magazine.

But tobacco, thank heaven, is not merely a
"commercial product."   Let us call on Salvation
Yeo for his immortal testimony:

"When all things were made none was made
better than this; to be a lone man's companion, a
bachelor's friend, a hungry man's food, a sad man's
cordial, a wakeful man's sleep, and a chilly man's
fire, sir; while for stanching of wounds, purging of
rheum, and settling of the stomach, there's no
herb like unto it under the canopy of heaven."

And by this time the bowl is naught but ash. Even my dear General Catalogue begins to blur before me. Slip it under the pillow; gently and kindly lay the pipe in the candlestick, and blow out the flame. The window is open wide: the night rushes in. I see a glimpse of stars . . . a distant chime . . . and fall asleep with the faint pungence of the Indian herb about me.

TIME TO LIGHT THE FURNACE

THE twenty-eighth of October. Coal nine dollars a ton. Mr. and Mrs. Blackwell had made a resolution not to start the furnace until Thanksgiving. And in the biting winds of Long Island that requires courage.

Commuters the world over are a hardy, valorous race. The Arab commutes by dromedary, the Malay by raft, the Indian rajah by elephant, the African chief gets a team of his mothers-in-law to tow him to the office. But wherever you find him, the commuter is a tough and tempered soul, inured to privation and calamity. At seven-thirty in the morning he leaves his bungalow, tent, hut, palace, or kraal, and tells his wife he is going to work.

How the winds whistle and moan over those Long Island flats! Mr. and Mrs. Blackwell had laid in fifteen tons of black diamonds. And hoping that would be enough, they were zealous not to start the furnace until the last touchdown had been made.

But every problem has more than one aspect. Belinda, the new cook, had begun to work for

them on the fifth of October. Belinda came
from the West Indies, a brown maiden still un-
spoiled by the sophistries of the employment
agencies. She could boil an egg without crack-
ing it, she could open a tin can without maiming
herself. She was neat, guileless, and cheerful.
But, she was accustomed to a warm climate.

The twenty-eighth of October. As Mr. and
Mrs. Blackwell sat at dinner, Mr. Blackwell
buttoned his coat, and began a remark about how
chilly the evenings were growing. But across the
table came one of those glances familiar to indiscreet husbands. Passion distorted, vibrant with
rebuke, charged with the lightning of instant
dissolution, Mrs. Blackwell's gaze struck him
dumb with alarm. Husbands, husbands, you
know that gaze!

Mr. Blackwell kept silence. He ate heartily,
choosing foods rich in calories. He talked of other
matters, and accepted thankfully what Belinda
brought to him. But he was chilly, and a vision
of coal bills danced in his mind.

After dinner he lit the open fire in the living
room, and he and Mrs. Blackwell talked in discreet tones. Belinda was merrily engaged in washing the dishes.

"Bob, you consummate blockhead!" said Mrs.

Blackwell, "haven't you better sense than to
talk about its being chilly? These last few days
Belinda has done nothing but complain about the
cold. She comes from Barbados, where the thermometer never goes below sixty. She said she
couldn't sleep last night, her room was so cold.
I've given her my old fur coat and the steamer
rug from your den. One other remark like that
of yours and she'll leave. For heaven's sake,
Bob, use your skull!"

Mr. Blackwell gazed at her in concern. The
deep, calculating wisdom of women was made
plain to him. He ventured no reply.

Mrs. Blackwell was somewhat softened by his
docility.

"You don't realize, dear," she added, "how
servants are affected by chance remarks they
overhear. The other day you mentioned the
thermometer, and the next morning I found
Belinda looking at it. If you must say anything
about the temperature, complain of the heat.
Otherwise we'll have to start the furnace at
once."

Mr. Blackwell's face was full of the admiration common to the simple-minded race of husbands.

"Jumbo," he said, "you're right. I was
crazy. Watch me from now on. Mental sug-

gestion is the dope. The power of the chance
remark!"

The next evening at dinner, while Belinda was
passing the soup, Mr. Blackwell fired his first gun.
"It seems almost too warm for hot soup," he
said. "All the men at the office were talking
about the unseasonable hot weather. I think
we'd better have a window open." To Mrs.
Blackwell's dismay, he raised one of the dining-
room windows, admitting a pungent frostiness
of October evening. But she was game, and
presently called for a palm-leaf fan. When
Belinda was in the room they talked pointedly of
the heat, and Mr. Blackwell quoted imaginary
Weather Bureau notes from the evening paper.

After dinner, as he was about to light the log
fire, from force of habit, Mrs. Blackwell snatched
the burning match from him just as he was setting it to the kindling. They grinned at each
other wistfully, for the ruddy evening blaze was
their chief delight. Mr. Blackwell manfully took
off his coat and waistcoat and sat in his shirt-
sleeves until Belinda had gone to bed. Then
he grew reckless and lit a roaring fire, by which
they huddled in glee. He rebuilt the fire before
retiring, so that Belinda might suspect nothing
in the morning.

The next evening Mr. Blackwell appeared **at**

dinner in a Palm Beach suit. Mrs. Blackwell
countered by ordering iced tea. They both
sneezed vigorously during the meal. "It was so
warm in town to-day, I think I caught a cold,"
said Mr. Blackwell.

Later Mrs. Blackwell found Belinda examining the thermometer with a puzzled air. That
night they took it down and hid it in the attic.
But the great stroke of the day was revealed when
Mrs. Blackwell explained that Mr. and Mrs.
Chester, next door, had promised to carry on a
similar psychological campaign. Belinda and
Mrs. Chester's cook, Tulip—jocularly known as
the Black Tulip—were friends, and would undoubtedly compare notes. Mrs. Chester had agreed
not to start her furnace without consultation with
Mrs. Blackwell.

October yielded to November. By good fortune the weather remained sunny, but the nights
were crisp. Belinda was given an oil-stove for
her attic bedroom. Mrs. Blackwell heard no
more complaints of the cold, but sometimes she
and her husband could hear uneasy creakings
upstairs late at night. "I wonder if Barbados
really is so warm?" she asked Bob. "I'm sure
it can't be warmer than Belinda's room. She
never opens the windows, and the oil-stove has
to be filled every morning."

"Perhaps some day we can get an Eskimo maid," suggested Mr. Blackwell drowsily. He wore his Palm Beach suit every night for dinner, but underneath it he was panoplied in heavy flannels.

Through Mr. Chester the rumour of the Blackwells' experiment in psychology spread far among suburban husbands. On the morning train less fortunate commuters, who had already started their fires, referred to him as "the little brother of the iceberg." Mr. and Mrs. Chester came to dinner on the 16th of November. Both the men loudly clamoured for permission to remove their coats, and sat with blanched and chattering jaws. Mr. Blackwell made a feeble pretence at mopping his brow, but when the dessert proved to be ice-cream his nerve forsook him. "N-no, Belinda," he said. "It's too warm for ice-cream to-night. I don't w—want to get chilled. Bring me some hot coffee." As she brought his cup he noticed that her honest brown brow was beaded with perspiration. "By George," he thought, "this mental suggestion business certainly works." Late that evening he lit the log fire and revelled by the blaze in an ulster.

The next evening when Mr. Blackwell came home from business he met the doctor in the hall.

"Hello, doc," he said, "what's up?"

"Mrs. Blackwell called me in to see your maid," said the doctor. "It's the queerest thing I've met in twenty years' practice. Here it is the 17th of November, and cold enough for snow. That girl has all the symptoms of sunstroke and prickly heat."

MY FRIEND

TO-DAY we called each other by our given names for the first time.

Making a new friend is so exhilarating an adventure that perhaps it will not be out of place if I tell you a little about him. There are not many of his kind.

In the first place, he is stout, like myself. We are both agreed that many of the defects of American letters to-day are due to the sorry leanness of our writing men. We have no Chestertons, no Bellocs. I look to Don Marquis, to H. L. Mencken, to Heywood Broun, to Clayton Hamilton, and to my friend here portraited, to remedy this. If only Mr. Simeon Strunsky were stouter! He is plump, but not yet properly corpulent.

My friend is a literary journalist. There are but few of them in these parts. Force of circumstances may compel him to write of trivial things, but it would be impossible for him not to write with beauty and distinction far above his theme. His style is a perfect echo of his person, mellow, quaint, and richly original. To plunder a phrase of

201

his own, it is drenched with the sounds, the scents, the colours, of great literature.

I, too, am employed in a bypath of the publishing business, and try to bring to my tasks some small measure of honest idealism. But what I love (I use this great word with care) in my friend is that his zeal for beauty and for truth is great enough to outweigh utterly the paltry considerations of expediency and comfort which sway most of us. To him his pen is as sacred as the scalpel to the surgeon. He would rather die than dishonour that chosen instrument.

I hope I am not merely fanciful: but the case of my friend has taken in my mind a large importance quite beyond the exigencies of his personal situation. I see in him personified the rising generation of literary critics, who have a hard row to hoe in a deliterated democracy. By some unknowable miracle of birth or training he has come by a love of beauty, a reverence for what is fine and true, an absolute intolerance of the slipshod and insincere.

Such a man is not happy, can never be happy, when the course of his daily routine wishes him to praise what he does not admire, to exploit what he does not respect. The most of us have some way of quibbling ourselves out of this dilemma. But he cannot do so, because more than comfort, more than clothes and shoe leather, more than wife or fireside, he must preserve the critic's self-respect. "I cannot write a publicity story about A. B.," he said woefully to me, "because I am convinced he is a bogus philosopher. I am not interested in selling books: what I have to do with is that strange and esoteric thing called literature."

I would be sorry to have it thought that because of this devotion to high things my friend is stubborn, dogmatic, or hard to work with. He is unpractical as dogs, children, or Dr. Johnson; in absent-minded simplicity he has issued forth upon the highway only half-clad, and been haled back to his boudoir by indignant bluecoats; but in all matters where absolute devotion to truth and honour are concerned I would not find him lacking. Wherever a love of beauty and a ripened judgment of men and books are a business asset, he is a successful business man.

In person, he has the charm of a monstrously overgrown elf. His shyly wandering gaze behind thick spectacle panes, his incessant devotion to cigarettes and domestic lager, his whimsical talk on topics that confound the unlettered—these are amiable trifles that endear him to those who understand.

Actually, in a hemisphere bestridden by the

crass worship of comfort and ease, here is a man whose ideal is to write essays in resounding English, and to spread a little wider his love of the niceties of fine prose.

I have anatomized him but crudely. If you want to catch him in a weak spot, try him on Belloc. Hear him rumble his favourite couplet:

> And the men who were boys when I was a boy
> Shall sit and drink with me.

Indeed let us hope that they will.

A POET OF SAD VIGILS

THERE are many ways of sitting down to an evening vigil. Unquestionably the pleasantest is to fortify the soul with a pot of tea, plenty of tobacco, and a few chapters of Jane Austen. And if the adorable Miss Austen is not to hand, my second choice perhaps would be the literary remains of a sad, poor, and forgotten young man who was a contemporary of hers.

I say "forgotten," and I think it is just; save for his beautiful hymn "The Star of Bethlehem," who nowadays ever hears of Henry Kirke White? But on the drawing-room tables of our grandmothers' girlhood the plump volume, edited with a fulsome memoir by Southey, held honourable place near the conch shell from the Pacific and the souvenirs of the Crystal Palace. Mr. Southey, in his thirty years' laureateship, made the fame of several young versifiers, and deemed that in introducing poor White's remains to the polite world he was laying the first lucifer to a bonfire that would gloriously crackle for posterity. No less than Chatterton was the worthy laureate's esti-

mate of his young foundling; but alas! Chatterton
and Kirke White both seem thinnish gruel to us;
and even Southey himself is down among the pinch
hitters.   Literary prognosis is a parlous sport.

The generation that gave us Wordsworth,
Scott, Coleridge, Lamb, Jane Austen, Hazlitt,
De Quincey, Byron, Shelley, and Keats, leaves us
little time for Kirke White considered purely as a
literary man.   His verses are grotesquely stilted,
the obvious conjunction of biliousness and overstudy, and adapted to the taste of an era when
the word female was still used as a substantive.
But they are highly entertaining to read because
they so faithfully mirror the backwash of roman-
ticism.   They are so thoroughly unhealthy, so
morbid, so pallid with moonlight, so indentured
by the ayenbite of inwit, that it is hard to believe
that Henry's father was a butcher and should presumably have reared him on plenty of sound beefsteak and blood gravy.   If only Miss Julia Lath-
rop or Dr. Anna Howard Shaw could have been
Henry's mother, he might have lived to write
poems on the abolition of slavery in America.
But as a matter of fact, he was done to death by
the brutal tutors of St. John's College, Cambridge, and perished at the age of twenty-one, in
1806.   As a poet, let him pass; but the story of
his life breathes a sweet and honourable fragrance,

and is comely to ponder in the midnight hours.
As Southey said, there is nothing to be recorded
but what is honourable to him; nothing to be
regretted but that one so ripe for heaven should so
soon have been removed from the world.

He was born in Nottingham, March 21, 1785,
of honest tradesman parents; his origin reminds
one inevitably of that of Keats.   From his earliest
years he was studious in temper, and could with
difficulty be drawn from his books, even at meal-
times.   At the age of seven he wrote a story of a
Swiss emigrant and gave it to the servant, being
too bashful to show it to his mother.   Southey's
comment on this is "The consciousness of genius
is always accompanied with this diffidence; it is a
sacred, solitary feeling."

His schooling was not long; and while it lasted
part of Henry's time was employed in carrying his
father's deliveries of chops and rumps to the prosperous of Nottingham.   At fourteen his parents
made an effort to start him in line for business
by placing him in a stocking factory.   The work
was wholly uncongenial, and shortly afterward
he was employed in the office of a busy firm of
lawyers.   He spent twelve hours a day in the office
and then an hour more in the evening was put upon
Latin and Greek.   Even such recreation hours as
the miserable youth found were dismally employed

in declining nouns and conjugating verbs. In a
little garret at the top of the house he began to
collect his books; even his supper of bread and
milk was carried up to him there, for he refused
to eat with his family for fear of interrupting his
studies.   It is a deplorable picture: the fumes of
the hearty butcher's evening meal ascend the stair
in vain, Henry is reading "Blackstone" and "The
Wealth of Nations."   If it were Udolpho or Conan
Doyle that held him, there were some excuse.
The sad life of Henry is the truest indictment of
overstudy that I know.   No one, after reading
Southey's memoir, will overload his brain again.
   At the age of fifteen we find the boy writing to
his older brother Neville: "I have made a firm
resolution never to spend above one hour at this
amusement [novel reading].   I have been obliged
to enter into this resolution in consequence of a
vitiated taste acquired by reading romances."
He is human enough to add, however, that "after
long and fatiguing researches in 'Blackstone'
or 'Coke,' 'Tom Jones' or 'Robinson Crusoe'
afford a pleasing and necessary relaxation.   Of
'Robinson Crusoe' I shall observe that it is
allowed to be the best novel for youth in the
English language."
   The older brother to whom these comments
were addressed was living in London, apparently a

fairly successful man of business. Henry permitted himself to indulge his pedagogical and
ministerial instincts for the benefit and improve-
ment of his kinsman. They seem to have carried
on a mutual recrimination in their letters:
Neville was inclined to belittle the divine calling
of poets in their teens; while Henry deplored his
brother's unwillingness to write at length and
upon serious and "instructive" topics. Alas, the
ill-starred young man had a mania for self-improve-
ment. If our great-grandparents were all like that
what an age it had been for the Scranton correspondence courses! "What is requisite to make
one's correspondence valuable?" asks Henry. "I
answer, *sound sense*." (The italics are his own.)
"You have better natural abilities than many
youth," he tells his light-hearted brother, "but
it is with regret I see that you will not give yourself the trouble of writing a good letter. My
friend, you never found any art, however trivial,
that did not require some application at first."
He begs the astounded Neville to fill his letters
with his opinions of the books he reads. "You
have no idea how beneficial this would be to
yourself." Does one not know immediately that
Henry is destined to an early grave?

Henry's native sweetness was further impaired
by a number of prizes won in magazine **compe-**

titions. A silver medal and a pair of twelve-inch
globes shortly became his for meritorious contributions to the *Monthly Mirror*. He was also
admitted a member of a famous literary society
then existing in Nottingham, and although the
youngest of the sodality he promptly announced
that he proposed to deliver them a lecture. With
mingled curiosity and dismay the gathering
assembled at the appointed time, and the inspired youth harangued them for two hours on
the subject of Genius. The devil, or his agent
in Nottingham, had marked Henry for de-
struction.

In such a career there can be no doubt as to
the next step. He published a book of poems.
His verses, dealing with such topics as Consumption, Despair, Lullaby of a Female Convict to Her
Child the Night Previous to Execution, Lines
Spoken by a Lover at the Grave of His Mistress,
The Eve of Death, and Sonnet Addressed by a
Female Lunatic to a Lady, had been warmly wel-
comed by the politest magazines of the time.
To wish to publish them in more permanent
form was natural; but the unfortunate young
man conceived the thought that the venture
might even be a profitable one. He had found
himself troubled with deafness, which threatened
to annul his industry in the law; moreover, his

spirit was canting seriously toward devotional matters, and thoughts of a college career and then the church were lively in his mind.

The winter of 1802-3 was busily passed in preparing his manuscript for the printer. Probably never before or since, until the Rev. John Franklin Bair of Greensburg, Pennsylvania, set about garnering his collected works into that volume which is the delight of the wicked, has a human heart mulled over indifferent verses with so honest a pleasure and such unabated certainty of immortality. The first two details to be attended to were the printing of what were modestly termed *Proposals*—i. e., advertisements of the projected volume, calling for pledges of subscription—and, still more important, securing the permission of some prominent person to accept a dedication of the book. The jolly old days of literary patronage were then in the sere and saffron, but it was still esteemed an aid to the sale of a volume if it might be dedicated to some marquis of Carabas. Accordingly the manuscript was despatched to London, and Neville, the philistine brother, was called upon to leave it at the residence of the Duchess of Devonshire. A very humble letter from honest Henry accompanied it, begging leave of her Grace to dedicate his "trifling effusions" to her.

Henry's letters to Neville while his book was in preparation are very entertaining, as those of minor poets always are under such circumstances. Henry was convinced that at least 350 copies would be sold in Nottingham. He writes in exultation that he has already got twenty-three orders even before his "proposals" are ready:

"I have got twenty-three, without making the affair public at all, among my immediate acquaintance: and mind, I neither solicit nor draw the conversation to the subject, but a rumour has got abroad, and has been received more favourably than I expected."

But the matter of the dedication unfortunately lagged far behind the poet's hopes. After the manuscript was left at the house of her Grace of Devonshire there followed what the Ancient Mariner so feelingly calls a weary time. Poor Henry in Nottingham hung upon the postman's heels, but no word arrived from the duchess. She was known to be assaulted from all sides by such applications: indeed her mail seems to have been very nearly as large as that of Mary Pickford or Theda Bara. Then, to his unspeakable anxiety, the miserable and fermenting Henry learned that all parcels sent to the duchess, unless marked with a password known only to her particular correspondents, were thrown into a closet

by her porter to be reclaimed at convenience, or
not at all. "I am ruined," cried Henry in agony;
and the worthy Neville paid several unsuccessful visits to Devonshire House in the attempt to
retrieve the manuscript. Finally, after waiting
four hours in the servants' hall, he succeeded.
Even then undaunted, this long-suffering older
brother made one more try in the poet's behalf:
he obtained a letter of introduction to the duchess,
and called on her in person, wisely leaving the
manuscript at home; and with the complaisance
of the great the lady readily acquiesced in Henry's
modest request. Her name was duly inscribed
on the proper page of the little volume, and in
course of time the customary morocco-bound
copy reached her. Alas, she took no notice of it,
and Mr. Southey surmises that "Involved as
she was in an endless round of miserable follies,
it is probable that she never opened the book."

"Clifton Grove" was the title Henry gave the
book, published in 1803.

It is not necessary to take the poems in this
little volume more seriously than any seventeen-
year-old ejaculations. It is easy to see what Henry's
reading had been—Milton, Collins, and Gray, evidently. His unconscious borrowings from Milton
do him great credit, as showing how thoroughly
he appreciated good poetry. It seeped into his

mind and became part of his own outpourings. *Il Penseroso* gushes to the surface of poor Henry's song every few lines; precious twigs and shreds of Milton flow merrily down the current of his thought. And yet smile as we may, every now and then friend Henry puts something over. One of his poems is a curious foretaste of what Keats was doing ten years later. Every now and then one pauses to think that this lad, once his youthful vapours were over, might have done great things. And as he says in his quaint little preface, "the unpremeditated effusions of a boy, from his thirteenth year, employed, not in the acquisition of literary information, but in the more active business of life, must not be expected to exhibit any considerable portion of the correctness of a Virgil, or the vigorous compression of a Horace."

The publishing game was new to Henry, and the slings and arrows found an unshielded heart. When the first copies of his poor little book came home from the printer he was prostrated to find several misprints. He nearly swooned, but seizing a pen he carefully corrected all the copies. After writing earnest and very polite letters to all the reviewers he dispatched copies to the leading periodicals, and sat down in the sure hope of rapid fame. How bitter was his chagrin when the *Monthly Review* for February, 1804, came out with a rather disparaging comment: in particular the critic took umbrage at his having put *boy* to rhyme with *sky*, and added, referring to Henry's hopes of a college course, "If Mr. White should be instructed by alma mater, he will, doubtless, produce better sense and better rhymes."

The review was by no means unjust: it said what any disinterested opinion must have confirmed, that the youth's ambitions were excellent, but that neither he, nor indeed any two-footed singer, is likely to be an immortal poet by seventeen. But Henry's sensitive soul had been so inflated by the honest pride of his friends that he could only see gross and callous malignity and conspiracy in the criticism. His theology, his health, his peace of mind, were all overthrown. As a matter of fact, however (as Southey remarks), it was the very brusqueness of this review that laid the foundation of his reputation. The circumstance aroused Southey's interest in the young man's efforts to raise himself above his level in the world and it was the laureate who after Henry's death edited his letters and literary remains, and gave him to us as we have him. Southey tells us that after the young man's death he and Coleridge looked over his papers with great emotion, and were amazed at the fervour of his industry and ambition.

Alas, we must hurry the narrative, on which one would gladly linger. The life of this sad and high-minded anchorite has a strong fascination for me. Melancholy had marked him for her own: he himself always felt that he had not a long span before him. Hindered by deafness, threatened with consumption, and a deadlier enemy yet—epilepsy—his frail and uneasy spirit had full right to distrust its tenement. The summer of 1804 he spent partly at Wilford, a little village near Nottingham where he took lodgings. His employers very kindly gave him a generous holiday to recruit; but his old habits of excessive study seized him again. He had, for the time, given up hope of being able to attend the university, and accordingly thought it all the more necessary to do well at the law. Night after night he would read till two or three in the morning, lie down fully dressed on his bed, and rise again to work at five or six. His mother, who was living with him in his retreat, used to go upstairs to put out his candle and see that he went to bed; but Henry, so docile in other matters, in this was unconquerable. When he heard his mother's step on the stair he would extinguish the taper and feign sleep; but after she had retired he would light it again and resume his reading. Perhaps the best things he wrote were composed in this period of extreme depression. The "Ode on Disappointment," and some of his sonnets, breathe a quiet dignity of resignation to sorrow that is very touching and even worthy of respect as poetry. He never escaped the cliché and the bathetic, but this is a fair example of his midnight musings at their highest pitch:—

TO CONSUMPTION

Gently, most gently, on thy victim's head,
Consumption, lay thine hand. Let me decay,
Like the expiring lamp, unseen, away,
And softly go to slumber with the dead.
And if 'tis true what holy men have said,
That strains angelic oft foretell the day
Of death, to those good men who fall thy prey,
O let the aerial music round my bed,
Dissolving sad in dying symphony,
Whisper the solemn warning in mine ear;
That I may bid my weeping friends good-bye,
Ere I depart upon my journey drear:
And smiling faintly on the painful past,
Compose my decent head, and breathe my last.

But in spite of depression and ill health, he was really happy at Wilford, a village in the elbow of a deep gully on the Trent, and near his well-beloved Clifton Woods. On the banks of the stream he would sit for hours in a maze of dreams, or wander among the trees on summer nights, awed by the sublime beauty of the lightning, and heedless of drenched and muddy clothes.

Later in the summer it was determined that he should go to college after all; and by the generosity of a number of friends (including Neville who promised twenty pounds annually) he was able to enter himself for St. John's College, Cambridge. In the autumn he left his legal employers, who were very sorry to lose him, and took up quarters with a clergyman in Lincolnshire (Winteringham) under whom he pursued his studies for a year, to prepare himself thoroughly for college. His letters during this period are mostly of a religious tinge, enlivened only by a mishap while boating on the Humber when he was stranded for six hours on a sand-bank. He had become quite convinced that his calling was the ministry. The proper observance of the Sabbath by his younger brothers and sisters weighed on his mind, and he frequently wrote home on this topic.

In October, 1805, we find him settled at last in his rooms at St. John's, the college that is always dear to us as the academic home of two very different undergraduates—William Wordsworth and Samuel Butler. His rooms were in the rearmost court, near the cloisters, and overlooking the famous Bridge of Sighs. His letters give us a pleasant picture of his quiet rambles through the town, his solitary cups of tea as he sat by the fire, and his disappointment in not being able to hear his lecturers on account of his deafness. Most entertaining to any one at all familiar with the life of the Oxford and Cambridge colleges is his account of the thievery of his "gyp" (the man-servant who makes the bed, cares for the rooms, and attends to the wants of the students). Poor Henry's tea, sugar, and handkerchiefs began to vanish in the traditional way; but he was practical enough to buy a large padlock for his coal bin.

But Henry's innocent satisfaction in having at last attained the haven of his desires was not long of duration. In spite of ill health, his tutors constrained him to enter for a scholarship examination in December, and when the unfortunate fellow pleaded physical inability, they dosed him with "strong medicines" to enable him to face the examiners. After the ordeal he was so unstrung that he hurried off to London to spend Christmas with his aunt.

The account of his year at college is very pitiful. His tutors were, according to their lights, very kind; they relieved him as far as possible from financial worries, but they did not have sense enough to restrain him from incessant study. Even on his rambles he was always at work memo-

'rizing Greek plays, mathematical theorems, or what not. In a memorandum found in his desk his life was thus planned: "Rise at half-past five. Devotions and walk till seven. Chapel and breakfast till eight. Study and lectures till one. Four and a half clear reading. Walk and dinner, and chapel to six. Six to nine reading. Nine to ten, devotions. Bed at ten."

In the summer of 1806 his examiners ranked him the best man of his year, and in mistaken kindness the college decided to grant him the unusual compliment of keeping him in college through the vacation with a special mathematical tutor, gratis, to work with him, mathematics being considered his weakness. As his only chance of health lay in complete rest during the holiday, this plan of spending the summer in study was simply a death sentence. In July, while at work on logarithm tables, he was over-taken by a sudden fainting fit, evidently of an epileptic nature. The malady gained strength, aided by the weakness of his heart and lungs, and he died on October 19, 1806.

Poor Henry! Surely no gentler, more innocent soul ever lived. His letters are a golden treasury of earnest and solemn speculation. Perhaps once a twelvemonth he displays a sad little vein of pleasantry, but not for long. Probably the

light-hearted undergraduates about him found
him a very prosy, shabby, and mournful young
man, but if one may judge by the outburst of
tributary verses published after his death he was
universally admired and respected. Let us close
the story by a quotation from a tribute paid him
by a lady versifier:

> If worth, if genius, to the world are dear,
> To Henry's shade devote no common tear.
> His worth on no precarious tenure hung,
> From genuine piety his virtues sprung:
> If pure benevolence, if steady sense,
> Can to the feeling heart delight dispense;
> If all the highest efforts of the mind,
> Exalted, noble, elegant, refined,
> Call for fond sympathy's heartfelt regret,
> Ye sons of genius, pay the mournful debt!

TRIVIA

The secret thoughts of a man run over all things, holy,
profane, clean, obscene, grave, and light, without shame or
blame. —HOBBES, *Leviathan*, Chap. VIII.

THE bachelor is almost extinct in America.
Our hopelessly utilitarian civilization
demands that a man of forty should be
rearing a family, should go to an office five times
a week, and pretend an interest in the World's
Series. It is unthinkable to us that there should
be men of mature years who do not know the
relative batting averages of the Red Sox and the
Pirates. The intellectual and strolling male of
from thirty-five to fifty-five years (which is what
one means by bachelor) must either marry and
settle down in the Oranges, or he must flee to
Europe or the MacDowell Colony. There is no
alternative. Vachel Lindsay please notice.

The fate of Henry James is a case in point.
Undoubtedly he fled the shores of his native
land to escape the barrage of the bonbonniverous
sub-deb, who would else have mown him down
without ruth.

But in England they still linger, these quaint, phosphorescent middle-aged creatures, lurking behind a screenage of muffins and crumpets and hip baths. And thither fled one of the most delightful born bachelors this hemisphere has ever unearthed, Mr. Logan Pearsall Smith.

Mr. Smith was a Philadelphian, born about fifty years ago. But that most amiable of cities does not encourage detached and meditative bachelorhood, and after sampling what is quaintly known as "a guarded education in morals and manners" at Haverford College, our hero passed to Harvard, and thence by a swifter decline to Oxford. Literature and liberalism became his pursuits; on the one hand, he found himself engrossed in the task of proving to the British electorate that England need not always remain the same; on the other, he wrote a Life of Sir Henry Wotton, a volume of very graceful and beautiful short stories about Oxford ("The Youth of Parnassus") and a valuable little book on the history and habits of the English language.

But in spite of his best endeavours to quench and subdue his mental humours, Mr. Smith found his serious moments invaded by incomprehensible twinges of esprit. Travelling about England, leading the life of the typical English bachelor, equipped with gladstone bag, shaving kit, evening clothes and tweeds; passing from country house to London club, from Oxford common room to Sussex gardens, the solemn pageantry of the cultivated classes now and then burst upon him in its truly comic aspect. The tinder and steel of his wit, too uncontrollably frictioned, ignited a shower of roman candles, and we conceive him prostrated with irreverent laughter in some lonely railway carriage.

Mr. Smith did his best to take life seriously, and I believe he succeeded passably well until after forty years of age. But then the spectacle of the English vicar toppled him over, and once the gravity of the Church of England is invaded, all lesser Alps and sanctuaries lie open to the scourge. Menaced by serious intellectual disorders unless he were to give vent to these disturbing levities, Mr. Smith began to set them down under the title of "Trivia," and now at length we are enriched by the spectacle of this iridescent and puckish little book, which presents as it were a series of lantern slides of an ironical, whimsical, and merciless sense of humour. It is a motion picture of a middle-aged, phosphorescent mind that has long tried to preserve a decent melancholy but at last capitulates in the most delicately intellectual brainslide of our generation.

This is no Ring Lardner, no Irvin Cobb, no Casey

at the bat. Mr. Smith is an infinitely close and
acute observer of sophisticated social life, tinged
with a faint and agreeable refined sadness, by an
aura of shyness which amounts to a spiritual vir-
ginity. He comes to us trailing clouds of glory
from the heaven of pure and unfettered speculation which is our home. He is an elf of utter
simplicity and infinite candour. He is a flicker
of absolute Mind. His little book is as precious
and as disturbing as devilled crabs.

Blessèd, blessèd little book, how you will run
like quicksilver from mind to mind, leaping—a
shy and shining spark—from brain to brain! I
know of nothing since Lord Bacon quite like these
ineffably dainty little paragraphs of gilded whim,
these rainbow nuggets of wistful inquiry, these
butterfly wings of fancy, these pointed sparklers
of wit. A purge, by Zeus, a purge for the wicked!
Irony so demure, so quaint, so far away; pathos
so void of regret, merriment so delicate that one
dare not laugh for fear of dispelling the charm—
all this is "Trivia." Where are Marcus Aurelius
or Epictetus or all the other Harold Bell Wrights
of old time? Baron Verulam himself treads a
heavy gait beside this airy elfin scamper. It is
Atalanta's heels. It is a heaven-given scenario of that shyest, dearest, remotest of essences—
the mind of a strolling bachelor.

Bless his heart, in a momentary panic of modesty at the thought of all his sacred spots laid bare, the heavenly man tries to scare us away. "These pieces of moral prose have been written, dear Reader, by a large, Carnivorous Mammal, belonging to that suborder of the Animal Kingdom which includes also the Orange-outang, the tusked Gorilla, the Baboon, with his bright blue and scarlet bottom, and the gentle Chimpanzee."

But this whimsical brother to the chimpanzee, despite this last despairing attempt at modest evasion, denudes himself before us. And his heart, we find, is strangely like our own. His reveries, his sadnesses, his exhilarations, are all ours, too. Like us he cries, "I wish I were unflinching and emphatic, and had big bushy eyebrows and a Message for the Age. I wish I were a deep Thinker, or a great Ventriloquist." Like us he has that dreadful feeling (now and then) of being only a ghost, a thin, unreal phantom in a world of bank cashiers and duchesses and prosperous merchants and other Real Persons. Like us he fights a losing battle against the platitudes and moral generalizations that hem us round. "I can hardly post a letter," he laments, "without marvelling at the excellence and accuracy of the Postal System." And he consoles himself, good man, with the thought of the meaningless creation crashing blindly through frozen space. His other great consolation is his dear vice of reading— "This joy not dulled by Age, this polite and unpunished vice, this selfish, serene, life-long intoxication."

It is impossible by a few random snippets to give any just figment of the delicious mental intoxication of this piercing, cathartic little volume. It is a bright tissue of thought robing a radiant, dancing spirit. Through the shimmering veil of words we catch, now and then, a flashing glimpse of the Immortal Whimsy within, shy, sudden, and defiant. Across blue bird-haunted English lawns we follow that gracious figure, down dusky London streets where he is peering in at windows and laughing incommunicable jests.

But alas, Mr. Pearsall Smith is lost to America. The warming pans and the twopenny tube have lured him away from us. Never again will he tread on peanut shells in the smoking car or read the runes about Phoebe Snow. Chiclets and Spearmint and Walt Mason and the Toonerville Trolley and the Prince Albert ads—these mean nothing to him. He will never compile an anthology of New York theatrical notices: "The play that makes the dimples to catch the tears." Careful and adroit propaganda, begun twenty years ago by the Department of State, might have won him back, but now it is impossible to repatriate him. The exquisite humours of our American life are faded from his mind. He has gone across the great divide that separates a subway from an underground and an elevator from a lift. I wonder does he ever mourn the scrapple and buckwheat cakes that were his birthright?

Major George Haven Putnam in his "Memories of a Publisher" describes a famous tennis match played at Oxford years ago, when he and Pearsall Smith defeated A. L. Smith and Herbert Fisher, the two gentlemen who are now Master of Balliol and British Minister of Education. The Balliol don attributed the British defeat in this international tourney to the fact that his tennis shoes (shall we say his "sneakers?") came to grief and he had to play the crucial games in stocking feet. But though Major Putnam and his young ally won the set of *patters* (let us use the Wykehamist word), the Major allowed the other side to gain a far more serious victory. They carried off the young Philadelphian and kept him in England until he was spoiled for all good American uses. That was badly done, Major! Because we needed Pearsall Smith over here, and now we shall never recapture him. He will go on calling an elevator a lift, and he will never write an American "Trivia."

PREFACES

IT HAS long been my conviction that the most graceful function of authorship is the writing of prefaces. What is more pleasant than dashing off those few pages of genial introduction after all the dreary months of spading at the text? A paragraph or two as to the intentions of the book; allusions to the unexpected difficulties encountered during composition; neatly phrased gratitude to eminent friends who have given gracious assistance; and a touching allusion to the Critic on the Hearth who has done the indexing— one of the trials of the wives of literary men not mentioned by Mrs. Andrew Lang in her pleasant essay on that topic. A pious wish to receive criticisms "in case a second edition should be called for"; your address, and the date, add a homely touch at the end.

How delightful this bit of pleasant intimacy after the real toil is over! It is like paterfamilias coming out of his house at dusk, after the hard day's work, to read his newspaper on the doorstep. Or it may be a bit of superb gesturing. No book is complete without a preface. Better a preface without a book. . . .

Many men have written books without prefaces. But not many have written prefaces without books. And yet I am convinced it is one of the subtlest pleasures. I have planned several books, not yet written; but the prefaces are all ready this many a day. Let me show you the sort of thing I mean.

PREFACE TO "THE LETTERS OF ANDREW MCGILL"

How well I remember the last time I saw Andrew McGill! It was in the dear old days at Rutgers, my last term. I was sitting over a book one brilliant May afternoon, rather despondent—there came a rush up the stairs and a thunder at the door. I knew his voice, and hurried to open. Poor, dear fellow, he was just back from tennis; I never saw him look so glorious. Tall and thin— he was always very thin, *see* p. 219 and *passim*— with his long, brown face and sparkling black eyes—I can see him still rambling about the room in his flannels, his curly hair damp on his forehead. "Buzzard," he said—he always called me Buzzard—"guess what's happened?"

"In love again?" I asked.

He laughed. A bright, golden laugh—I can hear it still. His laughter was always infectious.

"No," he said. "Dear silly old Buzzard, what

do you think? I've won the Sylvanus Stall fellowship."

I shall never forget that moment. It was very still, and in the college garden, just under my window, I could hear a party of Canadian girls deliciously admiring things. It was a cruel instant for me. I, too, in my plodding way, had sent in an essay for the prize, but without telling him. Must I confess it? I had never dared mention the subject for fear he, too, would compete. I knew that if he did he was sure to win. O petty jealousies, that seem so bitter now!

"Rude old Buzzard," he said in his bantering way, "you haven't congratulated!"

I pulled myself together.

"Brindle," I said—I always called him Brindle; how sad the nickname sounds now—"you took my breath away. Dear lad, I'm overjoyed."

It is four and twenty years since that May afternoon. I never saw him again. Never even heard him read the brilliant poem "Sunset from the Mons Veneris" that was the beginning of his career, for the week before commencement I was taken ill and sent abroad for my health. I never came back to New York; and he remained there. But I followed his career with the closest attention. Every newspaper cutting, every magazine article in which his name was mentioned, went into my scrapbook. And almost every week for twenty years he wrote to me—those long, radiant letters, so full of *verve* and *élan* and ringing, ruthless wit. There was always something very Gallic about his saltiness. "Oh, to be born a Frenchman!" he writes. "Why wasn't I born a Frenchman instead of a dour, dingy Scotsman? Oh, for the birthright of Montmartre! Stead of which I have the mess of pottage—stodgy, porridgy Scots pottage" (*see* p. 189).

He had his sombre moods, too. It was characteristic of him, when in a pet, to wish he had been born other-where than by the pebbles of Arbroath. "Oh, to have been born a Norseman!" he wrote once. "Oh, for the deep Scandinavian scourge of pain, the inbrooding, marrowy soul-ache of Ibsen! That is the fertilizing soil of tragedy. Tragedy springs from it, tall and white and stately like the lily from the dung. I will never be a tragedian. Oh, pebbles of Arbroath!"

All the world knows how he died. . . .

PREFACE TO AN HISTORICAL WORK
(In six volumes)

The work upon which I have spent the best years of my life is at length finished. After two decades of uninterrupted toil, enlivened only by those small bickerings over *minutiæ* so dear to all

scrupulous writers, I may perhaps be pardoned
if I philosophize for a few moments on the func-
tions of the historian.

There are, of course, two technical modes of
approach, quite apart from the preparatory con-
templation of the field. (This last, I might add,
has been singularly neglected by modern historians. My old friend, Professor Spondee, of Halle,
though deservedly eminent in his chosen lot, is
particularly open to criticism on this ground. I
cannot emphasize too gravely the importance of
preliminary calm—what Hobbes calls "the un-
prejudicated mind." But this by way of paren-
thesis.) One may attack the problem with the
mortar trowel, or with the axe. Sismondi, I think,
has observed this.

Some such observations as these I was privileged to address to my very good friend, Professor
Fish, of Yale, that justly renowned seat of learning, when lecturing in New Haven recently. His
reply was witty—too witty to be apt, "Piscem
natare doces," he said.

I will admit that Professor Fish may be free from
taint in this regard; but many historians of to-day
are, I fear, imbued with that most dangerous
tincture of historical cant which lays it down as a
maxim that contemporary history cannot be ju-
dicially written.

Those who have been kind enough to display some interest in the controversy between myself and M. Rougegorge—of the Sorbonne—in the matter of Lamartine's account of the elections to the Constituent Assembly of 1848, will remark several hitherto unobserved errors in Lamartine which I have been privileged to point out. For instance, Lamartine (who is supported *in toto* by M. Rougegorge) asserts that the elections took place on Easter Sunday, April 27, 1848. Whereas, I am able to demonstrate, by reference to the astronomical tables at Kew Observatory, that in 1848 Easter Day fell upon April 23. M. Rougegorge's assertion that Lamartine was a slave to opium rests upon a humorous misinterpretation of Mme. Lamartine's diary. (The matter may be looked up by the curious in Annette Oser's "Années avec les Lamartines." Oser was for many years the cook in Lamartine's household, and says some illuminating things regarding L.'s dislike of onions.)

It is, of course, impossible for me to acknowledge individually the generous and stimulating assistance I have received from so many scholars in all parts of the world. The mere list of names would be like Southey's "Cataract of Lodore," and would be but an ungracious mode of returning thanks. I cannot, however, forbear to mention

Professor Mandrake, of the Oxford Chair, *optimus maximus* among modern historians. Of him I may say, in the fine words of Virgil, "Sedet aeternumque sedebit."

My dear wife, fortunately a Serb by birth, has regularized my Slavic orthography, and has grown gray in the service of the index. To her, and to my little ones, whose merry laughter has so often penetrated to my study and cheered me at my travail, I dedicate the whole. *89, Decameron Gardens.*

PREFACE TO A BOOK OF POEMS

This little selection of verses, to which I have given the title "Rari Nantes," was made at the instance of several friends. I have chosen from my published works those poems which seemed to me most faithfully to express my artistic message; and the title obviously implies that I think them the ones most likely to weather the maëlstroms of Time. Be that as it may.

Vachel Lindsay and I have often discussed over a glass of port (one glass only: alas, that Vachel should abstain!) the state of the Muse to-day. He deems that she now has fled from cities to dwell on the robuster champaigns of Illinois and Kansas. Would that I could agree; but I see her in the cities and everywhere, set down to menial

taskwork. She were better in exile, on Ibsen's
sand dunes or Maeterlinck's bee farm. But in
America the times are very evil. Prodigious
convulsion of production, the grinding of mighty
forces, the noise and rushings of winds—and what
avails? *Parturiunt montes . . .* you know
the rest. The ridiculous mice squeak and scamper on the granary floor. They may play undis-
turbed, for the real poets, those great gray felines,
are sifting loam under Westminster. Gramercy
Park and the Poetry Society see them not.

It matters not. With this little book my task is
done. Vachel and I sail to-morrow for Nova
Zembla.
The Grotto, Yonkers.

A second edition of "Rari Nantes" having been
called for, I have added three more poems,
Esquimodes written since arriving here. Also the
"Prayer for Warm Weather," by Vachel Lindsay,
is included, at his express request. The success
of the first edition has been very gratifying to
me. My publishers will please send reviews to
Bleak House, Nova Zembla.

The rigorous climate of Nova Zembla I find
most stimulating to production, and therefore in

this new edition I am able to include several new poems. "The Ode to a Seamew," the "Fracas on an Ice Floe," and the sequence of triolimericks are all new. If I have been able to convey anything of the bracing vigour of the Nova Zembla *locale* the praise is due to my friendly and suggestive critic, the editor of *Gooseflesh*, the leading Nova Zemblan review.

Vachel Lindsay's new book, "The Tango," has not yet appeared, therefore I may perhaps say here that he is hard at work on an "Ode to the Gulf Stream," which has great promise.

The success of this little book has been such that I am encouraged to hope that the publisher's exemption of royalties will soon be worked off.

THE SKIPPER

I HAVE been reading again that most delightful of all autobiographies, "A Personal Record," by Joseph Conrad. Mr. Conrad's mind is so rich, it has been so well mulched by years of vigorous life and sober thinking, that it pushes tendrils of radiant speculation into every crevice of the structure upon which it busies itself. This figure of speech leaves much to be desired and calls for apology, but in perversity and profusion the trellis growth of Mr. Conrad's memories, here blossoming before the delighted reader's eyes, runs like some ardent trumpet vine or Virginia creeper, spreading hither and thither, redoubling on itself, branching unexpectedly upon spandrel and espalier, and repeatedly enchanting us with some delicate criss-cross of mental fibres. One hesitates even to suggest that there may be admirers of Mr. Conrad who are not familiar with this picture of his mind—may we call it one of the most remarkable minds that has ever concerned itself with the setting of English words horizontally in parallel lines?

The fraternity of gentlemen claiming to have

been the first on this continent to appreciate
the vaulting genius of Mr. Conrad grows numer-
ous indeed; almost as many as the discoverers of
O. Henry and the pallbearers of Ambrose Bierce.
It would be amusing to enumerate the list of those
who have assured me (over the sworn secrecy of a
table d'hôte white wine) that they read the proof-
sheets of "Almayer's Folly" in 1895, etc., etc. For
my own part, let me be frank. I do not think I ever
heard of Mr. Conrad before December 2, 1911. On
that date, which was one day short of the seven-
teenth anniversary of Stevenson's death, a small
club of earnest young men was giving a dinner to
Sir Sidney Colvin at the Randolph Hotel in
Oxford. Sir Sidney told us many anecdotes of
R. L. S., and when the evening was far spent I
remember that someone asked him whether there
was any writer of to-day in whom he felt the
same passionate interest as in Stevenson, any
man now living whose work he thought would
prove a permanent enrichment of English literature. Sir Sidney Colvin is a scrupulous and
sensitive critic, and a sworn enemy of loose statement; let me not then pretend to quote him exactly;
but I know that the name he mentioned was that
of Joseph Conrad, and it was a new name to
me.

Even so, I think it was not until over a year later

that first I read one of Mr. Conrad's books; and I am happy to remember that it was "Typhoon," which I read at one sitting in the second-class dining saloon of the *Celtic*, crossing from New York in January, 1913. There was a very violent westerly gale at the time—a famous shove, Captain Conrad would call it—and I remember that the barometer went lower than had ever been recorded before on the western ocean. The piano in the saloon carried away, and frolicked down the aisle between the tables: it was an ideal stage set for "Typhoon." The saloon was far aft, and a hatchway just astern of where I sat was stove in by the seas. By sticking my head through a window I could see excellent combers of green sloshing down into the 'tweendecks.

But the inspired discursiveness of Mr. Conrad is not to be imitated here. The great pen which has paid to human life "the undemonstrative tribute of a sigh which is not a sob, and of a smile which is not a grin," needs no limping praise of mine. But sometimes, when one sits at midnight by the fainting embers and thinks that of all novelists now living one would most ardently yearn to hear the voice and see the face of Mr. Conrad, then it is happy to recall that in "A Personal Record" one comes as close as typography permits to a fireside chat with the Skipper himself.

He tells us that he has never been very well acquainted with the art of conversation, but remembering Marlowe, we set this down as polite modesty only. Here in the "Personal Record" is Marlowe ipse, pipe in mouth, and in retrospective mood. This book and the famous preface to the "Nigger" give us the essence, the bouillon, of his genius. Greatly we esteem what Mr. Walpole, Mr. Powys, Mr. James, and (optimus maximus) Mr. Follett, have said about him; but who would omit the chance to hear him from his proper mouth? And in these informal confessions there are pieces that are destined to be classics of autobiography as it is rarely written.

One cannot resist the conviction that Mr. Conrad, traditionally labelled complex and tortuous by the librarians, is in reality as simple as lightning or dawn. Fidelity, service, sincerity—those are the words that stand again and again across his pages. "I have a positive horror of losing even for one moving moment that full possession of myself which is the first condition of good service." He has carried over to the world of desk and pen the rigorous tradition of the sea. He says that he has been attributed an unemotional, grim acceptance of facts, a hardness of heart. To which he answers that he must tell as he sees, and that the attempt to move others to the

extremities of emotion means the surrendering
one's self to exaggeration, allowing one's self to
be carried away beyond the bounds of normal
sensibility. Self-restraint is the duty, the dignity,
the decency of the artist. This, indeed, is the
creed of the simple man in every calling; and from
this angle it appears that it is the Pollyananiases
and the Harold Bell Wrights who are complicated and subtle; it is Mr. Conrad, indeed, who
is simple with the great simplicity of life and
death.

Truly in utter candour and simplicity no book
of memoirs since the synoptic gospels exceeds
"A Personal Record." Such minor facts as
where the writer was born, and when, and the
customary demonology of boyhood and courtship
and the first pay envelope, are gloriously ignored.
A statistician, an efficiency pundit, a literary ac-
countant, would rise from the volume nervously
shattered from an attempt to grasp what it was
all about. The only person in the book who is
accorded any comprehensive biographical résumé
is a certain great-uncle of Mr. Conrad, Mr.
Nicholas B., who accompanied Bonaparte on his
midwinter junket to Moscow, and was bitterly
constrained to eat a dog in the forests of Lith-
uania. To the delineation of this warrior, who
was a legend of his youth, Mr. Conrad devotes his

most affectionate and tender power of whimsical reminiscence; and in truth his sketches of family history make the tragedies of Poland clearer to me than several volumes of historical comment. In his prose of that superbly rich simplicity of texture —it is a commonplace that it seems always like some notable translation from the French—he looks back across the plains of Ukraine, and takes us with him so unquestionably that even the servant who drives him to his uncle's house becomes a figure in our own daily lives. And to our delicious surprise we find that the whole of two long chapters constitutes merely his musings in half an hour while he is waiting for dinner at his uncle's house. With what adorable tenderness he reviews the formative contours of boyish memories, telling us the whole mythology of his youth! Upon my soul, sometimes I think that this is the only true autobiography ever written: true to the inner secrets of the human soul. It is the passkey to the Master's attitude toward all the dear creations of his brain; it is the spiritual scenario of every novel he has written. What self-revealing words are these: "An imaginative and exact rendering of authentic memories may serve worthily that spirit of piety toward all things human which sanctions the conceptions of a writer of tales." And when one stops to consider, how essentially impious and irreverent to humanity are the novels of the Slop and Glucose school!

This marvellous life, austere, glowing, faithful to everything that deserves fidelity, contradictory to all the logarithms of probability, this tissue of unlikelihoods by which a Polish lad from the heart of Europe was integrated into the greatest living master of those who in our tongue strive to portray the riddles of the human heart—such is the kind of calculus that makes "A Personal Record" unique among textbooks of the soul. It is as impossible to describe as any dear friend. Setting out only with the intention to "present faithfully the feelings and sensations connected with the writing of my first book and with my first contact with the sea," Mr. Conrad set down what is really nothing less than a Testament of all that is most precious in human life. And the sentiment with which one lays it by is that the scribbler would gladly burn every shred of foolscap he had blackened and start all over again with truer ideals for his craft, could he by so doing have chance to meet the Skipper face to face.

Indeed, if Mr. Conrad had never existed it would have been necessary to invent him, the indescribable improbability of his career speaks so closely to the heart of every lover of literary truth. Who of his heroes is so fascinating to us

as he himself? How imperiously, by his own
noble example, he recalls us to the service of
honourable sincerity. And how poignantly these
memories of his evoke the sigh which is not a
sob, the smile which is not a grin.

A FRIEND OF FITZGERALD

"Loder is a Rock of Ages to rely on.
—EDWARD FITZGERALD.

IHEARD the other day of the death of dear old John Loder, the Woodbridge bookseller, at the age of ninety-two. Though ill equipped to do justice to his memory, it seems to me a duty, and a duty that I take up gladly. It is not often that a young man has the good fortune to know as a friend one who has been a crony of his own grandfather and great-grandfather. Such was my privilege in the case of John Loder, a man whose life was all sturdy simplicity and generous friendship. He shines in no merely reflected light, but in his own native nobility. I think there are a few lovers of England and of books who will be glad not to forget his unobtrusive services to literature. If only John Loder had kept a journal it would be one of the minor treasures of the Victorian Age. He had a racy, original turn of speech, full of the Suffolk lingo that so delighted his friend FitzGerald; full, too, of the delicacies of rich thought and feeling. He used to lament in his later years that he had not kept a diary as a young man. Alas that his Boswell came too late to do more than snatch at a few of his memories.

There is a little Suffolk town on the salt tidewater of the Deben, some ten miles from the sea. Its roofs of warm red tile are clustered on the hillslopes that run down toward the river; a massive, gray church tower and a great windmill are conspicuous landmarks. Broad barges and shabby schooners, with ruddy and amber sails, lie at anchor or drop down the river with the tide, bearing the simple sailormen of Mr. W. W. Jacobs's stories. In the old days before the railway it was a considerable ˌport and a town of thriving commerce. But now—well, it is little heard of in the annals of the world.

Yet Woodbridge, unknown to the tourist, has had her pilgrims, too, and her nook in literature. It was there that George Crabbe of Aldeburgh was apprenticed to a local surgeon and wrote his first poem, unhappily entitled "Inebriety." There lived Bernard Barton, "the Quaker poet," a versifier of a very mild sort, but immortal by reason of his friendships with greater men. Addressed to Bernard Barton, in a plain, neat hand, came scores of letters to Woodbridge in the eighteen-twenties, letters now famous, which

found their way up Church Street to Alexander's
Bank.   They were from no less a man than Charles
Lamb.   Also I have always thought it very much
to Woodbridge's credit that a certain Wood-
bridgian named Pulham was a fellow-clerk of
Lamb's at the East India House.   Perhaps Mr.
Pulham introduced Lamb and Barton to each
other.   And as birthplace and home of Edward
FitzGerald, Woodbridge drew such visitors as
Carlyle and Tennyson, who came to seek out the
immortal recluse.   In the years following Fitz-
Gerald's death many a student of books, some all
the way from America, found his way into John
Loder's shop to gossip about "Old Fitz."   In
1893 a few devoted members of the Omar Khay-
yam Club of London pilgrimaged to Woodbridge
to plant by the grave at Boulge (please pronounce
"Bowidge") a rosetree that had been raised from
seed brought from the bush that sheds its petals
over the dust of the tent-maker at Naishapur.
In 1909 Woodbridge and Ipswich celebrated the
FitzGerald centennial.   And Rupert Brooke's
father was (I believe) a schoolboy at Woodbridge;
alas that another of England's jewels just missed
being a Woodbridgian!

Some day, if you are wise, you, too, will take a
train at Liverpool Street, and drawn by one of
those delightful blue locomotives of the Great

Eastern Railway speed through Colchester and
Ipswich and finally set foot on the yellow-pebbled
platform at Woodbridge. As you step from the
stuffy compartment the keen salt Deben air will
tingle in your nostrils; and you may discover in
it a faint under-whiff of strong tobacco—the
undying scent of pipes smoked on the river wall
by old Fitz, and in recent years by John Loder
himself. If you have your bicycle with you, or
are content to hire one, you will find that rolling
Suffolk country the most delightful in the world
for quiet spinning. (But carry a repair kit, for
there are many flints!) Ipswich itself is full of
memories—of Chaucer, and Wolsey, and Dickens
(it is the "Eatanswill" of Pickwick), and it is
much pleasure to one of Suffolk blood to recall
that James Harper, the grandfather of the four
brothers who founded the great publishing house
of Harper and Brothers a century ago, was an
Ipswich man, born there in 1740. You will bike
to Bury St. Edmunds (where Fitz went to school,
and our beloved William McFee also!) and Aldeburgh, and Dunwich, to hear the chimes of the sea-
drowned abbey ringing under the waves. If you
are a Stevensonian, you will hunt out Cockfield
Rectory, near Sudbury, where R. L. S. first met
Sidney Colvin in 1872. (Colvin himself came
from Bealings, only two miles from Woodbridge.)

You may ride to Dunmow in Essex, to see the country of Mr. Britling; and to Wigborough, near Colchester, the haunt of Mr. McFee's painter-cousin in "Aliens." You will hire a sailboat at Lime Kiln Quay or the Jetty and bide a moving air and a going tide to drop down to Bawdsey ferry to hunt shark's teeth and amber among the shingle. You will pace the river walk to Kyson —perhaps the tide will be out and sunset tints shimmer over those glossy stretches of mud. Brown seaweed, vivid green samphire, purple flats of slime where the river ran a few hours before, a steel-gray trickle of water in the scour of the channel and a group of stately swans ruffling there; and the huddled red roofs of the town with the stately church tower and the waving arms of the windmill looking down from the hill. It is a scene to ravish an artist. You may walk back by way of Martlesham Heath, stopping at the Red Lion for a quencher (the Red Lion figurehead is supposed to have come from one of the ships of the Armada). It is a different kind of Armada that Woodbridge has to reckon with nowadays. Zeppelins. One dropped a bomb— a "dud" it was—in John Loder's garden; the old man had to be restrained from running out to seize it with his own hands.

John Loder was born in Woodbridge, August 3,

1825. His grandfather, Robert Loder, founded the family bookselling and printing business, which continues to-day at the old shop on the Thoroughfare under John Loder's son, Morton Loder. In the days before the railway came through, Woodbridge was the commercial centre for a large section of East Suffolk; it was a busy port, and the quays were crowded with shipping. But when transportation by rail became swift and cheap and the provinces began to deal with London merchants, the little town's prosperity suffered a sad decline. Many of the old Woodbridge shops, of several generations' standing, have had to yield to local branches of the great London "stores."

In John Loder's boyhood the book business was at its best. Woodbridgians were great readers, and such prodigal customers as FitzGerald did much to keep the ledgers healthy. John left school at thirteen or so, to learn the trade, and became the traditional printer's devil. He remembered Bernard Barton, the quiet, genial, brown-eyed poet, coming down the street from Alexander's Bank (where he was employed for forty years) with a large pile of banknotes to be re-numbered. The poet sat perched on a high stool watching young Loder and his superior do the work. And at noon Mr. Barton sent out to the Royal Oak Tavern near by for a basket of buns and a jug of stout to refresh printer and devil at their work.

Bernard Barton died in 1849, and was laid to rest in the little Friends' burying ground in Turn Lane. That quiet acre will repay the visitor's half-hour tribute to old mortality. My grandmother was buried there, one snowy day in January, 1912, and I remember how old John Loder came forward to the grave, bareheaded and leaning on his stick, to drop a bunch of fresh violets on the coffin.

Many a time I have sat in the quiet, walled-in garden of Burkitt House—that sweet plot of colour and fragrance so pleasantly commemorated by Mr. Mosher in his preface to "In Praise of Old Gardens"—and heard dear old John Loder tell stories of his youth. I remember the verse of Herrick he used to repeat, pointing round his little retreat with a well-stained pipestem:

> But walk'st about thine own dear bounds,
> Not envying others' larger grounds :
> For well thou know'st, 'tis not th' extent
> Of land makes life, but sweet content.

Loder's memory used to go back to times that seem almost fabulous now. He had known quite well an English soldier who was on guard over Boney at St. Helena—in fact, he once published in some newspaper this man's observations upon the fallen emperor, but I have not been able to trace the piece. He had been in Paris before the troubles of '48. I believe he served some sort of bookselling apprenticeship on Paternoster Row; at any rate, he used to be in touch with the London book trade as a young man, and made the acquaintance of Bernard Quaritch, one of the world's most famous booksellers. I remember his lamenting that FitzGerald had not dumped the two hundred unsold booklets of Omar upon his counter instead of Quaritch's in 1859. The story goes that they were offered by Quaritch for a penny apiece.

I always used to steer him onto the subject of FitzGerald sooner or later, and it was interesting to hear him tell how many princes of the literary world had come to his shop or had corresponded with him owing to his knowledge of E. F. G. Anne Thackeray gave him a beautiful portrait of herself in return for some courtesy he showed her. Robert H. Groome, the archdeacon of Suffolk, and his brilliant son, Francis Hindes Groome, the "Tarno Rye" (who wrote "Two Suffolk Friends" and was said by Watts Dunton to have known far more about the gipsies than Borrow) were among his correspondents.* John Hay, Elihu

*No lover of FitzGerald can afford not to own that exquisite tributary volume "Edward FitzGerald: An Aftermath," by Francis Hindes Groome, which Mr. Mosher published in 1902. It tells a great deal about Woodbridge, and is annotated by John Loder. Mr. Mosher was eager to include Loder's portrait in it, but the old man's modesty was always as great as his generosity: he would not consent.

Vedder, Aldis Wright, Canon Ainger, Thomas B. Mosher, Clement Shorter, Dewitt Miller, Edward Clodd, Leon Vincent—such men as these wrote or came to John Loder when they wanted special news about FitzGerald. FitzGerald had given him a great many curios and personal treasures: Mr. Loder never offered these for sale at any price (anything connected with FitzGerald was sacred to him) but if any one happened along who seemed able to appreciate them he would give them away with delight. He gave to me FitzGerald's old musical scrapbook, which he had treasured for over thirty years. This scrapbook, in perfect condition, contains very beautiful engravings, prints, and drawings of the famous composers, musicians, and operatic stars of whom Fitz was enivré as a young man. Among them are a great many drawings of Handel; FitzGerald, like Samuel Butler, was an enthusiastic Handelian. The pictures are annotated by E. F. G. and there are also two drawings of Beethoven traced by Thackeray. This scrapbook was compiled by FitzGerald when he and Thackeray were living together in London, visiting the Cave of Harmony and revelling in the dear delights of young intellectual companionship. Under a drawing of the famous Braham, dated 1831, Fitz has written: "As I saw and heard him many nights in the Pit of

Covent Garden, in company with W. M. Thackeray, whom I was staying with at the Bedford Coffee House."

When I tried, haltingly, to express my thanks for such a gift, the old man said "That's nothing! That's nothing! It'll help to keep you out of mischief. Much better to give 'em away before it's too late!" And he followed it with Canon Ainger's two volumes of Lamb's letters, which Ainger had given him.

Through his long life John Loder lived quietly in Woodbridge, eager and merry in his shop, a great reader, always delighted when any one came in who was qualified to discuss the literature which interested him. He and FitzGerald had long cracks together and perhaps Loder may have accompanied the Woodbridge Omar on some of those trips down the Deben on the *Scandal* or the *Meum and Tuum* (the *Mum and Tum* as Posh, Fitz's sailing master, called her). He played a prominent part in the life of the town, became a Justice of the Peace, and sat regularly on the bench until he was nearly ninety. As he entered upon the years of old age, came a delightful surprise. An old friend of his in the publishing business, whom he had known long before in London, died and left him a handsome legacy by will. Thus his last years were spared from anxiety **and** he was able to continue his unobtrusive and quiet generosities which had always been his secret delight.

Looking over the preceding paragraphs I am ashamed to see how pale and mumbling a tribute they are to this fine spirit. Could I but put him before you as he was in those last days! I used to go up to Burkitt House to see him: in summer we would sit in the little arbour in the garden, or in winter by the fire in his dining room. He would talk and I would ask him questions; now and then he would get up to pull down a book, or to lead me into his bedroom to see some special treasure. He used to sit in his shirt-sleeves, very close to the fire, with his shoe laces untied. In summer he would toddle about in his shaggy blue suit, with a tweed cap over one ear, his grizzled beard and moustache well stained by much smoking, his eyes as bright and his tongue as brisk as ever. Every warm morning would see him down on the river wall; stumping over Market Hill and down Church Street with his stout oak stick, hailing every child he met on the pavement. His pocket was generally full of peppermints, and the youngsters knew well which pocket it was. His long life was a series of original and graceful kindnesses, always to those who needed them most and had no reason to expect them. No recluse he, no fine scholar, no polished litterateur, but a hard-headed, soft-hearted human man of the sturdy old Suffolk breed. Sometimes I think he was, in his own way, just as great a man as the "Old Fitz," whom he loved and reverenced.

He died on November 7, 1917, aged ninety-two years three months and four days. He was extraordinarily sturdy until nearly ninety—he went in bathing in the surf at Felixstowe on his eighty-sixth birthday. Perhaps the sincerest tribute I can pay him is these lines which I copy from my journal, dated July 16, 1913:

"Went up to have tea with old John Loder, and said a cunningly veiled Good-bye to him. I doubt if I shall see him again, the dear old man. I think he felt so, too, for when he came to the door with me, instead of his usual remark about 'Welcome the coming, speed the parting guest,' he said, 'Farewell to thee' in a more sober manner than his wont—and I left with an armful of books which he had given me 'to keep me out of mischief.' We had a good talk after tea—he told me about the adventures of his brothers, one of whom went out to New Zealand. He uses the most delightful brisk phrases in his talk, smiling away to himself and wrinkling up his forehead, which can only be distinguished from his smooth bald pate by its charming corrugation of parallel furrows. He

took me into his den while he rummaged through
his books to find some which would be acceptable
to me—'May as well give 'em away before it's too
late, ye know'—and then he settled back in his
easy chair to puff at a pipe. I must note down
one of his phrases which tickled me—he has such
a knack for the proverbial and the epigrammatic.
'He's cut his cloth, he can wear his breeches,'
he said of a certain scapegrace. He chuckled over
the Suffolk phrase 'a chance child,' for a bastard
(alluding to one such of his acquaintance in old
days). He constantly speaks of things he wants
to do 'before I tarn my toes up to the daisies.'
He told me old tales of Woodbridge in the time
of the Napoleonic wars when there was a garrison
of 5,000 soldiers quartered here—this was one of
the regions in which an attack by Boney was
greatly feared. He says that the Suffolk phrase
'rafty weather' (meaning mist or fog) originates
from that time, as being weather suitable for the
French to make a surprise attack by rafts or flat-
boats.

"He chuckled over the reminiscence that he was
once a great hand at writing obituary notices for
the local paper. 'Weep, weep for him who cried
for us,' was the first line of his epitaph upon a
former Woodbridge town crier! I was thinking
that it would be hard to do him justice when the

time comes to write his. May he have a swift and painless end such as his genial spirit deserves, and not linger on into a twilight life with failing senses. When his memory and his pipe and his books begin to fail him, when those keen old eyes grow dim and he can no longer go to sniff the salt air on the river-wall—then may the quick and quiet ferryman take dear old John Loder to the shadow land."

A VENTURE IN MYSTICISM

I HAD heard so much about this Rabbi Tagore and his message of calm for our hustling, feverish life, that I thought I would try to put some of that stuff into practice.

"Shut out the clamour of small things. Withdraw into the deep quiet of your soul, commune with infinite beauty and infinite peace. You must be full of gladness and love for every person and every tiniest thing. Great activity and worry is needless—it is poison to the soul. Learn to reflect, and to brood upon eternal beauty. It is the mystic who finds all that is most precious in life. The flowers of meditation blossom in his heart."

I cut out these words and pasted them in my hat. I have always felt that my real genius lies in the direction of philosophic calm. I determined to override the brutal clamour of petty things.

The alarm clock rang as usual at 6.30. Calmly, with nothing but lovely thoughts in my mind, I threw it out of the window. I lay until eight o'clock, communing with infinite peace. I began to see that Professor Tagore was right. My wife asked me if I was going to the office. "I am brooding upon eternal beauty," I told her.

She thought I was ill, and made me take breakfast in bed.

I usually shave every morning, but a moment's thought will convince you that mystics do not do so. I determined to grow a beard. I lit a cigar, and replied "I am a mystic" to all my wife's inquiries.

At nine o'clock came a telephone call from the office. My employer is not a devotee of eternal calm, I fear. When I explained that I was at home reading "Gitanjali," his language was far from mystical. "Get here by ten o'clock or you lose your job," he said.

I was dismayed to see the same old throng in the subway, all the senseless scuffle and the unphilosophic crowd. But I felt full of gladness in my new way of life, full of brotherhood for all the world. "I love you," I said to the guard on the platform. He seized me by the shoulders and rammed me into the crowded car, shouting "Another nut!"

When I reached the office my desk was littered with a hundred papers. The stenographer was at the telephone, trying to pacify someone. "Here he is now," I heard her say.

It was Dennis & Company on the wire.

"How about that carload of Bavarian herrings we were to have yesterday without fail?" said Dennis.

I took the 'phone.

"In God's good time," I said, "the shipment will arrive. The matter is purely ephemeral, after all. If you will attune yourself——"

He rang off.

I turned over the papers on my desk. Looked at with the unclouded eye of a mystic, how mundane and unnecessary all these pettifogging transactions seemed. Two kegs of salt halibut for the Cameron Stores, proofs of the weekly ad. for the *Fishmongers' Journal*, a telegram from the Uptown Fish Morgue, new tires needed for one of the delivery trucks—how could I jeopardize my faculty of meditation by worrying over these trifles? I leaned back in my chair and devoted myself to meditation. After all, the harassing domination of material things can easily be thrown off by a resolute soul. I was full of infinite peace. I seemed to see the future as an ever-widening vista of sublime visions. My soul was thrilled with a universal love of humanity.

The buzzer on my desk sounded. That meant that the boss wanted to see me.

Now, it has always seemed to me that to put one's self at the beck and call of another man is essentially degrading. In the long perspective of eternity, was his soul any more majestic than mine? In this luminous new vision of my importance as a fragment of immortal mind, could I, should I, bow to the force of impertinent trivialities?

I sat back in my chair, full of love of humanity.

By and by the boss appeared at my desk. One look at his face convinced me of the truth of Tagore's saying that great activity is poison to the soul. Certainly his face was poisonous.

"Say," he shouted, "what the devil's the matter with you to-day? Dennis just called me up about that herring order——"

"Master," I said mildly, "be not overwrought. Great activity is a strychnine to the soul. I am a mystic. . . ."

A little later I found myself on the street with two weeks' pay in my pocket. It is true that my departure had been hasty and unpleasant, for the stairway from the office to the street is long and dusty; but I recalled what Professor Tagore had said about vicissitudes being the true revealers of the spirit. My hat was not with me, but I remembered the creed pasted in it. After pacing a block or so, my soul was once more tranquil.

I entered a restaurant. It was the noon hour, and the room was crowded with hurrying waiters

and impatient people.   I found a vacant seat in a
corner and sat down.   I concentrated my mind
upon the majestic vision of the brotherhood of
man.

Gradually I began to feel hungry, but no waiter
came near me.   Never mind, I thought: to shout
and hammer the table as the others do is beneath
the dignity of a philosopher.   I began to dream of
endless vistas of mystical ham and eggs.   I brooded upon these for some time, but still no corporeal
and physical units of food reached me.

The man next me gradually materialized into
my consciousness.   Full of love for humanity I
spoke to him.

"Brother," I said, "until one of these priestly
waiters draws nigh, will you not permit me to sus-
tain myself with one of your rolls and one of your
butter-balls?   In the great brotherhood of humanity, all that is mine is yours; and *per contra*,
all that is yours is mine."   Beaming luminously
upon him, I laid a friendly hand on his arm.

He leaped up and called the head waiter.
"Here's an attic for rent!" he cried coarsely.
"He wants to pick my pocket."

By the time I got away from the police station
it was dusk, and I felt ready for home.   I must
say my broodings upon eternal beauty were
beginning to be a little forced.   As I passed along

the crowded street, walking slowly and withdrawn into the quiet of my soul, three people trod upon my heels and a taxi nearly gave me a passport to eternity. I reflected that men were perhaps not yet ready for these doctrines of infinite peace. How much more wise were the animals —and I raised my hand to stroke a huge drayhorse by the pavement. He seized my fingers in his teeth and nipped them vigorously.

I gave a yell and ran full tilt to the nearest subway entrance. I burst into the mass of struggling, unphilosophic humanity and fought, shoved, cursed, and buffeted with them. I pushed three old ladies to one side to snatch my ticket before they could get theirs. I leaped into the car at the head of a flying wedge of sinful, unmystical men, who knew nothing of infinite beauty and peace. As the door closed I pushed a decrepit clergyman outside, and I hope he fell on the third rail. As I felt the lurching, trampling, throttling jam of humanity sway to and fro with the motion of the car, I drew a long breath. Dare I confess it?—I was perfectly happy!

AN OXFORD LANDLADY

IT WAS a crisp October afternoon, and along Iffley Road the wind was chivvying the yellow leaves. We stood at the window watching the flappers opposite play hockey. One of them had a scarlet tam-o'-shanter and glorious dark hair underneath it. . . . A quiet tap at the door, gentle but definite, and in came Mrs. Beesley.

If you have been at our digs, you know her by sight, and have not forgotten. Hewn of the real imperial marble is she, not unlike Queen Victoria in shape and stature. She tells us she used to dance featly and with abandon in days gone by, when her girlish slimness was the admiration of every greengrocer's assistant in Oxford—and even in later days when she and Dr. Warren always opened the Magdalen servants' ball together. She and the courtly President were always the star couple. I can see her doing the Sir Roger de Coverley. But the virgin zone was loosed long ago, and she has expanded with the British Empire. Not rotund, but rather imposingly cubic. Our hallway is a very narrow one,

266

and when you come to visit us of an evening,
after red-cheeked Emily has gone off to better
tilting grounds, it is a prime delight to see Mrs.
Beesley backing down the passage (like a stately
canal boat) before the advancing guest. Very
large of head and very pink of cheek, very fond of
a brisk conversation, some skill at cooking, slow
and full of dignity on the stairs, much reminiscent
of former lodgers, bold as a lion when she thinks
she is imposed upon, but otherwhiles humorous
and placable—such is our Mrs. Beesley.

She saw us standing by the window, and thought
we were watching the leaves twisting up the road-
way in golden spirals.

"Watching the wind?" she said pleasantly.
"I loves to see the leaves 'avin' a frolic. They en-
joys it, same as young gentlemen do."

"Or young ladies?" I suggested. "We were
watching the flappers play hockey, Mrs. Beesley.
One of them is a most fascinating creature. I
think her name must be Kathleen. . . ."

Mrs. Beesley chuckled merrily and threw up her
head in that delightful way of hers. "Oh, dear, Oh,
dear, you're just like all the other gentlemen," she
said. "Always awatchin' and awaitin' for the
young ladies. Mr. Bye that used to be 'ere was
just the same, an' he was engaged to be marrit.
'Ad some of 'em in to tea once, he did. I thought

it was scandalous, and 'im almost a marrit gentle-man."

"Don't you remember what the poet says, Mrs. Beesley?" I suggested:

> "Beauty must be scorned in none
> Though but truly served in one."

"Not much danger of you gentlemen bein' too scornful," said Mrs. Beesley. Her eyes began to sparkle now that she saw herself fairly embarked upon a promising conversation. She sidled a little farther into the room. Lloyd winked at me and quietly escaped behind her.

"Seeing as we're alone," said Mrs. Beesley, "I come to you to see about dinner to-night. I knows as you're the father of 'em all." (That is her quaint way of saying that she thinks me the leading spirit of the three who dig with her.) "How about a little jugged 'are? Nice little 'ares there are in Cowley Road now. I thinks 'are is very tender an' tasty. That, an' a nice 'ot cup o' tea?'

The last 'are had been, in Tennyson's phrase, "the heir of all the ages," so I deprecated the sug-gestion. "I don't think hare agrees with Mr. Williams," I said.

"'Ow about a pheasant?" said Mrs. Beesley, stroking the corner of the table with her hand as

she always does when in deep thought. "A
pheasant and a Welsh rabbit, not too peppery.
That goes well with the cider. Dr. Warren came
'ere to dinner once, an' he had a Welsh rabbit
and never forgot it. 'E allus used to say when 'e
saw me, ''Ow about that Welsh rabbit, Mrs.
Beesley?' Oh, dear, Oh, dear, 'e *is* a kind gentleman!
'E gave us a book once—''Istory of Magdalen
College.' I think he wrote it 'imself."

"I think a pheasant would be very nice," I
said, and began looking for a book.

"Do you think Mr. Loomis will be back from
town in time for dinner?" asked Mrs. Beesley.
"I know 'e's fond o' pheasant. He'd come if he
knew."

"We might send him a telegram," I said.

"Oh, dear, Oh, dear!" sighed Mrs. Beesley, over-
come by such a fantastic thought. "You know,
Mr. Morley, a funny thing 'appened this morning," she said. "Em'ly and I were making Mr.
Loomis's bed. But we didn't find 'is clothes all
lyin' about the floor same as 'e usually does.
'I wonder what's 'appened to Mr. Loomis's
clothes?' said Em'ly.

"'P'raps 'e's took 'em up to town to pawn 'em.'
I said. (You know we 'ad a gent'man 'ere once
that pawned nearly all 'is things—a Jesus gentleman 'e was.)

"Em'ly says to me, 'I wonder what the three balls on a pawnbroker's sign mean?'

"'Why don't you know, Em'ly?' I says. It means it's two to one you never gets 'em back."

Just then there was a ring at the bell and Mrs. Beesley rolled away chuckling. And I returned to the window to watch Kathleen play hockey.

October, 1912.

"PEACOCK PIE"

ONCE a year or so one is permitted to find some book which brings a real tingle to that ribbon of the spinal marrow which responds to the vibrations of literature. Not a bad way to calendar the years is by the really good books they bring one. Each twelve month the gnomon on the literary sundial is likely to cast some shadow one will not willingly forget. Thus I mark 1916 as the year that introduced me to William McFee's "Casuals of the Sea" and Butler's "Way of All Flesh"; 1915 most of us remember as Rupert Brooke's year, or the year of the Spoon River Anthology, if you prefer that kind of thing; 1914 I notch as the season when I first got the hang of Bourget and Conrad. But perhaps best of all, in 1913 I read "Peacock Pie" and "Songs of Childhood," by Walter de la Mare.

"Peacock Pie" having now been published in this country it is seasonable to kindle an altar fire for this most fanciful and delightful of present-day poets. It is curious that his work is so little known over here, for his first book,

"Songs of Childhood," was published in England in 1902. Besides, poetry he has written novels and essays, all shot through with a phosphorescent sparkle of imagination and charm. He has the knack of "words set in delightful proportion"; and "Peacock Pie" is the most authentic knapsack of fairy gold since the "Child's Garden of Verses."

I am tempted to think that Mr. de la Mare is the kind of poet more likely to grow in England than America. The gracious and fine-spun fabric of his verse, so delicate in music, so quaint and haunting in imaginative simplicity, is the gift of a land and life where rewards and fairies are not wholly passed away. Emily Dickinson and Vachel Lindsay are among our contributors to the songs of gramarye: but one has only to open "The Congo" side by side with "Peacock Pie" to see how the seductions of ragtime and the clashing crockery of the Poetry Society's dinners are coarsening the fibres of Mr. Lindsay's marvellous talent as compared with the dainty horns of elfin that echo in Mr. de la Mare. And it is a long Pullman ride from Spoon River to the bee-droned gardens where De la Mare's old women sit and sew. Over here we have to wait for Barrie or Yeats or Padraic Colum to tell us about the fairies, and Cecil Sharp to drill us in their dances and songs. The gentry are not native in our hearts, and we might as well admit it.

To say that Mr. de la Mare's verse is distilled in fairyland suggests perhaps a delicate and absent-minded figure, at a loss in the hurly burly of this world; the kind of poet who loses his rubbers in the subway, drops his glasses in the trolley car, and is found wandering blithely in Central Park while the Women's Athenaeum of the Tenderloin is waiting four hundred strong for him to lecture. But Mr. de la Mare is the more modern figure who might readily (I hope I speak without offense) be mistaken for a New York stock broker, or a member of the Boston Chamber of Commerce. Perhaps he even belongs to the newer order of poets who do not wear rubbers.

One's first thought (if one begins at the beginning, but who reads a book of poetry that way?) is that "Peacock Pie" is a collection of poems for children. But it is not that, any more than "The Masses" is a paper for the proletariat. Before you have gone very far you will find that the imaginary child you set out with has been magicked into a changeling. The wee folk have been at work and bewitched the pudding—the pie rather. The fire dies on the hearth, the candle channels in its socket, but still you read on. Some of the poems bring you the cauld grue of Thrawn Janet.

When at last you go up to bed, it will be with the shuddering sigh of one thrilled through and through with the sad little beauties of the world. You will want to put out a bowl of fresh milk on the doorstep to appease the banshee—did you not know that the janitor of your Belshazzar Court would get it in the morning.

One of the secrets of Mr. de la Mare's singular charm is his utter simplicity, linked with a delicately tripping music that intrigues the memory unawares and plays high jinks with you forever after. Who can read "Off the Ground" and not strum the dainty jig over and over in his head whenever he takes a bath, whenever he shaves, whenever the moon is young? I challenge you to resist the jolly madness of its infection:

> Three jolly Farmers
> Once bet a pound
> Each dance the others would
> Off the ground.
> Out of their coats
> They slipped right soon,
> And neat and nicesome,
> Put each his shoon.
> One—Two—Three—
> And away they go,
> Not too fast,
> And not too slow;
> Out from the elm-tree's

Noonday shadow,
Into the sun
And across the meadow.
Past the schoolroom,
With knees well bent
Fingers a-flicking,
They dancing went.   .   .   .

Are you not already out of breath in the hilarious escapade?

The sensible man's quarrel with the proponents of free verse is not that they write such good prose; not that they espouse the natural rhythms of the rain, the brook, the wind-grieved tree; this is all to the best, even if as old as Solomon. It is that they affect to disdain the superlative harmonies of artificed and ordered rhythms; that knowing not a spondee from a tribrach they vapour about prosody, of which they know nothing, and imagine to be new what antedates the Upanishads. The haunting beauty of Mr. de la Mare's delicate art springs from an ear of superlative tenderness and sophistication. The daintiest alternation of iambus and trochee is joined to the serpent's cunning in swiftly tripping dactyls. Probably this artifice is greatly unconscious, the meed of the trained musician; but let no singer think to upraise his voice before the Lord ere he master the axioms of prosody. Imagist journals please copy.

One may well despair of conveying in a few rough paragraphs the gist of this quaint, fanciful, brooding charm. There is something fey about much of the book: it peers behind the curtains of twilight and sees strange things. In its love of children, its inspired simplicity, its sparkle of whim and Æsopian brevity, I know nothing finer. Let me just cut for you one more slice of this rarely seasoned pastry.

THE LITTLE BIRD

My dear Daddie bought a mansion
  For to bring my Mammie to,
In a hat with a long feather,
  And a trailing gown of blue;
And a company of fiddlers
  And a rout of maids and men
Danced the clock round to the morning,
  In a gay house-warming then.
And when all the guests were gone, and
  All was still as still can be,
In from the dark ivy hopped a
  Wee small bird: and that was Me.

"Peacock Pie" is immortal diet indeed, as Sir Walter said of his scrip of joy. Annealed as we are, I think it will discompose the most callous. It is a sweet feverfew for the heats of the spirit. It is full of outlets of sky.

As for Mr. de la Mare himself, he is a modest

man and keeps behind his songs. Recently he
paid his first visit to America, and we may hope
that even on Fifth Avenue he saw some fairies.
He lectured at some of our universities and en-
dured the grotesque plaudits of dowagers and professors who doubtless pretended to have read his
work. Although he is forty-four, and has been
publishing for nearly sixteen years, he has evaded
"Who's Who." He lives in London, is married,
and has four children. For a number of years
he worked for the Anglo-American Oil Company.
Truly the Muse sometimes lends to her favourites
a merciful hardiness.

THE LITERARY PAWNSHOP

EXCELLENT Parson Adams, in "Joseph Andrews," is not the only literary man who has lamented the difficulty of ransoming a manuscript for immediate cash. It will be remembered that Mr. Adams had in his saddlebag nine volumes of sermons in manuscript, "as well worth a hundred pounds as a shilling was worth twelve pence." Offering one of these as a pledge, Parson Adams besought Mr. Tow-Wouse, the innkeeper, to lend him three guineas, but the latter had so little stomach for a transaction of this sort that "he cried out, 'Coming, sir,' though nobody called; and ran downstairs without any fear of breaking his neck."

As a whimsical essayist (with whom I have talked over these matters) puts it, the business of literature is imperfectly coördinated with life.

Almost any other kind of property is hockable for ready cash. A watch, a ring, an outworn suit of clothes, a chair, a set of books, all these will find willing purchasers. But a manuscript which happens not to meet the fancy of the editors must perforce lie idle in your drawer though it sparkle with the brilliants of wit, and five or ten years hence collectors may list it in their catalogues. No mount of piety along Sixth Avenue will accept it in pawn, no Hartford Lunch will exchange it for corned beef hash and dropped egg. This is a dismal thing.

This means that there is an amusing and a competent living to be gained by a literary agent of a new kind. Think how many of the most famous writers have trod the streets ragged and hungry in their early days. There were times when they would have sold their epics, their novels, their essays, for the price of a square meal. Think of the booty that would accumulate in the shop of a literary pawnbroker. The early work of famous men would fill his safe to bursting. Later on he might sell it for a thousand times what he gave. There is nothing that grows to such fictitious value as manuscript.

Think of Francis Thompson, when he was a bootmaker's assistant in Leicester Square. He was even too poor to buy writing materials. His early poems were scribbled on scraps of old account books and wrapping paper. How readily he would have sold them for a few shillings. Or Edgar Poe in the despairing days of his wife's illness. Or R. L. S. in the fits of depression caused by his helpless dependence upon his father for funds. What a splendid opportunity these crises in writers' lives would offer to the enterprising buyer of manuscripts!

Be it understood, of course, that the pawnbroker must be himself an appreciator of good things. No reason why he should buy poor stuff, even though the author of it be starving. Richard Le Gallienne has spoken somewhere of the bookstores which sell "books that should never have been written to the customers who should never have been born." Our pawnbroker must guard himself against buying this kind of stuff. He will be besieged with it. Very likely Mr. Le Gallienne himself will be the first to offer him some. But his task will be to discover new and true talent beneath its rags, and stake it to a ham sandwich when that homely bite will mean more than a dinner at the Ritz ten years later.

The idea of the literary pawnbroker comes to me from the (unpublished) letters of John Mistletoe, author of the "Dictionary of Deplorable Facts," that wayward and perverse genius who wandered the Third Avenue saloons when he might have been fêted by the Authors' League had he lived a few years longer. Some day, I hope, the full story of that tragic life may be told, and the manuscripts still cherished by his executor made public. In the meantime, this letter, which he wrote in 1908, gives a sad and vivid little picture of the straits of unadmitted genius:

"I write from Connor's saloon. Paunchy Connor has been my best—indeed my only—friend in this city, when every editor, publisher, and critic has given me the frozen mitt. Of course I know why . . . the author of "Vermin" deserves not, nor wants, their hypocritical help. The book was too true to life to please the bourgeois and yet not ribald enough to tickle the prurient. I had a vile pornographic publisher after me the other day; he said if I would rub up some of the earlier chapters and inject a little more spice he thought he could do something with it—as a paper-covered erotic for shop-girls, I suppose he meant. I kicked him downstairs. The stinking bounder!

"Until to-day I had been without grub for sixty hours. That is literally true. I was ashamed of sponging on Paunchy, and could not bring myself to come back to the saloon where he would willingly have fed me. I did get a job for two days as a deckhand on an Erie ferryboat, but they found out I did not belong to the union. I had two dollars in my pocket—a fortune—but while I was dozing on a doorstep on Hudson Street, waiting for the cafés to open (I was too done to walk half a dozen blocks to an all-night restaurant), some snapper picked my pocket. That night I slept in a big drain pipe where they were putting up a building.

"Why isn't there a pawnshop where one could hang up MSS. for cash? In my hallroom over Connor's saloon I have got stuff that will be bid for at auctions some day (that isn't conceit, I know it), but at this moment, July 17, 1908, I couldn't raise 50 cents on it. If there were a literary mount of piety—a sort of Parnassus of piety as it were—the uncle in charge might bless the day he met me. Well, it won't be for long. This cancer is getting me surely.

"This morning I'm cheerful. I've scrubbed and swept Paunchy's bar for him, and the dirty, patchouli-smelling hop-joint he keeps upstairs, bless his pimping old heart. And I've had a real breakfast: boiled red cabbage, stewed beef (condemned by the inspector), rye bread, raw onions, a glass of Tom and Jerry, and two big schooners of the amber. I'm working on my Third Avenue novel called 'The L.'

"I shan't give you my right address, or you'd send someone down here to give me money, you damned philanthropist. . . . Connor ain't the real name, so there. When I die (soon) they'll find Third Avenue written on my heart, if I still have one. . . ."

It is interesting to recall that the MS. of his poems "Pavements, and Other Verses" was bought by a private collector for $250 last winter.

Will not some literary agent think over this idea?

A MORNING IN MARATHON

ONE violet throbbing star was climbing in the southeast at half-past four, and the whole flat plain was rich with golden moonlight. Early rising in order to quicken the furnace and start the matinsong in the steampipes becomes its own reward when such an orange moon is dropping down the sky. Even Peg (our most volatile Irish terrier) was plainly awed by the blaze of pale light, and hopped gingerly down the rimy back steps. But the cat was unabashed. Cats are born by moonlight and are leagued with the powers of darkness and mystery. And so Nicholas Vachel Lindsay (he is named for the daring poet of Illinois) stepped into the moonshine without a qualm.

There are certain little routine joys known only to the servantless suburbanite. Every morning the baker leaves a bag of crisp French rolls on the front porch.. Every morning the milkman deposits his little bottles of milk and cream on the back steps. Every morning the furnace needs a little grooming, that the cheery thump of rising pressure may warm the radiators upstairs.

Then the big agate kettle must be set over the blue gas flame, for hot water is needed both for shaving and cocoa. Our light breakfast takes only a moment to prepare. By the time the Nut Brown Maid comes singing downstairs, cocoa, rolls, and boiled eggs are ready in the sunny little dining room, and the Tamperer is bathed and shaved and telephoning to Central for "the exact time." The 8:13 train waits for no man, and it is nearly a mile to the station.

But the morning I think of was not a routine morning. On routine mornings the Tamperer rises at ten minutes to seven, the alarm clock being set for 6:45: which allows five minutes for drowsy head. The day in question was early February when snow lay white and powdery on the ground, and the 6 o'clock train from Marathon had to be caught. There is an express for Philadelphia that leaves the Pennsylvania Station at 7:30 and this the Tamperer had to take, to make a 10 o'clock appointment in the Quaker City. That was why the alarm clock rang at half-past four.

I cannot recall a more virginal morning than that snowy twilight before the dawn. No description that I have ever read—not even the daybreak in "Prince Otto," or Pippa's dawn boiling in pure gold over the rim of night—would be just to that exquisite growth of colour in the eastern sky. The violet star faded to forget-me-not and then to silver and at last closed his weary eye; the flat Long Island prairie gradually lost its fairy-tale air of mystery and dream; the close ceiling of the night receded into infinite space as the sun waved his radiant arms over the horizon.

But this was after I had left the house. The sun did not raise his head from the pillow until I was in the train. The Nut Brown Maid was still nested in her warm white bed as I took her up some tea and toast just before departing.

The walk to the station, over the crisply frozen snow, was delicious. Marathon is famous for its avenue of great elms, which were casting deep blue shadows in the strange light—waning moon and waxing day. The air was very chill—only just above zero—and the smoking car seemed very cold and dismal. I huddled my overcoat about me and tried to smoke and read the paper. But in that stale, fetid odour of last night's tobacco and this morning's wet arctics the smoker was but a dismal place. The exaltation of the dawn dropped suddenly into a kind of shivering nausea.

I changed to another car and threw away the war news. Just then the sun came gloriously over the edge of the fields and set the snow afire. As we rounded the long curve beyond Woodside I could see the morning light shining upon the Metropolitan Tower, and when we glided into the basement of the Pennsylvania Station my heart was already attuned to the thrill of that glorious place. Perhaps it can never have the fascination for me that the old dingy London terminals have —King's Cross, Paddington, or Saint Pancras, with their delicious English bookstalls and those porters in corduroy—but the Pennsylvania is a wonderful place after all, a marble palace of romance and a gallant place to roam about. It seems like a stable without horses, though, for where are the trains? No chance to ramble about the platforms (as in London) to watch the Duke of Abercorn or the Lord Claude Hamilton, or other of those green or blue English locomotives with lordly names, being groomed for the run.

In the early morning the Pennsylvania Station catches in its high-vaulted roof the first flush of sunlight; and before the flood of commuters begins to pour in, the famous station cat is generally sitting by the baggage room shining his morning face. Up at the marble lunch counters the coloured gentlemen are serving hot cakes and coffee to stray travellers, and the shops along the Arcade are being swept and garnished. As I passed through on my way to the Philadelphia train I was amused by a wicker basket full of Scotch terrier puppies—five or six of them tumbling over one another in their play and yelping so that the station rang. "Every little bit yelps" as someone has said. I was reminded of the last words I ever read in Virgil (the end of the sixth book of the Aeneid)—*stant litore puppes*, which I always yearned to translate "a litter of puppies."

My train purred smoothly under the Hudson and under Jersey City as I lit my cigar and settled comfortably into the green plush. When we emerged from the tunnel on the other side of the long ridge (which is a degenerate spur from the Palisades farther north) a crescent of sun was just fringing the crest with fire. Another moment and we flashed onto the Hackensack marshes and into the fully minted gold of superb morning. The day was begun.

THE AMERICAN HOUSE OF LORDS

I AM not a travelling salesman (except in so far as all men are) so I do not often travel in the Club Car. But when I do, irresistibly the thought comes that I have strayed into the American House of Lords. Unworthily I sit among our sovereign legislators, a trifle ill at ease mayhap. In the day coach I am at home with my peers—those who smoke cheap tobacco; who nurse fretful babies; who strew the hot plush with sandwich crumbs and lean throbbing foreheads against the window pane.

But the Club Car which swings so smoothly at the end of a limited train is a different place, pardee. It is not a hereditary chamber, but it is none the less the camera stellata of our prosperous carnivora. Patently these men are Lords. In two facing rows, averted from the landscape, condemned to an uneasy scrutiny of their mutual prosperity, they sit in leather chairs. They curve roundly from neck to groin. They are shaven to the raw, soberly clad, derby hatted, glossily booted. Always they smoke cigars, those strange, blunt cigars that are fatter at one end than at the other. Some (these I think are the very prosperous) wear shoes with fawn-coloured tops.

Is it strange then that I, an ill-clad and pipe-smoking traveller, am faintly uneasy in this House of Lords? I forget myself while reading poetry and drop my tobacco cinders on the rug, missing the little silver gourd that rests by my left foot. Straight the white-jacketed mulatto sucks them up with a vacuum cleaner and a deprecating air. I pass to the brass veranda at the end of the car for a bracing change of atmosphere. And returning, the attendant has removed my little pile of books which I left under my chair, and hidden them in his serving grotto. It costs me at least a whiskey and soda to get them out.

It means, I suppose, that I am not marked for success. I am cigarless and derbyless; I do not wear those funny little white margins inside my vest. My scarf is still the dear old shabby one in which I was married (I bought it at Rogers Peet's, and I shall never forget it) and when I look up from Emily Dickinson's poems with a trembling thrill of painful ecstasy, I am frightened by the long row of hard faces and cynic eyes opposite me.

The House of Lords disquiets me. Even if I ring a bell and order a bottle I am not happy. Is it only the swing of the car that nauseates me? At any rate, I want to get home—home to that star-sown meadow and the two brown arms at the journey's end.

December, 1914.

COTSWOLD WINDS

SPRING comes late on these windy uplands, and indoors one still sits close to the fire. These are the days of booming gales over the sheepwolds, and the afternoon ride with Shotover becomes an adventure. I am not one of those who shirk bicycling in a wind. Give me a two-mile spin with the gust astern, just to loosen the muscles and sweep the morning's books and tobacco from the brain—and then turn and at it! It is like swimming against a great crystal river. Cap off, head up—no crouching over the handle-bars like the Saturday afternoon shopmen! Wind in your hair, the broad blue Cotswold slopes about you, every ounce of leg-drive straining on the pedals—three minutes of it intoxicates you. You crawl up-wind roaring the most glorious nonsense, ribaldry, and exultation into the face of the blast.

I am all for the Cotswolds in the last vacation before "Schools." In mid-March our dear gray Mother Oxford sends us away for six weeks while she decks herself against the spring. Far and wide we scatter. The Prince to Germany—the dons to Devon—the reading parties to quiet country

inns here and there. Some blithe spirits of my
acquaintance are in those glorious dingy garrets
of the Latin Quarter with Murger's "Scènes de la
Vie de Bohème" as a viaticum. Others are among
the tulips in Holland. But this time I vote for
the Cotswolds and solitude.

There is a straggling gray village which lies in
the elbow of a green valley, with a clear trout-
stream bubbling through it. There is a well-
known inn by the bridge, the resort of many
anglers. But I am not for inns nor for anglers
this time. It is a serious business, these last two
months before Schools, and I and my books are
camped in a "pensive citadel" up on the hill,
where the postman's wife cares for me and worries because I do not eat more than two normal
men. There is a low-ceilinged sitting room with
a blazing fire. From one corner a winding stair
climbs to the bedroom above. There are pipes
and tobacco, pens and a pot of ink. There are
books—all historical volumes, the only evidence
of relaxation being Arthur Gibbs' "A Cotswold
Village" and one of Bartholomew's survey maps.
Ten hours' work, seven hours' sleep, three hours'
bicycling—that leaves four hours for eating and
other emergencies. That is how we live on twenty-
four hours a day, and turn a probable Fourth in
the Schools into a possible Third.

And what could better those lonely afternoon
rides on Shotover? The valley of the Colne is
one of the most entrancing bits in England, I
think. A lonely road, winding up the green
trough of the stream, now and then crossing the
shoulder of the hills, takes you far away from
most of the things one likes to leave behind.
There are lambs, little black fuzzy fellows, on the
uplands; there are scores of rabbits disappearing
with a flirt of white hindquarters into their way-
side burrows; in Chedworth Woods there are
pheasants, gold and blue and scarlet, almost
as tame as barnyard fowls; everywhere there are
skylarks throbbing in the upper blue—and these
are all your company. Now and then a great
yellow farm-wagon and a few farmers in cordu-
roys—but no one else. That is the kind of
country to bicycle into. Up and up the valley,
past the Roman villa, until you come to the
smoking-place. No pipeful ever tasted better
than this, stretched on the warm grass watching
the green water dimpling over the stones. That
same water passes the Houses of Parliament by
and by. I think it would stay by Chedworth
Woods if it could—and so would I.

But it is four o'clock, and tea will be waiting.
Protesting Shotover is pushed up a swampy hillside through the trees—and we come out onto a

hilltop some 800 feet above the sea. And from there it is eight miles homeward, mostly downhill, with a broad blue horizon to meet the eye. Back to the tiny cottage looking out onto the village green and the old village well; back to four cups of tea and hot buttered toast; and then for Metternich and the Vienna Congress. *Solvitur bicyclando!*

And when we clatter down the High again, two weeks hence, Oxford will have made her great transformation. We left her in winter, mud and sleet and stormy sunsets. But a fortnight from now, however cold, it will be what we hopefully call the Summer Term. There will be white flannels, and Freshmen learning to punt on the Cher. But that is not for us now. There are the Schools. . . .

Bibury, April, 1913.

CLOUDS

WHO has ever done justice to the majesty of the clouds? Alice Meynell, perhaps? George Meredith? Shelley, who was "gold-dusty with tumbling amongst the stars?" Henry Van Dyke has sung of "The heavenly hills of Holland," but in a somewhat treble pipe; R. L. S. said it better—"The travelling mountains of the sky." Ah, how much is still to be said of those piled-up mysteries of heaven!

We rode to-day down the Delaware Valley from Milford to Stroudsburg. That wonderful meadowland between the hills (it is just as lovely as the English Avon, but how much more likely we are to praise the latter!) converges in a huge V toward the Water Gap, drawing the foam of many a mountain creek down through that matchless passway. Over the hills which tumble steeply on either side soared the vast Andes of the clouds, hanging palpable in the sapphire of a summer sky. What height on height of craggy softness on those silver steeps! What rounded bosomy curves of golden vapour; what sharpened pinnacles of nothingness, spiring in ever-changing contour

into the intangible blue! Man the finite, reveller
in the explainable and the exact, how can his eye
pierce or his speech describe the rolling robes of
glory in which floating moisture clothes itself!

Mile on mile, those peaks of midsummer
snow were marching the highways of the air.
Fascinated, almost stupefied, we watched their
miracles of form and unfathomable glory. It was
as though the stockades of earth had fallen away.
Palisaded, cliff on radiant cliff, the spires of the
Unseeable lay bare. Ever since childhood one
has dreamed of scaling the bulwarks of the clouds,
of riding the ether on those strange galleons.
Unconscious of their own beauty, they pass in
dissolving shapes—now scudding on that waveless
azure sea; now drifting with scant steerage way.
If one could lie upon their opal summits what
depths and what abysses would meet the eye!
What glowing chasms to catch the ardour of the
sun, what chill and empty hollows of creaming
mist, dropping in pale and awful spirals. Floating flat like ice floes beneath the greenish moon,
or beetling up in prodigious ledges of seeming
solidness on a sunny morning—are they not the
most superbly heart-easing miracles of our visible
world? Watch them as they shimmer down
toward the Water Gap in every shade of silver and
rose and opal; or delicately tinged with amber

when they have caught some jewelled chain of
lightning and are suffused with its lurid sparkle.
Man has worshipped sticks and stones and stars:
has he never bent a knee to the high gods of the
clouds?

There they wander, the unfettered spirits of
bliss or doom. Holding within their billowed
masses the healing punishments of the rain, chaliced
beakers of golden flame, lightnings instant and
unbearable as the face of God—dissolving into a
crystal nothing, reborn from the viewless caverns
of air—here let us erect one enraptured altar to
the bright mountains of the sky!

At sunset we were climbing back among the
wooded hills of Pike County, fifteen hundred feet
above the salt. One great castle of clouds that
had long drawn our eyes was crowning some in-
visible airy summit far above us. As the sun
dipped it grew gray, soft, and pallid. And then one
last banner of rosy light beaconed over its highest
turret—a final flare of glory to signal curfew to all
the other silver hills. Slowly it faded in the shadow of dusk.

We thought that was the end. But no—a
little later, after we had reached the farm,
we saw that the elfs of cloudland were still at play.
Every few minutes the castle glowed with a sudden gush of pale blue lightning. And while we

watched, with hearts almost painfully sated by beauty, through some leak the precious fire ran out; a great stalk of pure and unspeakable brightness fled passionately to earth. This happened again and again until the artery of fire was discharged. And then, slowly, slowly, the stars began to pipe up the evening breeze. Our cloud drifted gently away.

Where and in what strange new form did it greet the flush of dawn? Who knows?

UNHEALTHY

ON SATURDAY afternoons Titania and I always have an adventure. On Sundays we stay at home and dutifully read manuscripts (I am the obscure creature known as a "publisher's reader") but Saturday post meridiem is a golden tract of time wherein we wander as we list.

The 35th Street entrance to McQueery's has long been hallowed as our *stell-dich-ein*. We meet there at one o'clock. That is to say, I arrive at 12:59 and spend fifteen minutes in most animated reflection. There is plenty to think about. One may stand between the outer and inner lines of glass doors and watch the queer little creatures that come tumbling out of the cloak and suit factory across the street. Or one may stand inside the store, on a kind of terrace, beneath pineapple shaped arc lights, looking down upon the bustle of women on the main floor. Best of all, one may stroll along the ornate gallery to one side where all sorts and conditions of ladies wait for other ladies who have promised to meet them

at one o'clock. They divide their time between
examining the mahogany victrolae and deciding
what kind of sundae they will have for lunch. A
very genteel old gentleman with white hair and a
long morning coat and an air of perpetual irrita-
tion is in charge of this social gallery. He wears
the queer, soft, flat-soled boots that are suggestive
of corns. There is an information bureau there,
where one may learn everything except the time
one may expect one's wife to arrive. But I have
learned a valuable subterfuge. If I am waiting
for Titania, and beginning to despair of her
arrival, I have only to go to a telephone to call
her up. As soon as I have put the nickel in, she
is sure to appear. Nowadays I save the nickel
by going into a booth and *pretending* to telephone.
Sure enough, at 1:14, Ingersoll time, in she
trots.

We have a jargon of our own.

"Eye-polishers?" say I.

"Yes," says Titania, "but there was a block
at 42nd Street. I'm *so* sorry, Grump."

"Eye-polishers" is our term for the Fifth
Avenue busses, because riding on them makes
Titania's eyes so bright. More widely, the word
connotes anything that produces that desirable
result, such as bunches of violets, lavender ped-
dlers, tea at Mary Elizabeth's, spring millinery,

or finding sixpence in her shoe.   This last is a rite
suggested by the old song:

> And though maids sweep their hearths no less
>   Than they were wont to do,
> Yet who doth now for cleanliness
>   Find sixpence in her shoe?

A bright dime does very well as a sixpenny
piece.

We always lunch at Moretti's on Saturday: it is
the recognized beginning of an adventure.   The
Moretti lunch has advanced from a quarter to
thirty cents, I am sorry to say, but this is readily
compensated by the Grump buying Sweet Capo-
rals instead of something Turkish.   A packet of
cigarettes is another curtain-raiser for an adventure.   On other days publishers' readers smoke
pipes, but on Saturdays cigarettes are possible.

"Antipasto?"

"No, thanks."

"Minestrone or consommé?"

"Two minestrone, two prime ribs, ice cream and
coffee.   Red wine, please."   That is the formula.
We have eaten the "old reliable Moretti lunch"
so often that the routine has become a ritual.   Oh,
excellent savor of the Moretti basement!   Compounded of warmth, a pungent pourri of smells,
and the jangle of thick china, how diverting it is!

The franc-tireur in charge of the wine-bin watches us complaisantly from his counter where he sits flanked by flasks of Hoboken chianti and a case of brittle cigars.

How good Moretti's *minestrone* tastes to the unsophisticated tongue. What though it be only an azoic extract of intense potato, dimly tinct with sargasso and macaroni—it has a pleasing warmth and bulk. Is it not the prelude to an Adventure?

Well, where shall we go to-day? No two explorers dickering over azimuth and dead reckoning could discuss latitude and longitude more earnestly than Titania and I argue our possible courses. Generally, however, she leaves it to me to chart the journey. That gives me the pride of conductor and her the pleasure of being surprised.

According to our Mercator's projection (which, duly wrapped in a waterproof envelope, we always carry on our adventures) there was a little known region lying nor' nor'west of Blackwell's Island and plotted on the map as East River Park. I had heard of this as a picturesque and old-fashioned territory, comparatively free from footpads and lying near such places as Astoria and Hell Gate. We laid a romantic course due east along 35th Street, Titania humming a little snatch from an English music-hall song that once amused us:

> "My old man's a fireman
> Now what do you think of that?
> He wears goblimey breeches
> And a little goblimey hat."

She always quotes this to me when (she says) I wear my hat too far on the back of my head.

The cross slope of Murray Hill drops steeply downward after one leaves Madison Avenue. We dipped into a region that has always been very fascinating to me. Under the roaring L, past dingy saloons, animal shops, tinsmiths, and painless dentists, past the old dismantled Manhattan hospital. The taste of spring was in the air: one of the dentists was having his sign regilded, a huge four-pronged grinder as big as McTeague's in Frank Norris's story. Oysters going out, the new brew of Bock beer coming in: so do the saloons mark the vernal equinox.

A huge green chalet built on stilts, with two tiers of trains rumbling by, is the L station at 34th Street and Second Avenue. A cutting wind blew from the East River, only two blocks away. I paid two nickels and we got into the front car of the northbound train.

Until Titania and I attain the final glory of

riding in an aeroplane, or ascend Jacob's ladder,
there never will be anything so thrilling as soaring
over the housetops in the Second Avenue L.
Rocking, racketing, roaring over those crazy
trestles, now a glimpse of the leaden river to the
east, now a peep of church spires and skyscrapers
on the west, and the dingy imitation lace curtains
of the third-story windows flashing by like a
recurring pattern—it is a voyage of romance!
Did you ever stand at the front door of an Ele-
vated train, watching the track stretch far ahead
toward the Bronx, and the little green stations
slipping nearer and nearer? The Subway is a
black, bellowing horror; the bus a swaying, jolty
start-and-stop, bruising your knees against the
seat in front; but the L swings you up and over the
housetops, smooth and sheer and swift.

We descended at 86th Street and found ourselves in a new world. A broad, dingy street,
lined by shabby brown houses and pushbutton
apartments, led in a gentle descent toward the
river. The neighbourhood was noisy, quarrel-
some, and dirty. After a long, bitter March the
thaw had come at last: the street was viscous
with slime, the melting snow lay in grayish piles
along the curbs. Small boys on each side of the
street were pelting sodden snowballs which spat-
tered around us as we walked down the pavement.

But after two blocks things changed suddenly. The trolley swung round at a right angle (up Avenue A) and the last block of 86th Street showed the benefit of this manœuvre. The houses grew neat and respectable. A little side street branching off to the left (not recorded by Mercator) revealed some quaint cottages with gables and shuttered windows so mid-Victorian that my literary heart leaped and I dreamed at once of locating a novel in this fascinating spot. And then we rounded the corner and saw the little park.

It was a bit of old Chelsea, nothing less. Titania clapped her hands, and I lit my pipe in gratification. Beside us was a row of little houses of warm red brick with peaked mansard roofs and cozy bay windows and polished door knockers. In front of them was the lumpy little park, cut up into irregular hills, where children were flying kites. And beyond that, an embankment and the river in a dim wet mist. There was Blackwell's Island, and a sailing barge slipping by. In the distance we could see the colossal span of the new Iell Gate bridge. With the journalist's instinct or superlatives I told Titania it was the largest single span in the world. I wonder if it is?

As to that I know not. But it was the river that lured us. On the embankment we found benches and sat down to admire the scene. It was as picturesque as Battersea in Whistler's mistiest days. A ferryboat, crossing to Astoria, hooted musically through the haze. Tugs, puffing up past Blackwell's Island into the Harlem River, replied with mellow blasts. The pungent tang of the East River tickled our nostrils, and all my old ambition to be a tugboat captain returned.

And then trouble began. Just as I was planning how we might bilk our landlord on Long Island and move all our belongings to this delicious spot, gradually draw our friends around us, and make East End Avenue the Cheyne Walk of New York—we might even import an English imagist poet to lend cachet to the coterie—I saw by Titania's face that something was wrong.

I pressed her for the reason of her frown.

She thought the region was unhealthy.

Now when Titania thinks that a place is unhealthy no further argument is possible. Just on what data she bases these deductions I have never been able to learn. I think she can tell by the shape of the houses, or the lush quality of the foliage, or the fact that the garbage men collect from the front instead of from the back. But however she arrives at the conclusion, it is immutable.

Any place that I think is peculiarly amusing, or

quaint, or picturesque, Titania thinks is unhealthy.

Sometimes I can see it coming. We are on our
way to Mulberry Bend, or the Bowery, or Far-
rish's Chop House. I see her brow begin to
pucker. "Do you feel as though it is going to
be unhealthy?" I ask anxiously. If she does,
there is nothing for it but to clutch at the nearest
subway station and hurry up to Grant's Tomb.
In that bracing ether her spirits revive.

So it was on this afternoon. My utopian vision of a Chelsea in New York, outdoing the grimy
salons of Greenwich Village, fell in splinters at the
bottom of my mind. Sadly I looked upon the old
Carl Schurz mansion on the hill, and we departed
for the airy plateaus of Central Park. Desperately I pointed to the fading charms of East
River Park—the convent round the corner, the
hokey pokey cart by the curbstone.

I shall never be a tugboat captain. It isn't
healthy.

CONFESSIONS OF A SMOKER

TRUE smokers are born and not made. I remember my grandfather with his snowy beard gloriously stained by nicotine; from my first years I never saw my father out of reach of his pipe, save when asleep. Of what avail for my mother to promise unheard bonuses if I did not smoke until I was twenty? By the time I was eight years old I had constructed a pipe of an acorn and a straw, and had experimented with excelsior as fuel. From that time I passed through the well-known stages of dried bean-pod cigars, hayseed, corn silk, tea leaves, and (first ascent of the true Olympus) Recruits Little Cigars smoked in a lumberyard during school recess. Thence it was but a step to the first bag of Bull Durham and a twenty-five-cent pipe with a curved bone stem.

I never knew the traditional pangs of Huck Finn and the other heroes of fiction. I never yet found a tobacco that cost me a moment's unease —but stay, there was a cunning mixture devised by some comrades at college that harboured in its fragrant shreds neatly chopped sections of

rubber bands. That was sheer poison, I grant
you.

The weed needs no new acolyte to hymn her
sanctities. Where Raleigh, Pepys, Tennyson,
Kingsley, Calverley, Barrie, and the whimful
Elia best of all—where these have spoken so
greatly, the feeble voice may well shrink. But
that is the joy of true worship: ranks and hier-
archies are lost, all are brothers in the mystery,
and amid approving puffs of rich Virginia the
older saints of the mellow leaf genially greet the
new freshman, be he never so humble.

What would one not have given to smoke a
pipe out with the great ones of the empire! That
wainscoted back parlour at the Salutation and Cat,
for instance, where Lamb and Coleridge used to
talk into the small hours "quaffing egg flip,
devouring Welsh rabbits, and smoking pipes of
Orinooko." Or the back garden in Chelsea where
Carlyle and Emerson counted the afternoon well
spent, though neither one had said a hundred
words—had they not smoked together? Or Pis-
cator and Viator, as they trudged together to
"prevent the sunrise" on Amwell Hill—did not
the reek of their tobacco trail most bluely on the
sweet morning air? Or old Fitz, walking on the
Deben wall at Woodbridge, on his way to go sailing
with Posh down to Bawdsey Ferry—what mixture

did he fill and light?   Something recommended by
Will Thackeray, I'll be sworn.   Or, to come down
to more recent days, think of Captain Joseph
Conrad at his lodgings in Bessborough Gardens,
lighting that apocalyptic pipe that preceded the
first manuscript page of "Almayer's Folly."
Could I only have been the privileged landlady's
daughter who cleared away the Captain's breakfast dishes that morning!   I wonder if she remembers the incident?*

It is the heart of fellowship, the core and pith
and symbol of masculine friendship and good talk.
Your cigar will do for drummers, your cigarettes
for the dilettante smoker, but for the ripened,
boneset votary nothing but a briar will suffice.
Away with meerschaum, calabash, cob, and clay:
they have their purpose in the inscrutable order
of things, like crossing sweepers and presidents of
women's clubs; but when Damon and Pythias
meet to talk things over, well-caked briars are in
order.   Cigars are all right in fiction: for Prince
Florizel and Colonel Geraldine when they visit the
famous Divan in Rupert Street.   It was Leigh
Hunt, in the immortal Wishing Cap Papers (so
little read, alas!), who uttered the finest plea for
cigars that this language affords, but I will wager

*The reference here is to Chapter IV of Joseph Conrad's "A Personal Record." The author's allusions are often sadly obscure.—EDITOR.

not a director of the United Cigar Stores ever read it.

The fine art of smoking used, in older days, to have an etiquette, a usage, and traditions of its own, which a more hurried and hygienic age has discarded. It was the height of courtesy to ask your friend to let you taste his pipe, and draw therefrom three or four mouthfuls of smoke. This afforded opportunity for a gracious exchange of compliments. "Will it please you to impart your whiff?" was the accepted phrase. And then, having savored his mixture, you would have said: "In truth, a very excellent leaf," offering your own with proper deprecations. This, and many other excellent things, we learn from Mr. Apperson's noble book "The Social History of Smoking," which should be prayer book and breviary to every smoker con amore.

But the pipe rises perhaps to its highest function as the solace and companion of lonely vigils. We all look back with tender affection on the joys of tobacco shared with a boon comrade on some walking trip, some high-hearted adventure, over the malt-stained counters of some remote alehouse. These are the memories that are bittersweet beyond the compass of halting words. Never again perhaps will we throw care over the hedge and stride with Mifflin down the Banbury Road, filling the air with laughter and the fumes of Murray's Mellow. But even deeper is the tribute we pay to the sour old elbow of briar, the dented, blackened cutty that has been with us through a thousand soundless midnights and a hundred weary dawns when cocks were crowing in the bleak air and the pen faltered in the hand. Then is the pipe an angel and minister of grace. Clocks run down and pens grow rusty, but if your pouch be full your pipe will never fail you.

How great is the witching power of this sovereign rite! I cannot even read in a book of someone enjoying a pipe without my fingers itching to light up and puff with him. My mouth has been sore and baked a hundred times after an evening with Elia. The rogue simply can't help talking about tobacco, and I strike a match for every essay. God bless him and his dear "Orinooko!" Or Parson Adams in "Joseph Andrews"—he lights a pipe on every page!

I cannot light up in a wind. It is too precious a rite to be consummated in a draught. I hide behind a tree, a wall, a hedge, or bury my head in my coat. People see me in the street, vainly seeking shelter. It is a weakness, though not a shameful one. But set me in a tavern corner, and fill the pouch with "Quiet Moments" (do you know that English mixture?) and I am yours to the last ash.

I wonder after all what was the sweetest pipe I ever smoked? I have a tender spot in memory for a fill of Murray's Mellow that Mifflin and I had in the old smoking room of the Three Crowns Inn at Lichfield. We weren't really thirsty, but we drank cider there in honour of Dr. Johnson, sitting in his chair and beneath his bust. Then there were those pipes we used to smoke at twilight sitting on the steps of 17 Heriot Row, the old home of R. L. S. in Edinburgh, as we waited for Leerie to come by and light the lamps. Oh, pipes of youth, that can never come again!

When George Fox was a young man, sorely troubled by visions of the devil, a preacher told him to smoke tobacco and sing hymns.

Not such bad advice.

HAY FEBRIFUGE

OUR village is remarkable.

It contains the greatest publisher in the world, the most notable department store baron (and inventor of that new form of literary essay, the department store ad.), the most fragrant gas tanks in the Department of the East, the greatest number of cinders per eye of any arondissement served by the R—— railway, and the most bitterly afflicted hay fever sufferer on this sneezing sphere. Also the editor of the most widely circulated magazine in the world, and the author of one of the best selling books that ever was written.

Not bad for one village.

Your first thought is Northampton, Mass., but you are wrong. That is where Gerald Stanley Lee lives. For a stamped, addressed envelope I will give you the name of our village, and instructions for avoiding it. It is bounded on the north by goldenrod, on the south by ragweed, on the east by asthma and the pollen of anemophylous plants.

It is bounded on the west by a gray stone

facsimile of Windsor Castle, confirmed with but-
lers, buttresses, bastions, ramparts, repartees, feu-
dal tenures, moats, drawbridges, posterns, pasterns,
chevaux de frise, machicolated battlements, don-
jons, loopholes, machine-gun emplacements, cal-
trops, portcullises, glacis, and all the other travaux
de fantaisie that make life worth living for retired
manufacturers. The general effect is emetic in
the extreme. Hard by the castle is a spurious
and richly gabled stable in the general style of the
château de Chantilly. One brief strip of lawn
constitutes a gulf of five hundred years in archi-
tecture, and restrains Runnymede from Versailles.

Our village is famous for beautiful gardens. At
five o'clock merchants and gens de lettres return
home from office and tannery, remove the cinders,
and commune with vervain and bergamot. The
countryside is as lovely as Devonshire, equipped
with sky, trees, rolling terrain, stewed terrapin,
golf meads, nut sundaes, beagles, spare tires, and
other props. But we are equally infamous for
hideous houses, of the Chester A. Arthur era.
Every prospect pleases, and man alone is vile.

There is a large, expensive school for flappers
on a hill; and a drugstore or pharmacy where
the flappers come to blow off steam. It would
be worth ten thousand dollars to Beatrice Herford
to ambush herself behind the Welch's grape juice

life-size cut-out, and takes notes on flapperiana. Pond Lyceum Bureau please copy.

Our village was once famous also as the dwelling place of an eminent parson, who obtained a million signatures for a petition to N. Romanoff, asking the abolition of knouting of women in Siberia. And now N. Romanoff himself is gone to Siberia, and there is no knouting or giving in knoutage; no pogroms or ukases or any other check on the ladies. Knitting instead of knouting is the order of the day.

Knoutings for flappers, say I, after returning from the pharmacy or drugstore.

Dr. Anna Howard Shaw does not live here, but she is within a day's journey on the Cinder and Bloodshot.

But I was speaking of hay fever. "Although not dangerous to life," say Drs. S. Oppenheimer and Mark Gottlieb, "it causes at certain times such extreme discomfort to some of its victims as to unfit them for their ordinary pursuits. If we accept the view that it is a disease of the classes rather than the masses we may take the viewpoint of self-congratulation rather than of humiliation as indicating a superiority in culture and civilization of the favoured few. When the intimate connection of pollinosis and culture has been firmly grasped by the public mind, the complaint

will perhaps come to be looked upon like gout, as
a sign of breeding. It will be assumed by those
who have it not. . . . As civilization and culture advance, other diseases analogous to the
one under consideration may be developed from
oversensitiveness to sound, colour, or form, and
the man of the twenty-first or twenty-second
century may be a being of pure intellect whose
organization of mere nervous pulp would be
shattered by a strong emotion, like a pumpkin
filled with dynamite." (vide "Pollen Therapy in
Pollinosis," reprinted from the Medical Record,
March 18, 1916; and many thanks to Mr. H. L.
Mencken, fellow sufferer, for sending me a copy
of this noble pamphlet. I hope to live to grasp
Drs. Oppenheimer and Gottlieb by the hand.
Their essay is marked by a wit and learning that
proves them fellow-orgiasts in this hypercultivated
affliction of the cognoscenti.)

I myself have sometimes attempted to intimate
some of the affinities between hay fever and
genius by attributing it (in the debased form of
literary parody) to those of great intellectual
stature. Upon the literary vehicles of expression
habitually employed by Rudyard Kipling, Amy
Lowell, Edgar Lee Masters, and Hilaire Belloc I
have wafted a pinch of ragweed and goldenrod;
with surprising results. These intellectuals were

not more immune than myself. For instance, this is the spasm ejaculated by Mr. Edgar Lee Masters, of Spoon River:

> Ed Grimes always did hate me
> Because I wrote better poetry than he did.
> In the hay fever season I used to walk
> Along the river bank, to keep as far as possible
> Away from pollen.
> One day Ed and his brother crept up behind me
> While I was writing a sonnet,
> Tied my hands and feet,
> And carried me into a hayfield and left me.
> I sneezed myself to death.
> At the funeral the church was full of goldenrod,
> And I think it must have been Ed
> Who sowed that ragweed all round my grave.

The Lord loveth a cheerful sneezer, and Mr. Masters deserves great credit for lending himself to the cult in this way.

I am a fanatical admirer of Mr. Gerald Stanley Lee, and have even thought of spending fifty of my own dollars, privily and without collusion with his publisher, to advertise that remarkable book of his called "WE" which is probably the ablest and most original, and certainly the most verbose, book that has been written about the war. Now Mr. Lee (let me light my pipe and get this right) is the most eminent victim of words

that ever lived in New England (or indeed anywhere east of East Aurora). Words crowd upon
him like flies upon a honey-pot: he is helpless to
resist them. His brain buzzes with them: they
leap from his eye, distil from his lean and waving hand. Good God, not since Rabelais and
Lawrence Sterne, miscalled Reverend, has one
human being been so beclotted, bedazzled, and
bedrunken with syllables. I adore him for it,
but equally I tremble. Glowing, radiant, trans-
cendent vocables swim and dissolve in the porches
of his brain, teasing him with visions far more
deeply confused than ever Mr. Wordsworth's
were. The meanest toothbrush that bristles
(he has confessed it himself) can fill him with
thoughts that do often lie too deep for publishers.
Perhaps the orotund soul-wamblings of Coleridge
are recarnate in him, Scawfell become Mount
Tom. Who knows? Once I sat at lunch with
him, and though I am Trencherman Fortissimus
(I can give you testimonials) my hamburg steak
fell from my hand as I listened, clutching perilously
at the hem of his thought. Nay, Mr. Lee, frown
not: I say it in sincere devotion. If there is one
man and one book this country needs, now, it is
Gerald Stanley Lee and "WE." Set me upon
a coral atoll with that volume, I will repopulate
the world with dictionaries, and beget lusty tomes

It is a breeding-ground for a whole new philosophy of heaven, hell, and the New Haven Railroad.

But what I was going to say when I lit my pipe was this: had I the stature (not the leanness, God forbid: sweet are the uses of obesity) of Mr. Lee, I could find in any clodded trifle the outlets of sky my yearning mind covets: hay fever would lead me by prismatic omissions and plunging ellipses of thought to the vaster spirals and eddies of all-viewing Mind. So does Mr. Lee proceed, weaving a new economics and a new bosom for advertisiarchs in the mere act of brushing his teeth. But alas, the recurring explosions of the loathsome and intellectual disease keep my nose on the grindstone—or handkerchief. Do I begin to soar on upward pinion, nose tweaks me back to sealpackerchief.

The trouble with Mr. Lee is that he is a kind of Emerson; a constitutional ascete or Brahmin, battling with the staggering voluptuosities of his word-sense; a De Quincey needing no opium to set him swooning. In fact, he is a poet, and has no control over his thoughts. A poet may begin by thinking about a tortoise, or a locomotive, or a piece of sirloin, and in one whisk of Time his mind has shot up to the conceptions of Eternity, Transportation, and Nourishment: his cortex coruscates and suppurates with abstract thought;

words assail him in hordes, and in a flash he is
down among them, overborne and fighting for his
life. Mr. Lee finds that millionaires are bound
down and tethered and stifled by their limousines
and coupons and factories and vast estates.
But Mr. Lee himself, who is a millionaire and
landed proprietor of ideas, is equally the slave of
his thronging words. They cluster about him
like barnacles, nobly and picturesquely impeding
his progress. He is a Laocoon wrestling with
serpentine sentences. He ought to be confined to
an eight-hour paragraph.

All this is not so by the way as you think.
For if the poet is one who has lost control of his
thoughts, the hay fever sufferer has lost control
of his nose. His mucous membrane acts like
a packet of Roman candles, and who is he to say
it nay? And our village is bounded on the north
by goldenrod, on the south by ragweed, on the
east by chickweed, and on the west by a sleepless
night.

I would fain treat pollinosis in the way Mr. Lee
might discuss it, but that is impossible. Those
prolate, sagging spirals of thought, those grape-
vine twists of irremediable whim, that mind
shimmering like a poplar tree in sun and wind—
jetting and spouting like plumbing after a freeze-
up—'tis beyond me. I fancy that if Mr. Lee

were in bed, and the sheets were untucked at his feet, he could spin himself so iridescent and dove-throated and opaline a philosophy of the desirability of sleeping with cold feet, that either (1) he would not need to get out of bed to rearrange the bedclothes, or (2) he could persuade someone else to do it for him. Think, then, what he could do for hay fever!

And as Dr. Crothers said, when you mix what you think with what you think you think, effervescence of that kind always results.

APPENDIX

THIS book will be found exceedingly valuable for classroom use by teachers of theology, hydraulics, and applied engineering. It is recommended that it be introduced to students before their minds have become hardened, clotted, and skeptical. The author does not hold himself responsible for any of the statements in the book, and reserves the right to disavow any or all of them under intellectual pressure.

For a rapid quiz, the following suggested topics will be found valuable for classroom consideration:

1. Do you discern any evidences of sincerity and serious moral purpose in this book?
2. Why was fifty dollars a week not enough for Mr. Kenneth Stockton to live on? Explain three ways in which he augmented his income.
5. What is a "colyumist"? Give one notorious example.
4. Comment on Don Marquis's attitude toward
   (a) vers libre poets
   (b) beefsteak and onions
   (c) the cut of his trousers (Explain in detail)
   (d) The Republican Party

5. Who is Robert Cortes Holliday, and for what is he notable?
6. Where was Vachel Lindsay fumigated, and why?
7. Who is "The Head of the Firm"?
8. How much money did the author spend on cider in July, 1911?
9. Who was Denis Dulcet, and what did he die of?
10. When did William McFee live in Nutley, and why?
11. How are the works of Harold Bell Wright most useful in Kings, Long Island?
12. Where is Strychnine, and what makes it so fascinating to the tourist? Explain
    (a) The Gin Palace
    (b) Kurdmeister
    (c) unedifying Zollverein
13. What time did Mr. Simmons get home?
14. What is a "rarefied and azure-pedalled precinct?" Give three examples.
15. Who are the Dioscuri of Seamen, and what do they do?
16. How many pipes a day do sensible men smoke? Describe the ideal conditions for a morning pipe.
17. When did Mr. Blackwell light the furnace?
18. Name four American writers who are stout enough to be a credit to the profession.
19. "The fumes of the hearty butcher's evening meal ascend the stair in vain." Explain this. Who was the butcher? Why "in vain"?
20. In what order of the Animal Kingdom does Mr. Pearsall Smith classify himself?
21. "I hope he fell on the third rail." Explain, and give the context. Who was "he," and why did he deserve this fate?

22. Who was "Mr. Loomis," and why did he leave his clothes lying about the floor?

23. What are the Poetry Society dinners doing to Vachel Lindsay?

24. Why should the Literary Pawnbroker be on his guard against Mr. Richard Le Gallienne?

25. What is the American House of Lords? Who are "our prosperous carnivora"? Why do they wear white margins inside their waistcoats?

26. What is *minestrone*? Name three ingredients.

27. What are "publisher's readers," and why do they smoke pipes?

28. What was the preacher's advice to George Fox?

29. Give three reasons why Mr. Gerald Stanley Lee will not like this book.

30. Why should one wish to grasp Drs. Oppenheimer and Gottlieb by the hand?

31. In respect of Mr. Gerald Stanley Lee, comment briefly on these phrases:

(a) beclotted, bedazzled, and bedrunken with syllables

(b) the meanest toothbrush that bristles

(c) Scawfell become Mount Tom

FINIS CORONAT OPUS

/814M864S>C1/